Help us Rate this book...
Put your initials on the
Left side and your rating
on the right side.
1 = Didn't care for
2 = It was O.K.
3 = It was <u>great</u>

| | | Rating | DATE DUE | | |
|---|---|---|---|---|---|
| _dn_ | 1 2 ③ | | MAY 2 0 2019 | | |
| DV | 1 2 ③ | | **JUN 0 6 2019** | | |
| LR | 1 2 ③ | | JUN 2 8 2019 | | |
| | 1 2 3 | | JUL 1 9 2019 | | |
| | 1 2 3 | | JUL 2 2 2019 | | |
| | 1 2 3 | | SEP 2 5 2019 | | |
| | 1 2 3 | | OCT 2 1 2019 | | |
| | 1 2 3 | | AUG 0 6 2022 | | |
| | 1 2 3 | | | | |
| | 1 2 3 | | | | |
| | 1 2 3 | | | | |
| | 1 2 3 | | | | |
| | 1 2 3 | | | | |
| | 1 2 3 | | | | |
| | 1 2 3 | | | | |

PRINTED IN U.S.A.

# AS

## *Time*

# GOES BY

Center Point
Large Print

Also by Melody Carlson and available from
Center Point Large Print:

*Once Upon a Winter's Heart*
*Your Heart's Desire*

THE MULLIGAN SISTERS
Book Two

AS

*Time*

GOES BY

MELODY CARLSON

CENTER POINT LARGE PRINT
THORNDIKE, MAINE

This Center Point Large Print edition
is published in the year 2019 by arrangement with
WhiteFire Publishing.

The text of this Large Print edition is unabridged.
In other aspects, this book may vary
from the original edition.
Printed in the United States of America
on permanent paper.
Set in 16-point Times New Roman type.

ISBN: 978-1-64358-158-3

Library of Congress Cataloging-in-Publication Data

Names: Carlson, Melody, author.
Title: As time goes by : the Mulligan sisters / by Melody Carlson.
Description: Large Print edition. | Thorndike, Maine : Center Point
    Large  Print, 2019. | Series: The Mulligan sisters ; book 2 |
    Includes  bibliographical references and index.
Identifiers: LCCN 2019001654 | ISBN 9781643581583 (hardcover :
    alk. paper)
Subjects:  LCSH: Large type books.
Classification: LCC PS3553.A73257 A894 2019 | DDC 813/.54—dc23
LC record available at https://lccn.loc.gov/2019001654

# One

After six weeks of training and hard work, Colleen Mulligan finally felt like she could hold her own at the airplane factory. Or almost. It'd helped that she'd been befriended by a well-respected coworker during her first week. Audrey Lyons was not only accomplished at her job, she was big and tall—and tough enough that no one, not even the men, gave her much flack. But she was also bossy. That, Colleen decided, was the price she had to pay for her alliance with Audrey. And when Audrey got the management position in their department, Colleen appreciated their friendship even more.

For the most part, Colleen liked her job. She'd learned a lot about aviation electronics, and working on airplane instrument panels kept her busy enough that the days passed quickly. The pay wasn't bad either. But sometimes, like this morning when she'd suffered a painful burn from a careless coworker's soldering iron, Colleen seriously questioned why she'd chosen to be a factory worker . . . especially when she considered how she could've been an officer's wife instead.

On days like today, it wasn't hard to imagine living in a naval housing unit in San Diego. Sure, Geoff wouldn't be there with her, and she would miss her family. But compared to her demanding job at this factory, being a housewife was sounding more and more like a life of leisure. She could envision herself as a stylish sort of housewife, hobnobbing with other officers' wives, volunteering at the USO from time to time . . . Perhaps she'd even learn to play bridge.

"What're you daydreaming about?" Audrey elbowed her as she sat down at the lunch table, causing Colleen's forearm to throb all over again.

*"Ouch!"* Colleen scowled as she showed Audrey her bandaged arm. "Take it easy, will you? Some of us are injured."

Audrey's pale brows arched. "Well, if your burn is that bad, you should go home."

"It's not *that* bad." Colleen grimaced as she opened her lunch sack. "But thanks for caring, boss."

"Let me guess, you're fantasizing about your fiancé flyer again, aren't you?" Audrey rolled her eyes dramatically. "Probably romanticizing the idea that while you're in here building the planes . . . Lieutenant Lover Boy is out there flying them over the South Pacific, shooting down the Zeros." She chuckled. "You really should be in the movies, Hollywood."

Colleen was used to her "Hollywood" nickname by now. Audrey had given it to her on her first day at the plant. All because Colleen had been wearing a pretty silk scarf, dark glasses, and red lipstick when they'd initially met outside the building. Unfortunately, most of the other girls, and some of the men, had picked up on the nickname. So to avoid conflict, Colleen usually just played along. Even now, with her aching arm, she held her chin high as she gave a little up-pat to the back of her head—as if it was a stylish do, instead of a faded blue bandana wrapped around her blonde pin curls. "Thanks, darling. I couldn't agree more."

"So I'm right then. You *were* daydreaming about Lieutenant Lover Boy."

"Maybe I was . . . ." Colleen smiled coyly. She'd already seen a photo of Audrey's husband Harry. With his chubby cheeks and receding hairline, handsome he was not. Still, she knew Audrey loved him and that was all that mattered. Colleen couldn't help but singing Geoff's praises from time to time. "After all, you've seen pictures of my guy. You have to admit he's well worth daydreaming over." She had no intention of admitting she'd actually been imagining an easier line of work—playing housewife on the San Diego Naval Base. Not to Audrey anyway. It was okay to be teased for being overly glamorous, which seemed a further and further stretch, but she didn't want to be laughed at for being "weak." Not in this crowd.

Audrey tipped her head to one side as she noisily chewed a bite of apple. "I wasn't going to mention this, Hollywood." She lowered her voice. "But there may be an opportunity for a glamour girl like you."

"Huh?" Colleen stopped peeling waxed paper from her sandwich. "What do you mean?"

"I mean you should probably come to work looking your best tomorrow." She pointed to Colleen's cheek. "And maybe check your face from time to time."

Colleen grabbed her factory bag, which was really just an old purse big enough to carry her lunch and a few other necessities. She quickly removed a worn compact and examined her image in the mirror. Sure enough, she had several ugly black smears of soot or grease. In her early days of work here, she'd taken more care with her appearance. But it wasn't long before she realized it was pointless. She didn't even bother with lipstick anymore. Not with rationing making petroleum products more scarce. She planned to save what she had for more important occasions. Like playing bridge with the officers' wives.

Colleen peered curiously at Audrey as she used a napkin to wipe the smudge from her cheek. "What are you talking about, anyway? What kind of opportunity?"

"I can't say." Audrey glanced around the noisy

lunchroom. "Just make sure you look your best tomorrow." She held up a finger. "But in an appropriate-for-work sort of way, you know?"

"Okay . . ."

Audrey pointed at Colleen's sore arm. "Is that burn pretty bad?"

"Not really. Just painful. The nurse said it probably won't leave a scar."

"Wear long sleeves tomorrow."

"Right, boss."

"I heard it was Bernice who did it." Audrey narrowed her eyes slightly.

"That's right."

"Was it really an accident?" she whispered.

Colleen shrugged. She had her own suspicions but wasn't about to voice them—not even to Audrey. She knew enough about factory politics to know it was usually best not to get involved. She also knew Bernice Wagner's father was in management.

"Well, rumor has it that Bernice has been jealous of you. And it's not work related."

Colleen shrugged again, then took a bite of her liverwurst sandwich.

"It started out as soon as you were hired." Audrey chuckled. "You knocked her down from the top honors as the factory glamour girl. At least, she thought she was."

"Bernice is a very pretty girl," Colleen said brightly.

"Well, you better keep your eyes wide open," Audrey warned. "A burn on the arm is one thing, but if Bernice ever waves that soldering gun in your face, you better make a run for it, Hollywood."

Colleen forced a smile as she swallowed. "I'll keep that in mind." The truth was the same thought had occurred to her in the infirmary today. Bernice was probably a girl to watch out for. Just one more reason Geoff's proposal was growing more and more tempting. Colleen wondered when his next leave was due.

Margaret Hammond rejoiced when she finally started to fill out the maternity clothes she had meticulously begun sewing shortly after she discovered she was "in the family way." Mam and Colleen had teased her for donning the new garments so early in her pregnancy, but Margaret had simply felt more comfortable in them. Especially at work. The loose cotton dresses might not be stylish enough for Colleen's tastes, but they suited Margaret just fine. They didn't even look too bad with her grocer's apron on top of them. And several of her customers had inquired as to where she'd gotten them, making her wonder if there might be a future in sewing maternity dresses for sale.

Naturally, she always made sure that her wedding ring was clearly visible for the sake of her more *curious* customers. Not that anyone had questioned her pregnancy or her marriage to Brian. But some were aware that the couple had barely been married before the bridegroom shipped out. But that wasn't so unusual these days. And now with Brian so far away, she felt exceedingly grateful to be carrying his child. She was also glad to be nearly five months into her pregnancy, with a nicely rounded middle to show off. She knew some women went into hiding during their pregnancies. But she had no intention of doing anything like that. Like she kept telling everyone, she planned to manage the grocery store right up until the baby came. "And then I'll put him to work stacking canned goods like building blocks," she liked to joke with her customers.

"Look how big I am already," Margaret bragged to Mam and her sisters that evening. As usual, they were gathered in the kitchen after the workday, everyone helping to prepare dinner. She patted her swollen midsection, which always seemed to be larger by the end of the day. "I'll bet it's going to be a boy. A big boy too."

"Sit down," Mam insisted. "Take a load off your feet, Mary Margaret."

"That's right." Molly pulled out a kitchen chair for her. "According to Bridget's nursing textbook, an expectant mother shouldn't be standing all day."

"Oh, I don't mind," Margaret assured them as she sat down. "I feel more energetic than ever."

"That's fortunate." Mam filled the teapot with hot water. "We've been so busy since Goto's Grocery shut down."

"That's for sure," Margaret agreed. "I think sales have nearly doubled this past month. Although I must admit, it's sad to imagine the Goto family in an internment camp." She sighed. "They were nice people. And I miss Natsuko. I find it hard to believe they could've been a threat to our country."

"Except that they are Japanese," Mam said soberly.

"We discussed the internment camps in social studies this week," Molly added. "We decided that, even if it's unfair for some of the Japanese— the ones who have severed all ties to Japan and really consider themselves to be Americans— they may actually be safer in a camp. So many people hate them . . . simply because they are of Japanese descent." She paused from peeling a potato. "That would be like hating us because of something that's going on in Ireland. Even though we had nothing to do with it."

Mam let out a weary sigh. "I'm afraid that happens too . . . sometimes. Unfortunately, it is the way of the world. More than ever when we are at war."

Margaret knew this conversation could go

either direction. But she was determined to keep it as positive as possible. "Anyway," she said in a light tone, "I just really think pregnancy agrees with me. I hope that Brian and I have at least eight children. I mean, after the war ends."

"Eight babies?" Mam exclaimed. "You may reconsider after you give birth to your first one."

"Aren't you sad to lose your figure?" Colleen set a cup of steaming tea in front of Margaret, staring at her with a perplexed expression. "I sure would be." She stood up straight, striking a pose that showed off her own perfect shape.

Margaret considered this. "To be honest, I was a little concerned about that . . . at first. But I must say, it was a huge relief to stop wearing that confounded girdle." They all laughed. "I can understand why mothers let their figures go."

"*Well* then." Mam sounded slightly wounded.

"Present company excluded," Margaret reassured her. "You've managed to keep your figure, Mam. Even after five children. You're truly an inspiration."

"Thank you." Mam patted Margaret on the head.

The four females continued to chatter and joke as they prepared a simple dinner, finally setting it on the kitchen table. They'd taken to eating all their meals in here these past several months. Besides being easier and cozier, it made it less obvious that some family members were missing.

But as Margaret looked around the table, she couldn't help but miss them and long for their return. Although her older brother Peter would never come home again. Not after going down on the USS *Arizona* during the attack on Pearl Harbor. But Bridget and Brian, as well as Geoff and Patrick, would come home someday. At least, she hoped and prayed they would. And then there was Dad, still suffering from tuberculosis. Not so different than the Goto family . . . He was stuck in an "internment" camp—actually, a sanatorium in the mountains.

Margaret sighed as they bowed their heads, waiting for Molly to say the blessing, which as usual was positive and hopeful and bright. But Margaret knew as well as any of them that the last six months had taken a mighty toll on the Mulligan family. And although she wanted to believe, like Molly did, that life was going to get better for everyone—especially with a baby on the way—sometimes, especially with this horrible war tearing at all corners of the world, it was hard to be faithful. Just last week they'd heard the news of Germany's devastating air raids on Great Britain's cathedral cities. Knowing that Brian was in England right now brought no comfort. And who knew how long it would be until US troops would face the Germans? Margaret could hardly stand to think of it!

# Two

Molly Mulligan was eager to get the dinner dishes cleared from the table. Not because they still had some leftover apple pandowdy for dessert, but because this was what Mam called a "red-letter day." They'd come home to discover mail from Bridget and Brian and Geoff—and although Margaret had already read Brian's letter, and Colleen had read Geoff's—Bridget's V-mail letter remained unopened. Because after dinner was the official time for everyone to gather around to hear the letters read aloud.

"Who wants coffee or tea with dessert?" Molly called out, quickly filling their orders while Colleen and Mam dished up dessert. And then they all sat down at the table.

"I'll go first," Margaret offered. "Brian's letter was rather short. But he sounds well." She quickly read the letter, which had been mailed from some undisclosed location in Great Britain, deleting a sentence or two that she claimed was too personal to share. "Now it's Colleen's turn," she declared, carefully refolding the V-mail.

Geoff's letter was longer, but like Brian's it was vague in regard to specific locations or what exactly he was doing in the South Pacific. And any words that might've offered some clue were blacked out. They all knew Geoff flew navy planes off a gigantic aircraft carrier and that his was considered one of the most dangerous flying jobs in the armed forces. But, according to Colleen, Geoff wasn't only comfortable with it— he loved it. And Molly couldn't help but think it must be exciting. If women were ever allowed to be navy pilots, she might consider it herself. Although Mam would probably have other ideas.

"And now for Bridget's letter." Mam used a table knife to slit open the V-mail, then, clearing her throat, she began to read.

Dear Family,

I miss you all so very much, but I do believe I am exactly where I need to be right now. Thank you for your prayers and letters. Molly, thank you for the photos you sent in your last letter. I love and treasure them.

I know I already told you about being transported by ship to an island some- where in this big world. But, as you know, I cannot reveal the whereabouts. After we disembarked, we were herded like cattle onto army trucks, then transported to a hospital where we stayed for three days. During that time, we got our land legs back and prepared to be sent to another location. The roads here are very rough, and the long ride was uncomfortable. Our unit was extremely relieved to arrive at our destination, even though it's in a very remote place.

Our quarters are small tents directly across from the hospital, and we have a banana tree right beside us! I share my tent with two other nurses named Marsha and Judy. They're from Boston and speak with an interesting accent. They joined the ANC together and are fast friends. They remind me of Virginia and our plans to join the ANC together. But according to her last letter, she finally passed her boards. Pray that she gets assigned to my unit. It would be so wonderful to have a familiar face here.

My tentmates and I work different shifts at the hospital, which is actually a configuration of several very large wall tents divided into several wards. Because some of the tents have open sides, it's not unusual for chickens to wander right through the wards. But no one seems to mind.

As you can guess, the conditions here are very primitive, so we must rely on our ingenuity and limited resources. For instance, we use our steel helmets for numerous tasks, including as a wash basin, a laundry sink, or even as a stool to sit upon. Our uniform blouses are clean but wrinkled. It's very hot and humid and dirty here, but I am not complaining. It's hard to feel sorry for yourself when you see the condition of some of our patients. Yet few of them complain. I am learning so much about nursing too. Things I could never learn back home. Really, each day is a new adventure.

On our day off yesterday, my tentmates and I further explored the island. When we started out, the landscape was dry and dusty, but by the afternoon it began to rain in droves. Everything became muddy and the mosquitoes were relentless, but we still had fun, and I became much better acquainted with Marsha and Judy. They are good girls!

It is very rewarding caring for the wounded soldiers. They are so appreciative, and most of them are in good spirits and can't wait to return to the battlefront. I feel so fulfilled to be playing this small part in the war effort. And I thank you, my dear family, for making it possible for me to serve like this. I pray for all of you daily. Please, write and tell me how Dad is doing. No one mentioned him in the last letters I received, so I will simply assume that means he is getting better. I know it takes time.

Love and prayers,
Bridget

Molly let out a happy sigh. "It sounds like Bridget is having a great adventure!"

"Ugh, mud and mosquitoes!" Margaret wrinkled her nose. "Sounds awful."

"But she has a banana tree outside her door," Colleen said. "That sounds rather exotic."

"She sounds lonely to me." Mam slowly refolded the letter.

"Lonely?" Molly asked. "What about her new tentmates? Sounds like they're becoming friends."

"But she misses Virginia," Mam said.

"Don't worry so much," Colleen told Mam. "Bridget is doing exactly what she wants right now."

Mam frowned. "I just hope she's safe."

"Why wouldn't she be safe?" Molly questioned. "My social studies teacher was telling us about the Geneva Convention Rules this week. Did you know that hospitals are protected even if they're in war zones?"

"But how do we know Axis forces will honor the Geneva Convention?" Margaret asked her. "Do you really believe they can be trusted?"

No one said anything now . . . and Molly

19

suspected Margaret could be right about this. "But remember what our first lady said—we must rise above our fears."

"She's right," Colleen agreed. "If we give in to fear, we lose."

"Well, I will still be lighting candles for all of our loved ones tomorrow." Mam slowly stood. "And asking God to watch over them."

"And I am going to write Bridget a letter tonight," Molly announced. "Well, as soon as I finish helping with the dishes and finish my homework."

"Tell you what," Colleen said. "You write Bridget a nice long letter—and say it's from me too—and I'll do your portion of the dishes tonight."

Molly grinned. "It's a deal." She knew that, out of everyone in the family, even though she was the youngest—and only sixteen—everyone agreed she was the best letter writer. And since this war started, even before that when Peter went into the navy, she had probably written a hundred letters. Or close to that. Fortunately, Mam never complained about how many postage stamps Molly went through. And Molly suspected that before the war ended, she would go through a whole lot more.

Colleen got up an hour earlier than usual the next morning. Instead of wrapping a bandana around her pinned-up hair, she carefully brushed her platinum locks. Fortunately she'd just touched up her roots a few days ago. And since she'd been growing her hair out to resemble her favorite up-and-coming actress, young Lauren Bacall, it now curled gently on her shoulders. And in Colleen's opinion, it looked lovely.

Although Colleen normally wore her high-waist denim dungarees to work, topped with one of Dad's old plaid shirts, she decided to wear a skirt today. Some of the more conservative ladies, who disapproved of women in pants, only wore skirts to work. Of course, their skirts were long and unattractive and, combined with heavy hosiery and homely shoes, were decidedly unstylish.

Colleen always paid close attention to fashion, and even with the challenges of war rationing, she strived to be a trendsetter. When silk stockings became scarce because of the war in Asia Colleen had tried out the new nylon stockings that manufacturers produced to replace them. She quickly discovered the lightweight stockings were preferable to silk! But when Colleen heard that nylon was soon to be rationed—due to the material needed for parachutes for the paratroopers—she had the foresight to stock up on numerous pairs of stockings. She rationalized that she could share the hosiery with her sisters if needed.

Another fashion change, due to the war, was hemlines. Shortages of fabric meant women had been encouraged to shorten and streamline their skirts. Excess fabric removed from the old garments could be used to make children's clothes or other smaller items for the family or home. Consequently, Colleen had already altered many of her skirts. Today she put on a neat A-line navy skirt, short enough to expose her long legs, and topped this with a tidy powder blue blouse that nearly matched her eyes. To this working-girl ensemble she added a trim brown leather belt and matching brown pumps that she borrowed from Margaret. Her own pair had high heels that were unsuitable for the plant.

"Don't you look nice!" Mam exclaimed when Colleen joined them for breakfast.

"What's the special occasion?" Molly asked.

Colleen explained about Audrey's request for her to dress up. "I honestly don't know what it's about." She frowned. "I just hope I haven't overdone it. I'm so used to wearing dungarees to work, I feel a little silly."

Margaret laughed. "Imagine that! Our stylish sister feels like she's overdressed, and all she has on is a plain blue skirt and blouse." They all laughed.

"Yes, times have certainly been a-changing." Mam shook her head as she filled a bowl with oatmeal. "Hard to keep up."

"I wonder why Audrey wants you to look nice for the airplane factory," Molly said as she sat down at the table. "She's not playing a trick on you, is she? I remember when Pricilla Wright told Dottie Harris that she was having a formal birthday party, but she really wasn't. Dottie showed up in a gown and the rest of us had on everyday clothes." She chuckled as she stuck her spoon into her oatmeal. "Dottie wanted to kill Pris."

Colleen considered this. "I think I can trust Audrey. But just in case, I'll stick my dungarees and a head bandana in my purse. If she's pulled a fast one, I'll just do a quick change in the restroom—and then I'll never speak to her again!" But as Colleen poured coffee, she wondered. What if it *was* a trick or practical joke? Would she be able to take it graciously?

By the time Colleen was going into the plant, she decided she didn't care whether it was a trick or not. It felt good to look nice. And with an extra spring in her step and a nonchalant attitude, she held her head high as she put her handbag in her locker. And when someone whistled as she walked by, she simply smiled and held her head even higher. Fine, let them look . . . she could take it.

"Well, look at you, Hollywood." Audrey chuckled. "I'm glad you took my advice."

Colleen studied her closely. "So you were serious?"

"Of course."

"But you still won't tell me why?"

Audrey firmly shook her head. "Just try to keep that blouse clean this morning."

"So it will happen this morning?"

Audrey just shrugged. "I guess."

Colleen suspected this was all related to a visit from a photographer. Perhaps the plant had someone coming in this morning. Maybe for publicity to promote their war effort. Not so unusual these days. And if that was the case, Colleen would cooperate fully with them.

But the morning passed slowly and, other than a few catcalls from guys and some teasing from the women, nothing out of the ordinary transpired. Well, except that Bernice was acting even more superior than usual. She glowered at Colleen each time she passed by her station. And then finally, just before the noon whistle, Bernice stopped and leaned over to peer at Colleen as if she were on display.

"What's the special occasion?" Bernice demanded in a snippety tone.

"Whatever do you mean?" Colleen innocently asked.

"You're all dolled up." Bernice's smile was catty. "Like you think you're going to be photographed or something."

Colleen just shrugged, turning her attention back to the wire she was twisting into place. Her position on the assembly line didn't demand the most technical of skills, but it did require close attention. Something she took seriously. She knew her ability to do this detailed work was related to her years of experience with needle and thread. She was a perfectionist.

"So what's the special occasion?" Bernice demanded, making Colleen jump.

With the needle-nosed pliers held in the air, she frowned at Bernice. It hadn't slipped past her that her snooty coworker had taken extra care with her appearance as well. In fact, she looked rather stylish—in a factory sort of way. And then, suddenly hoping to bury the hatchet from yesterday, Colleen blinked, as if surprised. "Well, I must say, Bernice, you certainly do look nice today." She followed this with a bright smile. "Very stylish."

Bernice stepped back, seemingly caught off guard.

"That red blouse really sets off your dark hair." Colleen studied her more closely. "You look very pretty." And that was the truth. Despite her less than warm nature, Bernice was rather attractive in a Joan Crawford sort of way.

"Well, uh, thanks." Bernice gave her a nervous nod and then moved on.

Colleen smiled to herself as she turned back to her work. Maybe that was the best way to deal with Bernice—kill her with kindness. And if it worked, it would be well worth the effort. Still, Colleen couldn't help but wonder about Audrey's insistence that Colleen look extra nice this morning. As a result, when the lunch whistle blew, she felt a real sense of letdown. Nothing out of the ordinary had occurred, and her effort to fix herself up seemed pointless. Not only that, but having her hair loose like this was hampering her work. She had almost expected the plant manager to make a comment about it. But he hadn't made his rounds yet.

"So should I assume I dressed up for nothing?" Colleen asked Audrey as they walked to the employees' locker room after lunch.

"I'm sorry." Audrey frowned. "Maybe so."

"Then I'm changing into real work clothes." Colleen grabbed up her handbag and, making a beeline for the bathroom, quickly changed into dungarees, then secured her old blue bandana around her head to hold back her hair. She even rolled up her shirt sleeves, exposing the ugly white bandage on her forearm. So much for glamour in the workplace.

Her only goal now was to finish up that instrument panel by the end of the day. Because it was Friday, it would be nice to have it wrapped up before the weekend. And whatever pilot wound up having it in his plane would probably appreciate she'd given it her full and careful attention. Colleen took pride in her work, and she'd made no secret about being engaged to a navy pilot. She frequently reminded fellow workers that men's lives depended on their flying machines to function perfectly.

"Hold it right there, miss."

Colleen stopped what she was doing and started to look up.

"No, I mean it. Hold it right there. Don't stop what you're doing," the man's voice commanded with authority.

And so, feeling conspicuous, Colleen continued to tighten the tiny screw into place. But from the corner of her eye, she could see that several men were clustered around her station. And although she hadn't noticed it before, the light was brighter than usual. Plus, the nearby whirring sound indicated that someone was operating a movie camera. Despite her aggravation at having changed into her sloppy work clothes, she was determined to play this out—hopefully with some panache. Adjusting her posture and holding her chin at what she hoped was a good angle, she continued her task, hoping that she didn't have a smudge of grease on her nose.

"Cut," someone finally said. "That's perfect."

"May I look up now?" she asked tentatively.

"Yes, of course," a male voice answered.

She looked up to see several men in suits. One held a large motion picture camera, another a light bar, a third a clipboard, and an older portly

27

gentleman, who appeared to be in charge, simply looked on. She smiled brightly at him.

"Does this mean I'm going to be a star?" she said in a light and teasing tone.

"What's your name?" the man with the clipboard asked while the older man's forehead creased with what appeared to be disapproval. Perhaps she did have a smudge on her nose.

"Colleen Maureen Mulligan," she proudly told him, resisting the urge to rip off the ugly bandana and run it over her nose and cheeks.

"Is this *all* you do?" He pointed at the panel she was assembling with an unimpressed expression.

"Well, yes. But it's a very important job." She shook her small screwdriver at him. "Everything we do here is important. If any one of us fails to give our best effort, it could cost a serviceman his life." And now, feeling like she was on her soapbox again, she explained how her fiancé was a navy flyer and how she gave every task her full attention because of it.

"Stop!" The old man held up his hand, and she knew she'd said too much.

"Sorry," she mumbled in embarrassment. "I guess you can see I'm passionate about my work."

Ignoring her, the man turned to his crew. And, feeling dismissed and insignificant, she tried not to stare as they held an impromptu conference meeting nearby. Then, realizing it was getting late in the day, she returned to her work. She really wanted to ask them what their film footage would be used for, but based on her interaction with the old curmudgeon, she suspected her "performance" might end up on the cutting floor anyway. He clearly did not like her.

Colleen was just finishing up the last step on her panel when the head manager, Arnold Perry, walked up to her station. "I need to talk to you," he said solemnly.

"Uh, okay." She set down her pliers and nervously stood.

"Come to my office."

Colleen felt seriously worried as she followed the gangly middle-aged man across the factory floor. He must've observed her this morning, working with her hair down. She was well aware women were expected to either keep their hair tied back or covered with scarves, or else to use those hideous granny hairnets. But she'd thoroughly brushed her hair this morning, and she always kept a close eye on everything in her station while working. She felt certain that not a single hair had tumbled from her head. And being that her hair was so pale and platinum, she could easily spot a fallen lock. Still, she realized as she followed him up the stairs, it had been careless and irresponsible. Not to mention stupid! And if her recklessness had cost her this job, she would be truly devastated. Not to mention humiliated.

# Three

I'm so sorry," Colleen said as soon as they were in Mr. Perry's office. "I know I should've had on a scarf this morning and I'm—"

"A scarf?" He made a quizzical look.

"I should've had my—" Her words were interrupted by a sharp rap on the door.

"Come in," Mr. Perry called out. And suddenly the portly older man and his camera crew were standing in Mr. Perry's office and the next thing she knew, introductions were being exchanged, but Colleen was so taken aback that the only name she could remember belonged to the older gentleman. Apparently he was a film director and his name was Mr. Ramsay.

"We feel you are very photogenic," Mr. Ramsay told her after they were all seated around Mr. Perry's big desk. "And we would like to have your cooperation in our film."

She smiled brightly. "I'd love to help you. What is your film about?"

"It's a short promotional film called *Women of War, On the Home Front*," he explained. "The purpose is to elevate and encourage women of all ages and walks of life—the ones on the home front—to participate in the war effort. It will be shown in movie houses across the country, before and after major motion pictures. It will also be shown academically in high schools and colleges. The goal is to show how vital women are to attaining victory."

She nodded with approval. "I like the sound of that." Quickly, she told him about being part of a household of women. "We all do different things, but we like to think we're all participating in the war effort."

Mr. Ramsay looked genuinely interested. "Tell me more about your family, Miss Mulligan." He glanced at the man with the clipboard. "Take notes, Sid."

Now she explained about her oldest sister running the store and how she dealt with hoarders and enforced rationing. "Just this week, Margaret had to stand up to a greedy woman who threw a fit because Margaret wouldn't sell her sugar— the woman had no ration coupons. And Margaret's husband is a GI stationed in England right now. And she's expecting their first baby.

"Then there's my sister Bridget. She's an army nurse somewhere in the South Pacific, although that's probably not helpful for your home front movie. Except that it's because of Bridget that my younger sister Molly—she's sixteen—faithfully writes lots of letters. Molly says it's her part in the war effort to write to Bridget as well as a few others. She's the queen letter writer at our house—and she sends them photos too. But that's not her only part in the war effort. She recently planted a victory garden. It's not very far along and our backyard is tiny, but she works hard at it. She also collects all sorts of things, you know, for the various drives—like tin foil or bacon grease or bicycle tires. If something goes missing in our house, everyone asks Molly." She laughed remembering how Molly had confiscated the last of Mam's cold cream the other day.

"Am I saying too much?" she asked suddenly.

"Not at all. This is just the sort of thing we're looking for." Mr. Ramsay looked impressed. "Did you say your younger sister is just sixteen?"

"Molly's the youngest, but she's old for her age." She decided not to confess that Molly sometimes seemed more mature than Colleen. After all, hadn't Colleen been trying to become more responsible lately?

He turned to Sid. "Let's consider the young girl for our youth film." He looked back at Colleen. "Is Molly an attractive girl?"

Colleen flashed her best smile. "Everyone says Molly and I look a lot alike."

"Looks like we've found the right young woman," Mr. Ramsay told his crew. "Now we just need to work out a filming schedule with the management." He pointed his pen at Mr. Perry. "We'd like to film Miss Mulligan at a variety of tasks. Not only her usual job. She will be acting, of course, but it will be more impressive if we film her working with some of the larger power tools. I'd like to get her actually working on an airplane that's mostly assembled. Much more photogenic for the big screen."

"Kind of like Rosie the Riveter," Sid added.

"We can do that," Mr. Perry assured him. "But like I told you earlier, it will need to be after hours and we're already running two shifts, so that leaves the wee hours of the morning and Sundays. And I or someone else from management will need to supervise the filming."

"That's understandable." Mr. Ramsay turned to Colleen. "Do you mind working those late hours or on Sundays?"

Colleen had to contain herself from leaping from her chair and dancing around the room. Was this really happening? Was she truly going to be in a movie? "That would be fine," she calmly told him. "With my fiancé in the South Pacific, my social calendar isn't terribly full these days. Although I do like to visit the USO occasionally."

"The USO," he said eagerly. "Good idea! Let's plan for some footage there too." He pointed to Sid's clipboard. "What if we script the whole thing around Miss Mulligan here—*a day in the life of a woman on the home front?* We get her on the job, with her family at their store and in their home, and at the USO? You got all that, Sid?"

Sid just nodded as he continued to write. "Yeah, boss, I like that idea."

Suddenly Colleen felt a bit overwhelmed. Not so much for herself, but what would her family say about being involved? Mam might throw a fit. "I, uh, I'm not sure," she stammered. "I mean, about how much this, uh, project might entail. How much time are we talking about? And when do you plan to start film—"

"It'll take us a week or two to get the script ready and everything all set to roll," Mr. Ramsay told her. "And, naturally, you'll be reimbursed for your time, once we get started. We don't have a big budget. And all the filming shouldn't take too long." He turned to the man who'd been running the camera earlier. "What's your best guess, Henry? Couple of weeks?"

"At the most." Henry nodded. "We could wrap it up faster if we weren't restricted to non-working times here at the plant."

"We may be able to work around that," Mr. Perry offered. "Let me talk to the other managers to see."

"You'll have to work out the shooting schedule, Phil." Mr. Ramsay pointed at the fourth man. "Based on how much footage you think we'll need. But between filming at the family's grocery store and the Mulligan home and the USO, we should have plenty to choose from by the time it goes to editing—hopefully by the end of June. The studio wants it ready to release by next fall." He looked back at Colleen. "So, are you prepared to give us two, maybe three weeks of your life, young lady? Will you be ready to shoot by the end of May?"

Colleen nodded eagerly. That would give her almost two weeks to convince her family—particularly Mam—to participate. She would explain that this film was for the war effort. If necessary, she would remind Mam that their loved ones were overseas risking their very lives. Cooperating in a helpful promotional film was small potatoes compared to that—but it was better than nothing.

"So you're comfortable with this plan, Miss Mulligan?" Mr. Ramsay studied her closely. "We realize you're not a professional actress, but we didn't want any professional actors for this. At the same time, we don't want any shrinking violets either. You need to be able to do what we ask while the cameras are rolling. Just like you did earlier today."

She nodded. "That makes sense."

"And even though our film will be scripted, we want it to feel like real people doing real jobs. Understand?"

"Absolutely." She answered with confidence. "And although I'm not a professional actress, I did participate in some high school theatrical productions." She stopped herself from sharing about how she'd had Hollywood aspirations.

"Perfect." He grinned at his crew. "Can I pick

'em or what?" He stuck out his hand to her. "So we have a deal, Miss Mulligan?"

"As far as I'm concerned, we do." She firmly clasped his hand, shaking it.

"We'll have a contract for you to sign sometime next week," he assured her. "And a release form for your family members too."

Just as the whistle blew, signifying the end of her shift, they all stood up, agreeing to reconvene sometime next week. Colleen calmly thanked Mr. Ramsay and excused herself as if nothing out of the ordinary had just occurred. But as she exited the management department, going down the stairs to the main floor, she felt like she was floating on the air. *She was going to be in a film!* A real motion picture! Okay, maybe not a full-length film, but it was a start. Who knew what doors might open for her after this? Perhaps all her movie star dreams were about to come true! Anything was possible!

As she went into the employee locker room, she realized there was a small fly in her ointment . . . Geoff. What would her fiancé say about this new development? On some levels, he'd always sounded supportive of her dreams. He'd even defended her to his own mother. And he'd often told her that she was pretty enough to be in pictures. But was he just being nice? Or was it possible he truly had no qualms with a movie-star fiancée?

"What happened?" Audrey demanded as she came into the locker room. "Why did Perry call you into his office just now?"

"You will not believe it." Colleen grinned as she got her handbag.

"So you're not in hot water?" Audrey peeled off her work apron.

Colleen sighed dreamily. "Not at all."

"I want to hear everything," Audrey said eagerly. "I'll give you some gas money and you can give me a ride home. That way you can tell me the whole story."

Colleen agreed, but the truth was she would've gladly given Audrey a ride home anyway. Especially since Audrey was the one who'd told her to look her best today. And although she'd been wearing her work dungarees by the time the film crew arrived, she'd still looked nicer than usual.

Colleen had been using Dad's car to get to work every day, dropping Molly at school on her way to the plant. And she often gave other workers a ride in exchange for gas money contributions. But gas rationing would soon begin, and she knew she'd probably have to start exchanging rides for rationing coupons. As she drove, she told Audrey about the part she'd be playing in the upcoming promotional film.

"That's wonderful," Audrey said, "but you should watch your back when it comes to Bernice."

"Oh, I think Bernice and I are okay."

"Don't be so sure," Audrey warned. "From what I hear, Bernice can be a real pain when her nose is out of joint."

Colleen considered this as she pulled up to Audrey's apartment building. "Well, I suppose I'll just have to try even harder to win her over now. But, really, she'll just have to get over it."

Audrey laughed as she got out. "May be easier said than done." She waved good-bye, swinging her lunch pail as she walked up to the building. Not for the first time, Colleen was grateful for her friendship with Audrey. Thankfully, Audrey was not the type to be jealous about something like this. Perhaps there'd be a way to include Audrey in the actual filming. That is, if she wanted to be included. Colleen knew being in front of a camera wasn't for everyone. But she sure wouldn't complain!

On Friday after school, Molly sat on her back-porch steps staring in wonder at the tiny green sprouts in her victory garden. It was a gloriously sunny afternoon, and it felt slightly miraculous to see the tiny seeds she'd planted several weeks ago had broken through the soil, emerging as bright green seedlings. Was it possible that these fragile plants would really transform into edible food by the end of the summer? That was what her *Grow a Victory Garden* booklet had promised. So far she'd done everything by the book, including combining odd things like potato peels and coffee grounds and shredded news-papers to concoct a smelly compost mixture that made the soil more fertile.

"Your garden looks good."

"Thank you!" Molly went over to meet old Mrs. Bartley as her neighbor slowly made her way down her back-porch steps. "I can hardly believe the seeds I planted are really growing. And tomorrow I plan to transplant the seedlings that I've been growing on the back porch." She pointed to the window where her tomato and pepper plants were lined up. "It's time to get them in the ground."

"You must have a green thumb." Mrs. Bartley adjusted her wire-rimmed glasses to peer at the small, tidy garden. Each row was marked with a stick poked through a sun-faded empty seed packet. She pointed to some feathery green shoots. "Those appear to be carrots."

"That's right," Molly said eagerly. "And that row is radishes and those are turnips and . . . ." She went on to explain about everything she'd planted, telling Mrs. Bartley about the instruction booklet that had been her guide.

Mrs. Bartley nodded to her small flower-filled backyard. "Perhaps I should let you turn this space into a victory garden too."

Molly pursed her lips. "But your flowers are so pretty."

"Pretty, yes, but not edible."

Molly just nodded. "Well, if you really do want to give up your flowers, I'd be happy to help. And I had been wondering if I'd have room for my other plants. According to the book, tomatoes need lots of room. And I still have seeds that I haven't even planted because they need extra room too. I have bean and squash and cucumber and even pumpkin seeds." She frowned. "But I wonder if it's too late."

"Oh, I don't think so. I'm sure I've planted vegetables in late May before."

"You grew vegetables?" Molly was surprised.

"Oh, yes. I used to grow all sorts of things. And I canned them too."

"I want to learn how to can," Molly said eagerly. "Mam said she's never canned anything before. I think it's because she grew up with a grocery store in the family. They always had canned goods available."

"Well, I grew up on a farm and learned to can from my mother. I still have all my jars and lids and canning things. Perhaps I can teach you how to do it at harvest time."

"That'd be great!"

"Now, what to do about these flowers?" Mrs. Bartley picked a bloom from a bush, examining it. "I've never been that fond of these azaleas.

The plants just take over the entire yard, but they only bloom once a year. I won't miss them a bit. I'll tell my yardman to remove them when he comes tomorrow."

Molly studied Mrs. Bartley's yard. "What about your rosebushes? You don't want to get rid of them."

"Perhaps we can let them stay. Especially since they're on the edge of the yard." She waved her hand through the middle. "But I'll have Carlos get rid of all this. And he can work up the soil so that it's ready for you to plant."

Molly frowned at the bright flowers. Even though it seemed right to replace them with vegetables, she felt sad to see the flowers go. "Maybe we should pick some of the flowers before your yardman pulls them out."

"Good idea. We could make some lovely bouquets."

"If it was Memorial Day we could take some flowers to Golden Gate National Cemetery . . . to decorate war veterans' graves." Molly sighed sadly. "We had a stone placed there for Peter, even though he was lost in Pearl Harbor. It's a place we can go to remember him."

"I've been to the National Cemetery. With the view of the bridge, it's a lovely location." Mrs. Bartley's tone grew solemn. "And near enough to easily visit."

"Is your son buried there too?"

41

"No, no . . . That cemetery wasn't there during the Great War. Henry and his father are in a cemetery about twenty miles north of the city. I always drive up there to visit their graves on Memorial Day." Her brow creased as she removed her glasses, using the corner of her apron to wipe them. "But I won't be going this year."

"Why not?"

"My eye doctor says my vision is too deteriorated for driving. He told me to turn in my driver's license." She glumly shook her head. "I remember how proud I was to get it. I was nearly forty when my husband got his first car, but I insisted on driving too. I've been driving for more than thirty years . . . and now I must give it up."

"I'm sorry." Molly put a sympathetic hand on her shoulder. "Perhaps I could drive you to—"

"You drive?"

"I only have my learner's permit. Peter took me to get it . . . You know, before he joined the navy. And he was teaching me to drive too. I turned sixteen in March and both Colleen and Margaret let me drive with them sometimes. And I plan to take my driver's test after school lets out for the summer. Margaret said she'll let me deliver groceries in the car. But I have to get my license first. And to do that, I need to practice."

"I know what we'll do," Mrs. Bartley happily

declared. "We'll use these flowers to make floral arrangements to decorate our loved ones' graves. Then we'll take the bouquets to the cemeteries. I know we're a bit early for Memorial Day, but this way we can avoid the extra traffic. Are you comfortable with driving that far, Molly?"

"You bet." She grinned.

"How about if we go on Sunday? After church."

On Saturday morning, Molly and Mrs. Bartley began to salvage the condemned blooms. As the two of them cut flowers, setting the stems in buckets of water to keep them fresh until they made the arrangements, Molly felt it was touchingly appropriate that these sacrificed blooms would honor their fallen loved ones—the brave servicemen who'd laid down their lives for the good of others.

# Four

Despite her dismay that Mam had not been very supportive of her daughter's movie-star dreams, Colleen had not given up her campaign to win her mother over. And by Saturday evening, she felt like she was making a little progress.

"It's your choice to be in that movie business," Mam said as they cleared the table after dinner. "And I suppose I can give you permission to let them film in our house. Just don't expect me to participate."

"But it's for the war effort." Colleen repeated her best slogan. "Don't you want to do your part, Mam?"

"I do my part every day. I've already lost a son to this war. And then there's Bridget over there—living under such primitive conditions and—"

"But this movie is about the women on the home front," Colleen reminded her. "It's to encourage the females in our country to contribute to—"

"That is fine and well, Colleen, but I do not wish to see myself on a movie screen." She shook a dishtowel in Colleen's face. "Nor would anyone else. I'm a worn out old woman who—"

"Oh, Mam," Molly scolded her. "You're a beautiful woman. And if Dad were here, he would not put up with that kind of talk from you."

"That's right." Colleen pushed a strand of her mother's graying hair away from her forehead. "You are a lovely woman. Everyone always says so. And if you like, we can fix you up some before the cameras start to roll."

"On with you." Mam waved a dismissive hand. "But speaking of your father, I want to go see him tomorrow, Colleen. How about if you drive me?"

Colleen made a sly smile. "Sure, Mam. That'll give me more time to convince you how important it is for you to participate in this. And I'm sure Dad will agree with me."

"I wish I could go see Dad too," Molly said wistfully. "But I already promised Mrs. Bartley that we'd go decorate graves tomorrow."

"Yes, and that's a very nice thing to do with her," Mam reassured Molly. "Your dad will be glad to hear about it."

"But I have something for you to take to him," Molly said. "I'll go get it."

"I'm curious as to what Geoff is going to think about you being in a movie." Margaret looked doubtful as she set her plate by the sink.

"I'm sure he'll be happy for me."

45

"I don't know how you can be so sure. I don't think Brian would approve of me being in a movie."

"Do you mean you're not going to cooperate either?" Colleen frowned at her.

"I suppose I'll cooperate." Margaret picked up a washrag to wipe the kitchen table. "But I'm not the one who's already dreaming of going down to Hollywood for screen tests and so on."

Colleen rolled her eyes. "Oh, that was just me talking. Besides, a girl can dream, can't she?"

"But shouldn't your dreams include Geoff?" Margaret pointed to Colleen's engagement ring. "Or are you having second thoughts?"

"I'm not having second thoughts," Colleen declared. "I love Geoff. I plan to marry him . . . when the timing is right."

"Are you going to write Geoff about the movie?" Mam asked.

"Of course. Why wouldn't I?"

"I'm writing to Brian tonight." Margaret sat back down at the table. "Maybe you should write to Geoff too."

"Oh . . . I was thinking about going to the USO tonight." Colleen frowned as the sink filled with water.

"You'd rather go to the USO than write to your fiancé?" Margaret's tone sounded slightly accusatory.

46

"I didn't say that." Colleen poured soap powder into the sink.

"Margaret makes a good point," Mam said. "You need to tell Geoff about your movie plans. He deserves to know. And if he has any objections, you will need to respect them."

Colleen wanted to argue this but knew it was pointless. Mam was hopelessly old fashioned and provoking her only made matters worse.

"Here it is," Molly proclaimed as she returned to the kitchen with a paper folder. "I made this for Dad." She opened the folder to show them the folder contained stationery. "I addressed and stamped the envelopes. Most for Bridget, but some for Brian and Geoff and even Patrick. Dad can write them letters. It'll give him something to do."

"That's a lovely idea." Mam patted Molly on the head. "Your dad used to be a very good letter writer."

As Colleen returned her attention to washing the dishes, she wished she were a better letter writer herself. She knew that Mam and Margaret were right. Geoff did have a right to know about her part in the promotional film. And, really, she told herself as she scrubbed a water glass, he would probably be happy for her. Of course, his mother might not approve. But to be fair, his mother didn't approve of much of anything when it came to Colleen.

After Molly and Colleen finished the dishes, Colleen forced herself to sit down and write Geoff a quick letter. To her surprise, it wound up being three pages long—as she told him all about the film crew at work and how they'd chosen her to star in their project. "How about that?" She waved the three pages in front of Margaret, who was still working on her second page.

"Impressive." Margaret nodded.

"And just so you know, I told Geoff that I was going to the USO after I finished this letter. But I'll mail it on my way there." Colleen licked the stamp, sticking it onto the envelope. "Too bad you don't want to go with me."

Margaret just laughed. "I hardly think any servicemen would want to dance with me, in my condition."

As Colleen changed her clothes, she considered inviting Molly to go with her, but she knew her baby sister, for the most part, wasn't that comfortable going to the USO. Never mind that there were other girls not much older than her, or that Molly had enjoyed her previous visit there. And, as far as Colleen knew, Molly was still writing letters to the young soldier she'd met that time.

As Colleen got into the car, she reminded herself that encouraging the troops was just one more way women contributed to the war effort. But as she drove toward town, she felt a smidgeon of guilt. Despite Geoff saying he didn't mind if she went to the USO, she knew that he hadn't been fully supportive of this activity. Although it wasn't as if she went all the time. She hadn't been to the USO for a couple of weeks. And besides, she told herself as she parked on the street, this was her chance to reconnect with her girlfriends too. Just because Geoff was overseas didn't mean that she should have absolutely no social life. And tonight she had some fun news to share with her friends— Colleen Mulligan was going to be a movie star!

Molly tried not to feel nervous as she drove Mrs. Bartley's shiny DeSoto down the highway. Their plan was to go to the out-of-town cemetery first, then loop back to the National Cemetery. "Most of my driving practice has been in the city," she confessed. "I'm not very used to going this fast." She glanced at the speedometer to see she was going over fifty miles an hour. Even so, some cars had already passed her.

"City driving is much more challenging than highway driving," Mrs. Bartley assured her. "You're doing very well, dear."

As she glanced in the rearview mirror, like Peter had told her to do regularly, Molly wondered about Mrs. Bartley's deteriorating eyesight. Would the old woman even notice if Molly did something wrong—or broke the law?

Not that she planned to, but perhaps this wasn't such a good idea after all. Molly gripped the steering wheel even tighter.

"Just relax," Mrs. Bartley said gently. "You'll be fine."

Molly took a deep breath, loosening her grip slightly.

"My Henry loved to drive. He learned to drive a farm truck as a boy. Then he worked hard and saved up his money, and bought a car shortly after graduating high school."

"Just like Peter," Molly told her.

"Yes, I suspect my Henry and your Peter had much in common."

"Do you think they know each other?" Molly asked. "I mean in heaven."

Mrs. Bartley laughed a little. "Well, I suppose they just might."

To Molly's relief, they arrived at the cemetery with no problems and not even the slightest scratch on the DeSoto. She carried one of the two bouquets, watching as Mrs. Bartley reverently placed each one on the side-by-side graves and then bowed her head. Molly went to sit on a nearby bench as her elderly friend paid her respects. She didn't want her to feel rushed or watched. After about ten minutes, Mrs. Bartley rejoined her.

"I'm glad we did this today." Mrs. Bartley dabbed her eyes with a lace trimmed hanky. "It's much quieter here than it will be on Memorial Day. I like that."

Molly just nodded.

"Are you ready to drive back to the city?"

"Yes. And I don't feel as nervous as I did before."

"Well, you did a fine job of getting us here." Mrs. Bartley looped her arm into Molly's. "I'm sure you'll have no problem going back."

"Does it make you sad to come here?" Molly asked as they strolled back to the car.

"Not exactly. Oh, of course, I'm reminded of my loss. But it also makes me feel connected to my husband and son. And it's reassuring to know that someday I'll be laid to rest here too."

"But not anytime soon," Molly said quickly.

Mrs. Bartley chuckled. "Well, my own mother, bless her heart, only passed away last year. She was ninety-six. So if I take after her, I expect I'll be around for a good while longer."

"I'm glad." Molly squeezed her arm.

After about half an hour, Molly parked the DeSoto near Golden Gate National Cemetery. She'd visited Peter's memorial stone several times during the past few months. So much so that she thought she could easily find it. "There seem to be more stone markers," she commented as they made their way down a row.

"More servicemen have lost their lives." Mrs. Bartley sighed.

"I guess so."

"The price of war."

Molly stopped by the stone bearing her brother's full name and rank in the US Navy as well as his birth and death dates. Kneeling down to lay the bouquet of flowers beside the stone, she felt the familiar lump in her throat. She knew that everyone in the family missed Peter, but it seemed that as time passed, they mentioned his name less and less. Not that they'd forgotten him. That was impossible. But perhaps it was just easier not to talk about him too much. Besides that, everyone was so busy and distracted with the demands of life. Still, Molly didn't think a single day had gone by that she hadn't missed her brother. Hadn't felt that dull ache inside of her. She didn't know if it was even possible.

Closing her eyes, she took in a deep breath, then silently told Peter how much she loved him . . . and missed him . . . and thanked him for being such a great brother. Blinking back tears, Molly stood up and looked across the cemetery. So many stones . . . so many lives already lost. She wondered how many more would be lost before this crazy war was over. She hoped and prayed it wouldn't be any more of their loved ones. She just didn't think the Mulligans could take much more loss.

# Five

News of Colleen's upcoming role in the promotional film had circulated quickly around the airplane plant by Monday morning's coffee break. Not that Colleen minded the extra attention. In fact, she rather enjoyed it. Just one more reason to assume she was perfectly suited for a life of celebrity . . . and why she'd taken extra care in getting ready for work today. Oh, she was still sporting her dungarees, but she had on a feminine shirt, and her hair was styled and tied away from her face with a pretty pink scarf. She'd even put on lipstick.

"So it's true," Bernice said to Colleen as they were going into the lunchroom. "You really did steal the part from me."

"Steal?" Colleen blinked innocently. "The part from you?"

"My father practically promised me that I'd be chosen to star in that propaganda film."

"You mean the *promotional* film?" Colleen didn't appreciate Bernice calling it propaganda. Even if it was. "Well, apparently your father wasn't involved in the decision-making process." She smiled at Bernice, remembering her plan to kill her coworker with kindness.

"But I'm sure you would've done beautifully if you'd been picked, Bernice."

Bernice scowled darkly.

"And you never know . . . perhaps they'll need some extra people to be in it with me." Colleen tried to sound hopeful as she pulled out a cigarette. "I'd be happy to request you. I mean, if you're interested."

Bernice pursed her lips as if considering this. "Well, it's not a big deal to me. I just didn't like the idea of you pulling a fast one."

"Sorry, but it really wasn't up to me. Mr. Ramsay, the director, is in charge of casting." Colleen lit her cigarette.

"Anyway, no one cares about a silly propaganda film. I know I don't."

Colleen felt relieved as she took a slow drag on her cigarette. "Although I'm sure you'd be very photogenic, Bernice." She hoped a little honey would help keep the bitterness at bay.

*"Really?"* Bernice's eyes lit up. "Well, then I'll take you up on that offer. Maybe I would like to be in the movie after all."

Colleen wished she'd closed her mouth sooner about this. "Okay then. I'll be sure to let the filming crew know about your interest." She forced a smile.

Bernice's eyes narrowed slightly. "I guess we'll see how it goes then."

As Colleen went to sit with Audrey, she suppressed the urge to let out a loud groan. Why on earth had she gone and done that? Now Bernice would fully expect to be involved in Colleen's movie. And if she was not involved, she would probably hold Colleen personally responsible. With a daddy in management, Bernice probably had the means to make Colleen miserable.

"What's eating you, Hollywood?" Audrey gave her a catty smile as she lit her cigarette. "I figured you'd still be on top of the world."

"Bernice," Colleen whispered. "She's trying to hitch her wagon to my star."

Audrey just laughed. "So did you write Lieutenant Lover Boy about your upcoming film?"

"As a matter of fact, I did." She nodded. "And mailed it too. On my way to the USO dance."

"What are you going to the USO for, Colleen? You already have a man."

"I go to encourage the troops." She smiled smugly. "Geoff knows all about it. In fact, I wrote him about that in the letter I just mailed to him."

Audrey's grin faded. *"Really?* You aren't worried he might take it wrong? I mean, he's over there risking life and limb—meanwhile, you're playing party girl."

"I am *not* a party girl." Colleen scowled. "Not anymore, anyway. I suppose I used to be . . . sort of. But Geoff knew who I was when we met. He didn't seem to mind. And the only reason I go to the USO is to cheer up servicemen and catch up with my girlfriends there." She tapped Audrey on the shoulder. "In fact, I think you should go too."

Audrey snickered. "The one and only time I went to the USO, I hugged the wall all night. No one wants to dance with a giraffe like me."

"I don't know. There are some tall guys there. They might—"

"Stop with the smokescreen." Audrey held up a hand. "I meant what I said, Colleen. You should be more concerned about your fiancé's morale than the fellows at the USO. Can't you imagine how your guy feels to hear that you're running around like that?"

"You sound just like my big sister Margaret."

"I'll take that as a compliment."

"I've got family enough to tell me what to do." Colleen tried to block out her father's words of warning from yesterday. When she'd told him about the movie and going to the USO—just trying to fill up the quiet in the visitors' room— Dad had turned all fatherly, expressing concern for Geoff too. "Anyway, I'd rather have you for a friend, Audrey."

"Well, aren't friends supposed to straighten out friends from time to time?"

Colleen shrugged. "Don't worry about Geoff and me. We'll be fine. He understands me better than most people think."

"Maybe so, but I'd still think you'd be more

interested in keeping Geoff's morale up." She grimly shook her head. "I would never write something like that to Harry."

"That's because you're not me . . . and Harry is not Geoff." Colleen snuffed out her cigarette.

Audrey still looked unconvinced, but at least she nodded. And as Colleen returned to work, she wished everyone wouldn't make mountains out of molehills when it came to her life. Good grief, she was only eighteen. Sure, she was about to turn nineteen and, yes, she was engaged. But did that mean she shouldn't have a life? She didn't think so! She didn't think Geoff thought so either.

Molly felt a wave of satisfaction as she closed the letter box with a loud clank. "There," she said to her friend, Dottie Harris. They were on their way to Molly's house, where Dottie planned to spend the night.

"Who did you write to this time?" Dottie asked.

"One to Bridget and one to Patrick." Molly peeled off her cardigan—a hand-me-down from her sister. "In Bridget's letter, I told her all about Patrick's latest news on the aircraft carrier." She grinned. "And in Patrick's letter, I told him about Bridget's work in the tent hospital. I can't tell him where she's stationed because we don't know. But I have shared their military addresses with each other. And I encouraged them to stay in touch." She laughed. "They probably think I'm playing matchmaker."

"Sounds like you are."

"Not any more than Mam and Mrs. Hammond do. I heard Mrs. Hammond saying that if Bridget and Patrick have children, they'll be double cousins with Margaret and Brian's children."

"Why doesn't Bridget just write to Patrick herself?" Dottie asked her.

"I don't know. I guess she's too busy."

"But she writes to you."

"She writes to our family. It's just that I'm the one who writes back the most. Mam calls me the family correspondent."

"How many letters do you write every week?"

Molly grinned at her best friend. "A lot."

"No, really, how many?" Dottie persisted.

Molly considered this. "Well, I usually write Bridget about twice a week." She held up two fingers. "But I only write Brian and Geoff about once a week, and their letters are usually just one page." She added two fingers. "And I write Tommy about once a week." She held up five fingers now.

"Is Tommy your sweetheart?" Dottie teased.

"No, I already told you all about him. He's just a lonely guy. We became friends that time my sisters took me to the USO. Poor Tommy was an orphan . . . with no family or anyone to write to him."

"Well, he probably thinks you're his sweet-heart."

"No, he doesn't. I made it clear I wasn't. But I sent him some photos." She giggled as she unlocked the front door. "To show off to his army buddies."

"I'll bet he pretends you're his sweetheart with them."

"That's okay. As long as he understands we're just friends." Molly led Dottie inside.

"What about Patrick?" Dottie's tone turned even more teasing. "How many times do you write to him?"

"Once or twice a week." Molly held up seven fingers, then added an eighth one. "And I write to Dad about once a week too. So that's about eight letters in total."

"Wow, you really are a good letter writer." Dottie set her overnight bag on Molly's bed, then went over to the dresser, examining all the photos that Molly had taped around the edges of her mirror.

"So you write to him *twice* a week?" She pointed at a photo of Patrick in his navy uniform. Molly had taken it at the drugstore soda fountain the day he'd shipped out. She had to admit it was a great photograph. His smile was dazzling.

"I guess so. Maybe not every week."

Dottie turned to Molly, locking eyes with her. "You're sweet on Patrick, aren't you?"

"No, I'm not," Molly said defensively. "That's ridiculous."

"I don't think it's ridiculous." Dottie smiled smugly. "I think I guessed your secret, Molly Mulligan. You're in love with Patrick Hammond."

"I am not!" she declared hotly. "Patrick is like my big brother. You know how close he and Peter were . . . before. Anyway, Patrick treats me really nice . . . like Peter would . . . if he were here."

"Even more reason for you to be sweet on Patrick. He's *so nice* to you." Dottie's teasing tone was starting to aggravate Molly.

"You're loony, Dottie." Molly rolled her eyes. "Like I already told you, our whole family wants Patrick and Bridget to get married. Our parents have been planning it for ages."

"But Patrick is so dreamy . . . ." Dottie turned back to ogle Patrick's photograph. "He's so handsome in his officer's uniform. It's no wonder you write letters to him. He would make a perfect sweetheart."

"I already told you he is *not* my sweetheart," Molly said indignantly.

"Fine and dandy, Molly. If you say so. But methinks thou dost protest too much."

Molly scowled at her friend, wondering if she'd made a mistake to invite Dottie here for a sleepover. When had she turned into such a boy-crazy tease? In some ways she reminded

Molly of Colleen. Except that Colleen was nicer.

"So if you're truly not in love with Patrick . . . then maybe I'll start writing to him too. That way he can become *my* sweetheart." Dottie had a sly look in her eyes now. Molly couldn't tell if she was teasing or serious. Either way, she didn't like it.

"You better not!" Molly felt a funny wave of jealousy as she scolded Dottie. "Patrick is a grown man. He'll be twenty-three in September."

Dottie's dark brows arched with interest. "Only twenty-three?"

"That is way too old for you, Dottie Harris!"

"I don't agree. After all, my dad is almost ten years older than my mom. Patrick's only six years older than me. And I'll be seventeen in November. My mom was only eighteen when she got married. Patrick and I could get engaged and—"

"Dottie Harris, you are incorrigible!"

"I'm just toying with you." Dottie put her arm around Molly. "I wouldn't really chase after Patrick." She laughed. "But I wouldn't complain if he chased after me."

"I hardly think that will happen." Molly still felt aggravated.

"I'm sorry I made you so mad." Dottie gave her a squeeze. "Although I do think I may've touched a nerve."

"It's just that I feel sort of protective of Patrick,"

Molly explained. "It probably makes no sense. But it's the same way I would be about Peter."

"I know." Dottie smiled. "You're a very loyal person, Molly."

"Besides . . . everyone thinks Patrick and Bridget will end up together. It's like it's meant to be. You know? Sometimes I imagine them meeting up in the South Pacific. On some exotic South Seas island. Probably in a hospital where Bridget is working. Not that I want Patrick to get hurt, but he could suffer a small non-life-threatening wound—just bad enough to need medical attention. And Bridget, looking all grand in her uniform, would nurse him back to health . . . and they could fall in love. That would be romantic, wouldn't it?"

"Yeah." Dottie nodded with wide eyes. "Like right out of movie. You know, I've secretly dreamed of becoming a nurse ever since I saw my first Dr. Kildare film." She went over to stare at herself in Molly's mirror. "Don't you think I look like Laraine Day? She makes such a gorgeous nurse in those movies. I really think Dr. Kildare should marry her."

Molly laughed. "You do know they're fictional people, right?"

Dottie rolled her eyes. "Anyway, I think I'll be like Bridget. And I'll become an army nurse. Do you think the war will still be on by the time I'm old enough to enlist?"

"I sure hope not." Molly grimly shook her head.

"That's not fair." Dottie folded her arms in front of her as she sat down on Molly's bed. "I want it to keep going so that we can participate too. Don't you think it would be glamorous to wear a uniform? To have a military romance? I think maybe I'll fall in love with an army doctor and—"

"You can't possibly mean that, Dottie."

"Why not? My mom would love for me to marry a doctor. She's always saying—"

"No, not that. I mean you can't want the war to last that long. Don't you understand that the longer this war lasts, the more soldiers and sailors—more people—will die." Molly shuddered to remember the multitudes of grave markers in the cemetery last Sunday. All week long, she'd been haunted by the thought that each marker represented a fallen young man—maybe a few women too—and their grieving families. It was almost too much to even think about. And she really didn't want to talk about it.

"You should see my victory garden," she said suddenly. Hoping to change the subject, she told Dottie about her victory garden, probably building it up too much.

"I want to see it," Dottie declared.

So Molly took Dottie outside and showed off her fledgling garden. She told her about the various plants and how soon she'd be able to start harvesting. As she pulled some stray weeds, she explained how Mrs. Bartley had volunteered her yard. "That almost doubles the size of the garden." She stood, brushing the dirt off her hands. "It's more work. But I love it."

"Maybe I'll make a victory garden too," Dottie said. "My dad has been nagging me to get involved in the war effort." She smiled sheepishly. "I can't even tell him about all the stuff you've been doing, Molly. He already thinks I'm lazy."

"Well, you were just saying that you wanted to be involved in the war effort. There are lots of ways to help." She pointed to her collection piles near the back porch, explaining how they would be recycled and used to make military equipment. "I really like doing my part to help us win this war. And the sooner it's over, the happier I'll be."

"Well, no one will ever accuse you of being lazy." Dottie slowly shook her head. "And you really get to be in that movie with Colleen?"

"Yeah, I guess so." Molly wasn't sure she wanted to be filmed for a movie. She actually preferred being on the other side of the camera lens. But she had promised Colleen to cooperate when the time came.

"You're so lucky!" Dottie playfully punched Molly in the forearm. "You make me so jealous."

"You're lucky too, Dottie." Molly grew more solemn. "Be thankful that your brother is still alive."

Dottie slowly nodded. "Yeah . . . that's true. Hopefully Warren will live through the war too."

"And see, that's just another part of the war effort you can participate in," Molly said as they went up the porch stairs. "You can pray for your brother to remain safe." As they went into the kitchen, Molly thought about her loved ones in the service. She knew that, like Warren, they were in harm's way. And she prayed for them—every single day and not only when she went to church to light candles for them. Her prayers were always the same—that each one of them would make it safely home. The sooner the better.

# Six

Margaret didn't like feeling angry at anyone. Particularly a family member. But for the past two weeks—ever since the big announcement about the propaganda film—she'd been growing more and more irked at Colleen. It wasn't that Margaret opposed the film project—although she wasn't overly thrilled at the prospects of being part of a movie while not looking her best. Oh, she looked fine . . . for a pregnant woman. But, as Colleen liked to point out, Margaret was getting quite "thick around the middle." As offensive as insensitive comments like that felt, though, that wasn't why she was losing her patience with her sister.

What really irritated Margaret was how nonchalant Colleen appeared to be in regard to her fiancé. Geoff was a good guy. And unlike Margaret's husband Brian, who was still stationed in Great Britain, Geoff was involved in active duty. Margaret had just read a disturbing news story about the dangers navy pilots faced in the South Pacific on a daily basis. But despite that Geoff was risking life and limb for his country, Colleen acted as if his reaction—or non-reaction—to her soon-to-be acting career was of no consequence. She didn't even care that

Geoff hadn't written back to her. Never mind that he'd faithfully written her at least twice a week. Not that her sister managed to match that.

"You still haven't heard from Geoff?" Margaret had demanded just this morning while waiting for Colleen to evacuate the bathroom.

Colleen had merely shrugged, carefully applying a bright red coat of lipstick—as if it weren't eight o'clock in the morning and as if the government hadn't placed all petroleum based items on a ration list. "Navy mail is slow sometimes." Colleen blotted her lips on a tissue, making a wide smile like she thought cameras were rolling or Margaret would be impressed.

"Not all the navy mail has been slow," Molly injected from down the hall. "I got a letter from Patrick yesterday. And it only took a few days to get here."

"That's just my point!" Margaret exclaimed. "You should've heard from Geoff by now, Colleen. He's had plenty of time to react about your stupid movie. And the fact that he hasn't written should concern you. It's probably because he disapproves."

"Well, it doesn't concern me. And I seriously doubt Geoff would disapprove of anything I do. He's probably just too busy to write." Colleen continued primping in front of the mirror, barely moving out of the way to let Margaret to the wash basin to cleanse her face. More obsessed than ever about her appearance this past week, Colleen acted like she thought she was the Queen Bee . . . or a movie star. And Margaret had to bite her tongue to keep from saying something truly childish.

But it was harder than ever when, during breakfast, Colleen had paraded around the kitchen, showing off another one of the new outfits she'd recently acquired. "For my movie," she'd informed them. Margaret almost pointed out that Colleen's bright head scarf clashed with the pale pink skirt and jacket—except she knew Colleen never planned to wear the two together.

But the last straw came when Margaret asked Colleen to come to work with her, since it was Saturday—but Colleen had turned up her nose. "I already put in *my* work week," she'd said in a superior way. "And I still need to do my nails. Besides, I want to look fresh and rested for tonight's filming at the USO. Not like I've been grinding meat all day."

Margaret had controlled herself from yelling at her smug sister. But only for Mam's sake, since she was having one of her headaches and seemed unduly worried about Dad this past week. Consequently, Molly had volunteered to come to work with her today. Between Molly and Jimmy Sullivan, they were somehow managing to serve their customers. Although the waiting line had probably been longer than usual all morning, at least it had slowed down some in the afternoon. Right now, Margaret felt overdue for a break. Even more so when she spied Mrs. Jones approaching the checkout stand.

The cranky older woman was the most difficult customer, and Margaret just didn't have the patience for her today. Jimmy was in the back of the store cleaning up the produce section—but where was Molly?

"I'd like a pound of sugar," Mrs. Jones informed Margaret.

Margaret smiled stiffly as she held out her hand. "Your ration booklet, please?"

Mrs. Jones glanced over her shoulder, as if to see if anyone else was listening. "I—ahem—left it home," she said quietly.

"I'm sorry." Margaret pursed her lips, trying to keep her voice pleasant as she repeated the line she'd gotten accustomed to using this past month. "As you know, due to the war, sugar is in short supply. It's been placed on the ration list, and it's illegal for me to sell it without your ration booklet."

"So you would send an old woman like me all the way home to get a silly coupon?"

"I'm sorry but—"

"I'll have you know that I have been a good customer to your family's store for decades. Even before you were born, Margaret Mulligan—"

"Hammond," Margaret corrected. "I'm married."

"Well! I cannot believe this is the treatment I get from—"

"If memory serves, I believe you purchased a pound of sugar earlier this week." Margaret studied the woman closely. Was it possible Mrs. Jones was selling her sugar on the black market? Or did she just have a ferocious sweet tooth? The bell on the door jingled, and Margaret looked up to see Mrs. Spencer and Mrs. O'Brian entering the store. She smiled at the two older women, calling out a friendly greeting.

"I walked all the way up the hill." Mrs. Jones was attempting to sound sympathetic now. "In the hot sun too. And all I want is a pound of sugar—and you would turn me away like this?"

"As I said, it would be illegal for me to sell sugar without your ration—"

"Oh, that is perfectly ridiculous. Do you really expect a policeman will march in here and arrest you for selling an old woman sugar? I'm sure I could get some from the Goto Market . . . if it were open. They might've been Japanese but at least they knew how to treat their customers with respect."

"If you think another grocery store can better serve you than us . . ." Margaret locked eyes with the old woman. ". . . feel free to take your business there."

"Well, I never!" Mrs. Jones turned to the other women. "Did you hear how she speaks to me?"

"It sounds to me that Margaret is simply obeying the rationing laws," Mrs. Spencer said pleasantly. "We all have to do our part."

"But I could bring my ration book back up here tomorrow," Mrs. Jones said with irritation. "If only she would sell me my sugar today."

"That seems reasonable to me," Mrs. O'Brian told Margaret. "Why can't you do that for her?"

Margaret pointed to the corner of the ration booklet sticking out of Mrs. O'Brian's shiny black handbag. "Perhaps you could be a good neighbor and loan Mrs. Jones your sugar coupon—and she could pay you back later. That would resolve this—"

"No, no . . . I don't think that's a good idea." Mrs. O'Brian tucked the booklet more snugly in her handbag. "For all I know, that may be illegal."

Margaret tried not to look overly smug as she turned back to Mrs. Jones. "Is there anything else I can help you with today?"

"No, thank you!" Mrs. Jones said angrily. "And the next time I see your mother, I will be sure to give her a full report of how you treat your customers!"

"I will give her my own full report today!" Margaret used a tone that she knew was too sharp—but she didn't even care. Stupid old Mrs. Jones deserved it.

"And from now on I will take my business

elsewhere!" the old lady shouted as she marched toward the front door.

"And if another store sells you sugar without your ration booklet, I hope they get reported!" Margaret turned on her heel and stomped into the backroom.

"What happened?" Molly stuck a price-sticker on a can of peaches, setting it back into the case she was working on.

"Can you please take over out there?" Margaret hissed at her. "I need a break."

"Sure." Molly quickly stood. "You should probably sit down, Margaret. Mam doesn't like it when you're on your feet all day."

"Yeah." Margaret nodded. "Thanks." She went into the tiny office and sat down in her desk chair, putting her feet on the apple crate that doubled as her ottoman, and tried not to seethe. As she rubbed her hands over her swollen midsection, she reminded herself of all she had to be thankful for.

Sure, life hadn't gone exactly the way she'd hoped it would. She remembered how she'd hoped to be planning her big June wedding by now. But at least she and Brian had been able to get married before he shipped halfway around the world. And although they hadn't been able to get a small place of their own, at least she was able to be at home with Mam and her sisters.

By autumn she would welcome a sweet little baby into this world. Hopefully a boy. Was this the ideal way to start one's family? Of course not. But thanks to the war, no one's life was exactly ideal these days. One simply had to make the best of it. And she knew she needed to count her blessings. Didn't she?

What good did it do to be so angry? So what if nasty old Mrs. Jones wanted to throw a fit over sugar rationing? Let the law take care of her. Furthermore, what did it matter how Colleen lived her life? At least she wasn't doing anything illegal. And if Geoff decided that Colleen wasn't great wife material, why should Margaret trouble herself over it? At least they hadn't gotten married. And perhaps Colleen would never be the marrying kind. Maybe she was about to launch a big movie star career after all. Really, Margaret should simply be happy for her glamorous sister.

But the truth was, Margaret felt a tiny bit envious of Colleen. Maybe even more than a tiny bit. Oh, it was unreasonable and ridiculous. But it was hard to ignore the fact that, compared to the rest of them, Colleen really seemed to be enjoying this war.

After all, Colleen had been the first one to get engaged. Margaret remembered how jealous she'd felt seeing Colleen flash that fancy diamond ring under their noses. And as fate would have it, Colleen had managed to snag herself a handsome navy officer. Naturally, he was from a wealthy family too. And Colleen wasn't even nineteen yet.

And then Colleen got an exciting job—and it paid well too. Even when she complained about it, she managed to make work at the airplane factory sound glamorous and fun. Like it was some kind of social club. If that weren't enough, Colleen would take off whenever she felt like it—dressing to the nines and dancing the night away at the USO. Acting free as a bird . . . like she wasn't even engaged. And now the way she'd been lording over the rest of them due to that movie business. Well, sometimes it just didn't seem fair. Colleen was basically selfish and shallow and just plain silly . . . yet the best things in life seemed to always come her way.

Colleen hadn't expected the film crew to show up at her house on Saturday afternoon. But as Mr. Ramsay explained on the front porch, they just wanted to "get some footage of the home front women at home."

"But it's only my mother and me," she explained, trying to hide behind the door and wishing she didn't look so frumpy right now. Why hadn't anyone called to warn her? "My sisters, uh, they won't be home for dinner for a while. Not for about an hour."

"That's perfect," Mr. Ramsay assured her. "Just what I'd hoped for. May we come in?"

She reluctantly let them inside. Fortunately, Mam had recovered from her headache by now, but she hadn't gotten properly dressed yet. And Colleen, fresh out of the bathtub, had on a faded gingham dress and not a drop of makeup. And she was barefoot! Not to mention that her hair, still in pin-curls, was covered by an old blue bandana. This was a nightmare!

To make matters worse, thanks to Mam's head-ache, the living room was strewn with newspapers and other clutter. And the smell of cooked cabbage was wafting from the kitchen. Not exactly glamorous. Colleen wanted to die!

Instead, she scurried about the living room, apologizing while collecting the clutter and opening some windows to let fresh air inside. Meanwhile, she needed a way to prepare Mam for their unexpected guests.

"Excuse me," she said as the camera crew began unpacking their equipment.

With her arms still full of newspapers, Colleen burst into the kitchen. "I'm so sorry, Mam," she said quickly.

"Sorry for what?" Mam frowned. "Oh, are you cleaning up. Thank you—"

"I'm sorry. I didn't realize the film crew was coming today and—"

*"What?"* Mam stopped stirring a bowl of batter.

"They're in the living room."

"*What?*" Mam looked aghast. "Colleen Maureen Mulligan!"

"I'm sorry, Mam. I thought they planned to meet me at the USO later tonight." Colleen was on the verge of tears herself. "And look at me! I'm not ready to be filmed."

Mam waved at herself. "And me still in my housecoat—and it's nearly five o'clock. This is so humiliating!"

Colleen shoved the newspapers into the trash can. "I'll see if I can distract them while you make a beeline for your bedroom."

Mam glared at Colleen as they inched through the dining room, moving toward the doorway that led to the front room. "I cannot believe my own daughter puts me through such madness," she hissed at Colleen. "What would your dad say?"

"Shh." Colleen pressed her fingers to her lips. "I'll get their attention and you make a run for it." She stepped out and, trying to appear confident, strutted to the other side of the room. "I really must apologize," she said brightly to the crew. "We hadn't expected you fellows to show up here in our home today." She forced a big smile as she patted her bandana-wrapped head. Meanwhile Mam scurried unnoticed across the other side of the room. "Obviously, if I'd known you were coming, I would've done something about my appearance. Or baked you a cake." She laughed, hoping it sounded more genuine than it felt.

"We're sorry to catch you off guard," Mr. Ramsay told her. "But I must admit this is exactly what we were hoping for. We'd like to get some footage of you cooking in the kitchen. We like that you look like a normal working girl." He turned to his crew. "Are you ready?"

"But I need to fix up—"

"Nonsense," he said. "You look like a wholesome American girl. Just what we want."

"But I don't even have on shoes," she pointed out.

He frowned. "Well, yes, shoes might be good. But nothing fancy. And don't change anything else about your appearance. And don't dilly-dally. We have a lot to accomplish in the next couple of hours."

As Colleen slid her bare feet into a simple pair of black pumps, she was tempted to remove the detestable bandana and style her hair, but knew it would take too long. Although she did compromise with a quick swipe of lipstick. And she pinched her cheeks. Then, feeling like a complete failure as a starlet, she returned to discover they had already set up their equipment in the kitchen.

"Now it's time for you to cook," Mr. Ramsay instructed her.

"Cook?" she said meekly.

"You do know how to cook, don't you?"

"Oh, yes." She forced a guilty smile. "Of course I do." And the truth was she could boil water and peel potatoes. But anyone in her family would laugh if they thought she was passing herself off as a cook. She picked up the bowl of batter that Mam had been working on and cautiously proceeded to stir it, smiling for the cameramen with each turn of the wooden spoon . . . and wondering what on earth she thought she was doing.

# Seven

"Just act natural," Mr. Ramsay instructed Colleen. "No need to smile. Just maintain a pleasant expression . . . as if you're delighted to be making your family's dinner tonight. But perhaps you're a bit worn out after a long day working at the airplane factory."

She simply nodded, dimming down her bright smile and even using the back of her hand, feigning to daub a damp forehead. She knew from the meeting they'd had last week that they didn't expect her to actually speak for the film. She'd been informed that there would be a narrative voice-over throughout the movie as well as a lot of editing to make it flow smoothly. But they did want facial expressions from her—and she'd been practicing in front of her mirror every evening.

"What are you making?" Sid the script man asked her, his pencil ready to record her answer for his notes.

"I, uh, biscuits." She frowned at the batter, realizing it was too runny for biscuits. She wished that Mam had used a cookbook for a change. And then she noticed the greased muffin tin nearby. "I mean muffins."

"What kind of muffins?" he asked.

She glanced over the kitchen counter and saw an unopened can of blueberries by the sink. "Blueberry muffins."

"And what else?" He pointed his pencil to the big cast iron pot on the stove.

Fortunately, she knew the answer to this one. "Corned beef and cabbage." As she stirred the batter, she explained how the Mulligans were Irish and how this meal was one of her father's favorite dishes.

"You told us that your father suffers from tuberculosis." Sid said. "And that he's in a sanatorium. But you didn't mention how long. Or when he'll come home."

Colleen's pleasant expression faded. "He's been there about six months, and we don't know for sure when he'll be home."

"Never mind that now," Mr. Ramsay said quickly. "Just focus on the muffins, Colleen. I'd like to get her filling the muffin tin. And then checking on the corned beef and cabbage. And when the sisters come home, we can get them all working together. Setting the table and such." He clasped his hands with a grin. "This is all just perfect. Absolutely perfect."

"I think that's enough stirring," the head cameraman said. "How about filling the muffin tin now."

"But she needs to put in the blueberries," Mr. Ramsay pointed out.

"Get her opening the can," Sid said. "We'll tie that to the grocery store somehow."

And so, using her pleasant but weary expression, Colleen opened the can. This was a kitchen skill she was comfortable with. She stared down at the dark purple contents in the can, then shrugged. Carrying it over to the bowl, she proceeded to dump it into the batter. But now as she stirred, it all turned purple and the batter became very runny. But instead of registering her concern, she just continued to stir with the cameras running.

"Oh, there you are," Mr. Ramsay smiled at Mam as she came into the kitchen.

"Uh, yes." Mam looked uneasy as she came over to where Colleen was still stirring. "What have you done?" she demanded.

Colleen made a sheepish smile for the cameras. "Actually, my mom is the cook."

"You've ruined the muffins!" Mam shook her head. "Give me that."

"Keep the cameras running," Mr. Ramsay said. "This will be good. The mother showing her daughter how to cook."

"Except that I arrived too late." Mam scowled down at the runny purple mess. "I don't even know if I can salvage this."

"I'm sorry." Colleen stepped back, embarrassed and ready to bolt from the kitchen. This wasn't going at all how she'd imagined.

"I'll see what I can do," Mam muttered.

"Let's get some footage of Colleen checking on that corned beef and cabbage now," Mr. Ramsay said.

"Just don't ruin it," Mam warned her. "You know as well as anyone that you are *not* a cook."

The crew just laughed as Colleen, thoroughly humiliated, proceeded to lift up the lid and peek in the covered pot. Trying to ignore their amusement, she even dipped a spoon in, just like she'd often seen Mam do, and pretended to taste the broth.

"No, no," Mr. Ramsay told her. "I like that you did that, Colleen, but make it look natural. Act like there are no cameras rolling."

Colleen tried again, but Mr. Ramsay still didn't like it. And the third time she ended up slopping hot broth on the front of her dress. She was doing it for about the fifth time, and fighting real frustration, when she heard the back door open. Suddenly Margaret and Molly were bursting into the kitchen.

"There," Mr. Ramsay called out. "I think we can use that one. Cut." Suddenly the kitchen was extremely crowded and noisy and Colleen was trying to maintain some composure as she introduced her sisters to Mr. Ramsay and the crew.

"You're just in time," Mr. Ramsay told the newcomers. "I think Colleen here needs a break."

He winked at her. "How about we get some footage of these other lovely young ladies while you go fix your hair for the rest of the filming." He held up a finger. "But don't overdo it. I want you to look like you're really helping to fix dinner. You can get dolled up before we head over to the USO. And don't take too long either."

As she hurried upstairs to her bedroom, Colleen was grateful to get out of the kitchen. None of this was going the way she'd planned. And when she saw her bedraggled image in the mirror, she wanted to scream! Had she really allowed them to film her looking like this? She would have to convince Mr. Ramsay not to use it. And now, despite his warning not to overdo it, Colleen quickly applied full makeup. Somehow she had to put her best foot forward here.

As she hurriedly styled her platinum blonde hair, one of her best assets, she decided to wear her navy blue skirt along with her pale blue cashmere sweater set. Slightly matronly, but understated enough for the kitchen. By the time she returned to the kitchen, Mam, Margaret, and Molly had everything—including the film crew—under control. Mam was setting corned beef and cabbage on a serving plate and Margaret was removing muffins from the tin.

"Wait right there, Colleen." Mr. Ramsay pointed to the dining room. "We need to finish off this sequence before we can use you again."

Colleen lingered in the doorway, feeling a bit jealous as she watched the cameras continuing to roll. Were her sisters stealing her thunder?

"Let's do that again, Molly," Mr. Ramsay commanded. "Just like you did it before, but I want a camera getting you from the other side. Henry, reposition yourself by the backdoor. There, that looks like a good angle. This little girl has a pretty profile. I want to catch it just right."

Molly returned to gathering dishes from the cupboard, as if she were preparing to set the table. But she looked relaxed and natural, as if she were oblivious to the crowded film crew that had invaded the overly warm kitchen.

"Keep going," Mr. Ramsay told them. "Molly, you go ahead and carry the dishes into the dining room." He backed up now, nearly stepping on Colleen. "Oh, you!" he exclaimed. "Get out of the way. Hurry!"

Colleen moved out of the doorway, watching as Molly proceeded with the stack of dishes in her hands.

"Colleen, please! Out of way! Leave the dining room," Mr. Ramsay barked.

"Maybe she could help set the table," Molly said as she continued coming into the dining room, setting the plates down on the big table.

"Not this time," Mr. Ramsay moved out of the way of the second cameraman. "Keep rolling."

Standing in the living room and peering around the corner into the dining room, Colleen watched as her baby sister proceeded to set the table. She had on a hand-me-down plaid dress that Colleen had refashioned for herself several years ago by adding a crisp white collar and cuffs. But it still looked good. And Molly, with her cheeks slightly flushed from the warm kitchen and her hair curling naturally on her shoulders, actually looked rather pretty. And probably photogenic too. Judging by Mr. Ramsay's expression, he thought so. This did not bode well for Colleen.

"Cut," he yelled. "Let's try it again. This time Colleen can help Molly." He tossed out some instructions on where to stand and what to do and Colleen attempted to follow them. But as she was reaching for a dinner plate, Mr. Ramsay yelled "Cut!" again. Then, shaking a finger at her, he chastised her for reaching across Molly. "Let her hand you the plate," he said.

They tried it a second time, but once again, Mr. Ramsay was displeased. "Don't block Molly from the camera," he told her. By the fourth time they got it right but Colleen felt thoroughly flustered. Nothing about this was going as it ought.

"Okay, now," Mr. Ramsay called out. "I want to get the whole family eating dinner at the table together." He instructed how the women would sit on three sides of the table, positioning the cameras opposite them.

"You're going to film us *eating?*" Mam sounded slightly horrified.

"We just need some footage of you all sitting together with food on the table. We don't actually need to film you eating. Just visiting happily, passing the dishes around. And, oh yes, someone should say a blessing to start with." He pointed to Molly. "You can do that, young lady. And don't worry about what you say. We don't have sound. You can just pretend."

"But if I'm asking a blessing, it's not pretend," Molly told him.

He chuckled. "Yes, good. I like that."

By the time they were all seated at the table, trying to act natural, Colleen was seething inside. But, reminding herself that a real actress would conceal her true emotions, she tried to maintain a pleasant expression as they all bowed their heads.

Finally, Mr. Ramsay yelled "Cut" and, excusing himself and his crew, they removed themselves from the dining room. "You girls go ahead and enjoy your dinner. The boys and I will go grab a bite to eat in town. But we'll be back here by seven-thirty to film Colleen getting ready for the USO dance." He pointed at Margaret. "You will play the older sister, helping Colleen with her hair and makeup. Maybe we'll make it look like you're loaning her your dress." He pointed at Colleen. "So don't change into it until we've filmed Margaret handing it over to you." He turned to Molly. "You can be looking on. Maybe sharing some beauty tips. Or loaning some jewelry. This scene will be about the other sisters helping Colleen for her big night out."

"Just like real life." Margaret's tone was tinged with sarcasm as the men were leaving.

Molly giggled. "Isn't that funny, Colleen? Margaret and me helping you get ready for a date. As if you've ever *needed* our help."

"This is a fiasco," Colleen declared as she laid down her fork. "And I'm not hungry." She stood to leave.

"Your manners, Colleen Maureen?" Mam demanded.

"I'm sorry," Colleen muttered. "Please, excuse me."

"You are excused. And don't you forget that we are cooperating with these men because of *you,*" Mam reminded her in a sharp tone. "A little gratitude would be nice."

"Thank you." Colleen turned away from them, rolling her eyes upward with aggravation as she exited the dining room. The sooner this evening was over, the happier she would be. She went up to her room, where she'd already laid out the gown she planned to wear tonight. The gown that Margaret was going to pretend to "loan" her? Really? Colleen sat down at her dressing table and stared into the mirror. Her rushed hair and makeup had been an improvement from the earlier filming, but she knew she could bring it up several notches now. As she carefully lined her eyes, she reminded herself that there was still time to salvage her film career. She just needed to keep calm and follow Mr. Ramsay's directions as best she could. She knew by now that he was not the most patient man.

As promised, the crew returned by seven-thirty. By now Colleen had regained her composure. And still wearing her skirt and sweater, she pretended to be very grateful as Margaret handed over the gown. And she pretended to appreciate Molly's "loan" of earrings.

"Just like Cinderella," Mr. Ramsay declared as they filmed the three sisters in Colleen's bed-room. "Very nice." He nodded to the cameramen. "Cut. Now we'll let Colleen get ready for the dance. When she's done, we'll get her coming down the staircase."

"Too bad the other sisters aren't going to the USO too," Sid said. "That may be more interesting."

Mr. Ramsay rubbed his chin. "Not a bad idea."

"Oh, I can't possibly." Margaret put a hand over her midsection. "Not in my condition."

"Yes, that's probably true." Mr. Ramsay turned

to Molly. "But maybe you could go. Is she old enough for the USO?"

"She's gone before," Margaret offered. "She's already registered as a junior hostess."

"Perfect." Mr. Ramsay clapped his hands. "We'll get some footage similar to what we just did for Colleen."

Although Colleen appeared fully cooperative on the outside, handing over her pale blue gown to Margaret so that she could "loan" it to Molly, she was seething on the inside. Oh, it wasn't that she was mad at Molly. But the whole thing was just becoming more and more irksome. Wasn't this movie supposed to be about her? That was the way Mr. Ramsay had presented it. And now she was getting upstaged by her baby sister again!

The camera crew had to use lighting outside as Colleen and Molly got into the car. Mr. Ramsay's plan was to show these strong women, fully capable behind the wheel as they prepared to drive to the USO dance. But as she started Peter's car, Colleen was fed up and ready to hear the final "Cut!"

"Are you all right?" Molly asked quietly, after Colleen had driven in stony silence for several blocks.

"What?" Colleen glanced at her. "Yes, of course. I'm fine."

"It feels like you're mad about something."

Colleen blew out a loud sigh, longing for a cigarette. "I guess I'm just frustrated."

"You didn't want me to come with you to the USO tonight, did you?"

"It's not that." Colleen frowned. "It's just that none of this has turned out like I expected. I'll be relieved when it's all over with. Movie making is not what I'd call fun. And I'm sick of getting yelled at."

"Maybe you should just do what Mr. Ramsay says."

"What do you mean?" Colleen glared at her as she waited for the light to turn green. "Isn't that what I've been doing?"

"Not exactly." Molly grimaced. "He keeps telling us to pretend the cameras aren't rolling."

"So?"

"So it seems like you keep trying to *perform* for the cameras. I think that's bothering Mr. Ramsay."

"*You* are giving me acting advice now?" Colleen didn't know whether to laugh or scream.

"No, not exactly. It's just that you'd probably enjoy it more if you weren't so aware of the cameras all the time. Just be yourself, Colleen. Pretend they're not filming you. You're so pretty and lively and fun. But I don't think the cameras are catching that."

"Really? So you're saying you can tell that I'm, uh, well, a little perturbed?" Colleen bit her lip. Here she thought she'd been doing a good job acting, hiding her vexation.

"Sure . . . I can see it in your face. And I'm guessing Mr. Ramsay can see it too."

Colleen let out a loud moan.

"So why not forget about the cameras? Just be yourself. Laugh and have fun. What can it hurt?"

Colleen nodded with realization. "Okay, you may be onto something, Molly. I'll take your advice. Because honestly, I can't imagine how this evening could get any worse."

As it turned out, Molly was right. When Colleen loosened up and forgot about the cameras, not only was it more fun, but everything went much more smoothly. And when the cameramen moved about the USO dance floor, filming many of the other hostess volunteers and servicemen, Colleen didn't even feel envious. In fact, she felt relieved. And by the time the evening was over and she was driving Molly home, Colleen felt like her old self again. Well, except for one thing. Her old dream of becoming an actress felt tarnished. The limelight had lost its sparkle.

# Eight

Sometimes Margaret felt guilty for not following the war developments more closely. Early on she'd paid close attention to the military news on the radio and had read the daily reports in the newspapers. But so much of the news was disturbing—and even more so with the knowledge that Brian would eventually see active duty. After all, his army training wouldn't last forever. And the thought of her baby's father getting injured—or worse—well, it was more than she could bear. So she simply quit paying attention altogether.

Perhaps she was a silly ostrich with her head in the sand, but ignoring the news seemed the best way to get through this war. If the entire world were to continue falling apart like this, well, she just didn't want to hear about it. Her pregnancy became her excuse for not keeping up with current events. It wasn't good for the baby.

"I'll bet Brian is going to Algiers," Molly announced as they sat around the living room after dinner on Sunday night.

"Where is Algiers?" Mam asked absently.

"Africa," Molly informed her.

"Africa?" Colleen looked up from her magazine. "Why would Brian be sent to Africa?"

Molly held up a geography book so they could all see. "Algiers is in North Africa." She pointed to a spot on a colorful map. "Right here. My social studies teacher is predicting that US troops will be going there. Maybe as soon as this summer. Or early fall."

"Why do they want troops in Africa?" Colleen asked. "I thought we were supposed to fight against the Axis in Europe."

Margaret bristled to hear Colleen's interest. She used to be the one who never wanted to hear about these things. But it seemed working at the airplane factory and being engaged to a pilot had gotten Colleen more and more involved.

"Algiers is a key location." Molly pointed to the map again. "See, it's not that far from Spain. If the Allies can get control of key places like this, we can block shipments to the Axis. Plus, it puts us closer to the potential battlefield. Maybe even positioned for an invasion of—"

"Please." Margaret laid down her knitting. "If you're determined to talk about this stupid war, I will have to excuse myself to my room."

"Oh, Margaret." Molly closed her book. "I forgot that it bothers you to hear details about the war. I just find it so interesting."

Margaret looked down at her rounded midsection. "Well, I find it very disturbing. For both me and the baby."

Molly came over, placing a hand on Margaret's

shoulder. "I'm sorry." She pointed to the knitting. "What's that going to be?"

Margaret held up the yellow piece she was working on. "A baby sweater. This is a sleeve. I'm almost done with it. I just need to bind off."

Molly examined it, turning it so that the cuff came together. "It's so little and sweet. Can you imagine your baby's chubby little hand popping out of here?"

Margaret smiled. "Yes, I can."

"I can't wait to become an auntie."

"And I'm sorry I can't tolerate these discussions of war." Margaret sighed.

"No, no, I understand," Molly assured her. "I totally forgot." She set the geography book aside. "Anyway, I need to write a letter to Patrick tonight. I guess I better get to it."

"Are you going to tell him that you went to the USO with me last night—or that you were filmed for the movie?" Colleen used a teasing tone. "You know he probably won't approve."

Molly's brow creased. "I'll do my best to make him understand I was simply trying to do my part for the war effort." She brightened. "At least I'll have something interesting to write to him about for a change."

"That's a good point." Margaret put her materials back into the knitting bag. "Maybe I should write to Brian about it too."

Molly went over to Colleen. "How about you?

Are you going to tell Geoff about how it went?"

Colleen just shrugged. "Maybe I'll wait until I'm all done with it, then give him the full report."

"You still haven't heard from him, have you?" Margaret asked.

"You know I haven't." Colleen's voice was sharp. "No mail on Sunday."

"But I saw you light a candle for him at mass this morning," Molly said gently.

"He's probably just too busy to write." Colleen flipped a page, acting as if the cigarette advertisement was extremely interesting. "Maybe I am too."

As Margaret stood, she considered challenging Colleen about this ridiculous statement, but she knew she'd already goaded her enough these past few days. Still, as Margaret went for her stationery set, Colleen's lackadaisical attitude aggravated her. It was just plain selfish, not to mention disrespectful to Geoff. Sometimes Margaret had half a mind to write Geoff herself— and to tell him what a mistake he'd made in engaging himself to someone like Colleen and encourage him to find another girl, someone who could be loyal and supportive. But she knew that would be wrong. Sisters didn't do that to each other.

Before long, Molly and Margaret were sitting across from each other at the kitchen table—

their favorite place to write letters. Although it had been warm today, a breeze off the bay had cooled everything nicely. When Molly offered to make them tea, Margaret happily accepted. So with the radio quietly playing a classical musical program and with no more talk of the war raging all around the world, Margaret relaxed, simply soaking up the homey moment. And as usual, as she started her letter to Brian, she said a prayer for him to remain safe throughout the war . . . and to come home to her and their child. It didn't seem too much to ask.

After having had a whole day to consider how the filming had gone, Colleen felt a bit more enthusiasm as she went into the airplane factory on Monday. Perhaps she'd made a mountain out of a molehill about the whole thing. After all, once she'd taken her baby sister's advice— to relax and have fun—it hadn't been so bad. And having the cameras following her around at work might be interesting.

At least she'd had time to get herself fixed up this morning. Even with her hair tied back with a scarf—a pretty one—and wearing trousers and a cute gingham shirt as well as full makeup, she felt much more photogenic than she had on Saturday when the film crew had caught her off guard. *But today is a new day,* she told herself as she put her handbag in her locker.

"Hello, Hollywood." Audrey grinned at her. "I just saw your camera crew."

"They're here already?" Colleen checked her image in the small foggy mirror next to the door, making sure no lipstick was on her teeth.

"Yep. They were heading upstairs. Probably talking to management. How did it go this weekend? Did they film you at the USO like you'd planned?"

"Not exactly like I'd planned." Colleen frowned and quickly told her about being surprised by the film crew on Saturday afternoon.

Audrey laughed. "Now that's a movie I'd like to see."

"Hopefully those scenes will end up on the cutting room floor." She adjusted her scarf, securing a bobby pin to hold it in place. "I plan to ask Mr. Ramsay to make sure that they do."

Audrey's pale brows arched as she opened the door. "You really think you have that kind of pull?"

"I sure hope so." Colleen held her head high as the two of them walked through the factory, where other workers were going to their stations.

"Well, good luck, Hollywood." Audrey chuckled.

Colleen stopped at her station, unsure as to whether she was really supposed to work now or be ready to cooperate with the film crew. But when no one showed up, she felt guilty for being idle and started her tasks. She was still working when the noon whistle blew for lunch break. Catching up with Audrey in the locker room, she quietly asked her if she'd seen the film crew around.

"You didn't hear?" Audrey looked surprised.

"Hear what?"

"I assumed they told you."

"Told me what?" Colleen asked in irritation.

"They decided to use Bernice for the airplane factory part of their film."

"Instead of me?" Colleen felt her cheeks growing hot.

"Yes. I heard it's because she actually works with the big tools. You know, like a real Rosie the Riveter."

"Oh." Colleen slowly nodded.

"Or . . ." Audrey lowered her voice. "Maybe her dad intervened."

Colleen felt utterly deflated as she got her lunch sack from her locker. If she'd had a tail, she would've tucked it between her legs as she went over to a table.

"At least you'll be in part of the movie," Audrey said gently.

Colleen barely nodded.

Audrey patted her on the shoulder. "Poor Hollywood."

Colleen attempted a smile. "It's okay. To be honest, I kind of discovered that being in a film wasn't nearly as glamorous as I'd imagined it would be. The truth is, it's a lot of work. I think I'm actually relieved to know I'm done."

"Colleen." Bernice waved eagerly at her. "Did you hear the news?"

Colleen forced a bigger smile as she peeled waxed paper from her liverwurst sandwich. "Yes. I'm so glad you get to be in the movie too. I was just telling Audrey that I was a little worn out from all the filming we did this weekend. It's a relief that they found someone else to do the factory filming." She gave a tired sigh. "I found it rather exhausting."

"Exhausting?" Bernice's brown eyes grew big. "I think it's exciting and invigorating."

"Oh, well, of course. But you've only been doing it a few hours." Colleen took a bite.

"Maybe. But I'll be doing it for the rest of the day. Maybe even into the evening shift. And I'm looking forward to it." She patted her hair, which was devoid of any hairnet or scarf. "Mr. Ramsay keeps saying I'm a natural." She giggled. "And that I may even have a future in film. Can you imagine?"

Colleen nearly choked. Instead of responding, she simply nodded.

"That's all well and good," Audrey said. "But you'll excuse us to eat our lunch, Bernice." She pointed to Bernice's lunchbox. "You should have yours too. You may need your strength for later."

Bernice just laughed. "I'm not the least bit hungry. I think I'm too excited to eat." But at least she took the hint and left.

*"I'm too excited to eat,"* Colleen mimicked her quietly.

Audrey laughed.

"Do you think Mr. Ramsay really said that?" Colleen whispered to Audrey.

"Said what?" Audrey paused from peeling her orange.

"That Bernice is a natural."

Audrey shrugged.

Colleen suppressed the urge to throw her sandwich across the lunchroom. This was so unfair! What about the contract she'd signed with Mr. Ramsay? Didn't that mean anything? What right did he have to get her hopes up and then to drop her like this? It was wrong. Wrong. Wrong. Wrong!

"Are you okay?" Audrey peered closely at Colleen.

"Yeah, just fine." Colleen wadded up her bag, which still contained some uneaten lunch, and tossed it into the nearby trash can. "I'm just too excited to eat," she said again. "I'm going back to work."

"But it's not even—"

"I don't care," she snapped at Audrey. "What? Are you going to discipline me for working during my lunch hour now?"

"No, of course not." Audrey shook her head. "Just take it easy, Hollywood."

"And quit calling me that!" Colleen turned on her heel, storming out of the lunchroom and feeling like a spoiled five-year-old. She knew her coworkers were watching her with amusement. But, really, what did she care what they thought?

The afternoon seemed to crawl along at a snail's pace. Every time Colleen looked at her watch it seemed only a few minutes had passed. Would this workday ever end? Several times she had to resist the urge to march through the factory—to wherever Mr. Ramsay and the film crew were working—and demand to know why they thought they could treat her like this. Fortunately, she didn't.

But when she saw Bernice walking through the factory, with the film crew following her like devoted fans, it took every ounce of Colleen's self-control to keep her head down and pretend to focus on her work. Taking in a long deep breath, she slowly counted to ten. Then exhaled. And then she counted to ten again. And again. Until Bernice's entourage finally moved on.

By the time the whistle blew, signifying the end of the workday, Colleen was exhausted. As she went to her car, her head was throbbing and her feet felt like someone had tied lead weights to them. Fortunately, Audrey had the good sense to keep quiet while Colleen drove her home.

And then, instead of going home herself, Colleen drove down toward Golden Gate Park.

Before long, she was walking through the National Cemetery and finally standing in front of the stone that served as a memorial to her brother's short-lived life. "Oh, Peter." Her voice choked in a sob. "I miss you so much. I know if you were still here, you would've told me I was being silly about that movie. You would've tried to straighten me out. Just like you always used to do. But I probably wouldn't have listened." She pulled a handkerchief from her pocket, wiping her eyes. "But if you were here right now . . . I think I'd be ready to listen. I'd agree with you and say you were right. Even if you told me that I'm just a flibbertigibbet, I would agree." She pulled out a cigarette, sighing as she lit it. "Is that what you'd tell me?

"Okay, I know what you'd say." She held out the cigarette. "You'd tell me to stop smoking." She took a long drag then dropped the cigarette to the ground, grinding it out with her heel. "And maybe I will, Peter. Maybe I'll quit for you."

Her tears started to flow even more freely now. Partly for Peter and partly for herself. "I miss you, Peter," she whispered. "I miss you so much it hurts deep inside of me." She blew her nose. "I hate this stupid war. I hate that it took you from us. I know you were a hero—you gave

102

your life for your country. But I still hate it."
She sighed deeply, still longing for a cigarette.
"But I love you, Peter. I will always love you.
And maybe I will start growing up now. Maybe I
will become more sensible . . . like you were. I'll
try." She shoved her wet handkerchief into her
trouser pocket. "I love you, big brother."

As she walked back to the car, she felt calmer.
And stronger too. Her thoughts moved on to
Geoff while she drove home. She wondered what
he would say to her right now. Would he just
laugh this whole thing off, like she'd told
Margaret he would do? Or would he be
disappointed in her? What if he really had reacted
to her letter the way Margaret kept claiming any
"normal" man would do? What if Geoff had
fallen out of love and no longer wanted to marry
her? What if she'd hurt him too much?

Colleen felt sick with worry by the time she
got home. Suddenly she missed Geoff more than
ever. If only there was a V-mail letter waiting for
her in the mailbox. But, although there was one
for Molly—from her soldier friend Tommy—
there was nothing for Colleen. What a fool she'd
been! A shallow little fool. What if her stupidity
had cost her everything?

Relieved that no one else was home yet, Colleen
grabbed her box of stationery. As she opened it,
the familiar scent of Chanel No. 5 wafted around
her. She had liberally doused the pretty stationery

before writing her first letter to Geoff. That seemed so long ago now. With trembling hands, she removed a blank sheet, then picked up her fountain pen and started to write, pouring out her heart so quickly that the page soon filled.

Dear Geoff,
I want to apologize for the last letter I wrote to you. I bragged about how I was going to be in a movie. As if I had become some famous film star, which turned out to be completely wrong. I was a great big flop. I have no interest in Hollywood now. I also told you about going to the USO and dancing with the servicemen, acting like that was such a valiant war effort on my part. I know I must've sounded just like the flibbertigibbet that my family has always accused me of being. I'm sorry.

Meanwhile you're across the ocean, facing all sorts of dangers, risking your life, fighting for our country. You are so brave and fine and good, Geoff. Margaret is right—you really do deserve someone better than me. I wouldn't blame you if you went out looking for her. I think about my sister Bridget and how she's on some South Pacific island working so hard to help wounded soldiers. Maybe she is in a hospital near you somewhere.

Anyway, I know you deserve a good girl like Bridget. And I know there are plenty of wonderful girls to choose from. Especially for a guy like you. I still wonder why you picked someone like me, Geoff. You could have any girl. And you really do deserve a good one! Someone who's a better letter writer too!

Even so, I desperately hope you won't go looking for a better girl. Because I do love you, Geoff. And if you still love me, I am willing to marry you whenever you want. I know that I was the one who wanted to wait, but I have changed my mind. If you still want me, all you need to do is to pick the day. You tell me when and where, and I will be there. With bells on!

But if you don't love me anymore, Geoff, I will try to understand. Please, darling, just tell me. Don't be silent. I keep looking for your letter. But it's not there. So I tell my family that it's just because you are so busy flying around and fighting this blasted war. But I know it could be something else. It could be that you are done with me. And even though it would break my heart to hear that, I would rather hear it than continue not knowing.

I'm so sorry, Geoff. I'm sorry I didn't appreciate you enough. I'm sorry I wrote you that stupid, stupid letter. And I'm sorry I'm not a better letter writer. I should ask Molly to give me lessons! But if you still love me, I will try to do better. I promise I will, darling. I'm ready to grow up now. Please, be safe, Geoff. Don't let this horrid war take you away from me. Not like it took my brother. I need you. I want to be your wife. I love you with all my heart.

Yours truly,
Colleen

P.S. I have given up smoking cigarettes.

# Nine

*Mid-June 1942*

Colleen knew that it could take a couple of weeks before she received a response from Geoff. However, she sincerely believed that he would respond. And she hoped that he would respond favorably. In the meantime, she was determined to think positively—and true to her promise to her brother, she really had quit smoking. Sure, it was only five days so far—and it wasn't easy to resist those urges. Especially at work, where so many of the employees liked to light up during break times. Sometimes Colleen had to just go outside and take a little walk. During these strolls she would often say a prayer for Geoff—asking God to keep him safe . . . for her. Praying like this was another new habit for her. But she liked it. For the first time, Colleen felt like perhaps she really was going to grow up into a responsible adult.

"Are you nervous?" she asked Molly as she drove her to the Department of Motor Vehicles to take her driver's license test. It was Molly's last day of school, and since it was Friday and a busy day at the store, Colleen had gotten off work early just to do this for Molly.

"Yeah." Molly nodded. "Maybe I should've driven there like you'd suggested."

"It's not too late." Colleen looked for a spot to pull over.

"Do you think I should practice parking again?" Molly asked after she got behind the wheel.

"That's up to you."

Molly prudently decided to parallel park. Due to the hour, traffic was busy, but to Colleen's relief, Molly aced it. "That was fabulous," Colleen told her. "I can't even park that well. Nice work."

"Thanks. Mrs. Bartley has been coaching me on it."

"You're going to do just fine on your test," Colleen assured her as Molly pulled up to the DMV building. "You're much better prepared than I was when I took mine. And I passed." Colleen chuckled as they got out. "Although I think the guy testing me went easy on me. I mean, considering I ran a stop sign."

Molly laughed. "That's probably because he was smitten by your beauty."

"Well, you go smite them too." Colleen nodded to the waiting area. "I'll be right here. Come get me if you need anything."

"I should be okay." Molly held up her paper-work. "Mam already signed the permission form."

"Good luck!" Colleen glanced through the dog-eared magazines as she sat down and, not seeing anything she liked, picked up the newspaper instead. It wasn't the *Herald*, like they got at home, but one of the more "liberal" newspapers. Like the *Herald*, though, these headlines were all related to the war. Colleen wondered if the time would come when front pages would cover other items of interest. Not until this war was over.

She skimmed over a story related to the Battle of Midway. Midway had been the hottest news for the past week. Everyone at work was still talking about how the US Navy dealt a severe blow to the Imperial Japanese Navy by seizing a very strategic island in the center of the Pacific—and almost exactly six months after the attack on Pearl Harbor. As more news stories surfaced, the victory just seemed to get better and better. People had been in a celebratory mood. There was great satisfaction to hear that numerous Japanese ships were successfully sunk. Many news sources claimed Midway as a turning point in the war.

However, this article reported how the Japanese military was seeking brutal revenge in other parts of the South Pacific, suggesting that as a result of the Battle of Midway, Japan wanted to unleash all its powers to attack and destroy every US military base in and around the Philippines. All US servicemen, the newspapers seemed to say, were in grave danger just now. Colleen laid down the newspaper with a shudder. She didn't want to read another word. Was she starting to act like Margaret? Perhaps ignorance truly would be blissful.

"Bad news?" A middle-aged gentleman picked up the paper she'd just discarded, his brows arching with interest.

"Oh . . . I just don't like hearing about the Japanese retaliation for the Battle of Midway." She pointed to the newspaper. "Nasty stuff."

He adjusted his glasses as he scanned the article, then finally laid down the newspaper with a sigh. "That's disheartening."

"Especially if you've got loved ones serving over there," she said sadly.

"And you do?" he asked.

"Yes. My sister is an army nurse and my fiancé is a navy pilot. I don't know exactly where they're stationed, but we think it's near the Philippines."

He frowned. "I hear it's been pretty rough around the Philippines. My son is in the navy too, but he's still stationed in Honolulu."

"My brother was there," Colleen said quietly. "He didn't survive Pearl Harbor."

"I'm sorry." He grimly shook his head. "But from what I've been reading about some of our less fortunate servicemen"—he nodded to the newspaper—"especially near the Philippines, being held captive in a Japanese prison camp sounds like a fate worse than death. Deplorable conditions. Inhumane treatment. Needless to say, the Imperial Japanese military have no regard for the Geneva Convention."

Thanks to Bridget, Colleen knew a bit about the Geneva Convention—that it was supposed to be a set of rules that governed war, supposedly to keep things running "fairly." If that were even possible. "What's the use of the Geneva Convention if countries like Japan, and probably Germany too, don't even abide by those rules?"

"Good question." He waved over a young man, who was grinning happily from the counter area. "That's my boy," he said proudly. "Looks like he just passed his driver's test."

"Good for him. My sister is taking her test right now."

The man's smile faded. "I'm just thankful Larry is only sixteen—and I pray to God this war gets wrapped up before he turns eighteen."

"Two whole years . . ." She sighed to think of waiting that long before life returned to normal. "I sure hope it ends sooner than that."

He looked grim. "I wouldn't count on it."

Molly literally danced out the door of the DMV. "I can drive all by myself," she announced. "I'm legal."

Colleen patted her back. "Nice work, Molly. I knew you'd ace it."

"I didn't even run a stop sign." Molly poked Colleen in the arm.

"Go ahead, rub it in. Pretty soon you'll probably be a better driver than me too." Colleen was digging through her handbag.

"Looking for cigarettes?" Molly teased.

"No." Colleen wrinkled her nose. "Keys."

Molly jingled the keys in front of her. "Can I drive?"

"Sure." Colleen snapped her handbag closed.

"You can smoke if you want to," Molly told her as they got in the car. "It doesn't really bother me. Not like it does Margaret and Mam."

"For your information—and if you can keep it under your hat—I have given up smoking."

Molly turned to stare at her sister. "Are you kidding?"

"It's been less than a week, but I think I can do it. Just don't tell, okay?"

"Loose lips sink ships." Molly repeated a slogan from one of the posters that hung in her school. Now she patted Colleen on the back. "Congratulations on quitting smoking. Mam and Dad and Margaret will be glad to hear it. Bridget will be too. I'll write to her about it this weekend."

Colleen seemed extra quiet as Molly drove toward home. "Are you feeling okay?" Molly carefully parked Dad's car in front of the house, handing Colleen the keys.

Colleen's smile looked weak, but instead of answering, she got out of the car, hurrying up to the house.

Molly paused to check the mailbox, which was empty. "You seem sad, Colleen." She studied her sister as they went inside. "Is it because you gave up cigarettes?"

Colleen rolled her eyes. "No, that's not it."

"Then what is it?"

"I don't know." Colleen sighed as she set her handbag on the hall-tree by the front door. "Probably this war. It gets me down."

"Have you heard from Geoff?" Molly asked quietly.

"What do you think?"

Molly shrugged. "I don't know. I guess I was hoping you'd gotten a letter but had kept it to yourself. Kind of like quitting smoking."

Colleen stood up straighter. "Well, I plan on hearing from him. To be honest—and here's another thing you can keep to yourself—I wrote him a heartfelt letter on Monday. I feel certain he'll write me back as soon as he reads it. In the meantime, I'll just have to be patient. And"—she held up a finger—"I shall follow your fine example, Molly. Even though I haven't heard back yet, I'm going to write him again. Just a pleasant little letter about the recent goings-on here." She pointed to Molly. "Like how my baby sister is a licensed driver now."

Molly let out a happy sigh. "I feel like I'm almost grown-up."

"Just don't be in too much of a hurry."

Margaret was glad to have Molly available to work at the store during her summer vacation. Between Mam, Molly, and Jimmy during the week, plus Colleen sometimes on Saturdays, they were handling the work load fairly well. The trouble was that she wasn't sure how long they could manage like this. And come September, Molly would be back in school . . . and in October the baby would come. Margaret knew that somehow, they would have to hire another full-time employee. The problem was that, according to her bookkeeping, that was nearly impossible.

Thanks to shortages, government rationing, increased wholesale costs, and the wartime frugality of the average customer, the store's profit line was shrinking. Not only that, but Margaret kept hearing boasts of thriving victory gardens and home-preserving plans, which suggested that the store might be doing even less business by summer's end. Add to that—rather subtract from it—the cost of Dad's ongoing treatment at the sanatorium, and the Mulligans' rocky little boat felt like it was slowly but surely sinking. Not that Margaret cared to admit this much to anyone.

If Mam were stronger, Margaret would broach

the subject with her. But lately Mam had seemed more anxious than usual—about everything. She could worry herself nearly sick over Bridget if the lapse between letters grew ever so slightly. Mam was fearful that Bridget had either contracted some dreaded tropical disease or gotten captured by the Japanese. Then they'd receive a cheerful letter from Bridget, and Mam would start fretting over Dad's condition— *would he ever get well?* Or else Mam would worry—as did Margaret—that Colleen's silly stubbornness had "lost her a good man." On top of all else, if Margaret showed the even slightest sign of weariness, Mam would instantly get worked up over the fact that she was "slaving away—and in her condition!" and would question what effect this might have on the baby. Margaret would reassure her that all was well with her and the baby—and that even the obstetrician was pleased with her condition— and then Mam's worries would move on to the Hammond boys.

For a while Margaret thought the only person safe from Mam's long worry list was Molly. Oh, Mam would comment that Molly's childhood was being taken from her—by this war! But at least she hadn't seemed too concerned over Molly's general welfare. That was, until Molly got her license and began doing deliveries for the store.

"But I can't help but think something is wrong," Mam said for the second time.

Margaret looked up from the ledger she was trying to balance. "Mam," she said with impatience, "you just need to—"

"But I'm afraid she's gotten into an automobile accident." Mam was wringing her hands with a deep crease in her brow.

"What makes you think that?" Margaret wiggled the pencil back and forth between her fingers.

"I heard sirens just now. I think it was an ambulance."

"That doesn't mean it was for Molly, Mam."

Mam motioned to the wall clock. "But she should've been back by now."

"I'm sure Molly is fine. She's probably just stuck in traffic." Margaret pointed her pencil up to the clock. "It's rush hour, you know." Then, to her relief, Jimmy called out for help in the store and Mam was forced to return to the cash register.

Margaret stared at the column of numbers, trying to determine an answer to what was becoming a perplexing question. *How to make ends meet?* Not just this month, but in the upcoming months. Already Colleen contributed some to the household budget. But she could easily contribute more. It was a shame that her sister hadn't married Geoff when she had the

116

chance. An officer's pay wasn't much, but it certainly helped. Margaret knew she could ask Bridget to help out, but Bridget was working so hard and getting paid so little—it seemed miserly to expect her to send it home.

If Dad were healthier, Margaret might go to him for advice. But she knew that would only load him down with more guilt. He already felt terrible for being so helpless right now. Plus he had no idea how much his expensive stay at the sanatorium was costing his family. And she hoped he never did! Nor did she want him to know how the family business was actually faring. When she went to visit him, which wasn't much once she'd discovered she was pregnant, Margaret had always painted a cheery picture for how well the store was doing. If Dad could see this ledger, it would probably set him back in his treatment. It might even kill him. No, this seemed to be Margaret's burden to carry alone. Even though Brian was a sharp businessman, she wouldn't write to him about it—it would only worry him.

"I'm back," Molly sang out as she came in through the backdoor.

"Oh, good." Margaret went out to meet her. "Go show yourself to Mam. She has practically given you up for dead."

Molly laughed. "I got stuck in a traffic jam on the bridge. I think maybe there was a wreck in the city, but it must've gotten cleared up before I got there."

"Well, don't tell Mam about the wreck. It'll just plant more worry seeds in her head."

Molly nodded vigorously. "Don't I know it! I'll just tell her about the lovely view I had while sitting on the Golden Gate Bridge for almost an hour on a clear, bright, and beautiful day."

"Perfect." Margaret turned back to her book-keeping.

"Margaret?" Molly was still standing by her desk.

"Huh?" Margaret looked up.

"Are you okay?" Molly frowned. "I don't want to sound like Mam, but you've seemed, well, sort of blue lately. Are you missing Brian?"

Margaret forced a smile. "Of course I'm missing Brian, you silly goose!"

"But is it something more?" Molly peered down at the ledger. "Is the store in trouble?"

Margaret put her hand over the figures, wanting to protect her baby sister from the harsh realities of life, but knowing that Molly was too sharp and too quick. "Molly," she said slowly. "I don't want to burden you, but the store is, well, it could be . . . in a little trouble."

"What kind of trouble?"

To Margaret's relief, Molly's question was calm and even. And so, without going into all the details, Margaret explained.

"I've thought about how many people are growing victory gardens," Molly finally said. "And it gave me an idea."

"What's that?"

"We should stock in a lot of canning supplies to sell to customers, Margaret. Mrs. Bartley was showing me some things about canning, and she told me she needs some of the newer jars and lids and rings and paraffin and all sorts of things. Because hers are old and undependable. And you don't want to waste your time and vegetables only to have them spoil. And Mam's never canned, so we don't have any of those things in our house. I'll bet a lot of people in town will need them too."

"That's an excellent idea, Molly." Margaret made a note to look into canning supplies.

"And I've wondered about something else," Molly said with hesitation.

"What's that?"

"What if we were more than just a grocery store?"

"What do you mean? What would we carry?"

"Mr. Alder said rubber is on the ration list. He predicts boots and shoes with rubber soles will be hard to come by before long. What if we stocked up with some of those?"

Margaret frowned. "Shoes and boots and groceries?"

Molly shrugged. "Maybe we could divide the store. Have one side for groceries and one side for dry goods. And then we'd try to be really smart about what we stocked. Make sure we've got the things people will need and want."

Margaret considered this. "I'll give this some thought." She gave Molly a little nudge. "In the meantime, go reassure Mam that you're still in one piece, okay?"

Molly grinned. "Okay. But can we talk about this again later? I have some other ideas too."

"I'll bet you do!" Margaret couldn't help but laugh. "Yes, for sure, we will talk more later. But don't mention any of this to Mam."

"Loose lips sink ships." Molly giggled.

Margaret sighed. And returning to her ledger, she wondered if her baby sister might actually come up with a viable solution for saving the Mulligan's sinking boat.

# Ten

*Late June 1942*

Molly was the first one to the mailbox when they all came home after a long Saturday working at the store. But when she saw all three V-mail letters in the mailbox were addressed to her, she immediately felt guilty and, tucking the letters under her arm, hurried into the house.

"Hey, not so fast." Colleen put her hand on Molly's shoulder. "Are all three of those really for you?"

"Yes." Molly nodded.

"None for me?" Margaret said in a forlorn tone.

"Sorry." Molly held up the V-mail for everyone to see.

"Who are they from?" Mam asked.

"Well, this one's from Bridget," Molly said brightly. "So that's kind of like for the whole family. And this one's from Patrick, which is kind of to the whole family too. And the last one is from Tommy."

"Isn't that one for the whole family too?" Colleen teased.

"Sure." Molly nodded. "I'll read all of them to everyone after dinner."

"Which reminds me." Mam took off her hat.

121

"The Hammonds are coming tonight. Louise is bringing a tuna casserole—and cherry pie for dessert. Goodness, they will be here any minute now."

Suddenly all four of them were rushing around, setting the table, cooking green beans, making tea, and generally freshening up. And before long all six of them were seated around the big dining room table. Molly let out a happy sigh as they bowed their heads for the blessing. It almost felt like old times.

"It's such a treat not to have to cook dinner," Mam said gratefully as she put a generous serving of tuna casserole on a plate and handed the dish to Mr. Hammond.

"We should do this more often," Mrs. Hammond told her. "It gets a little lonely around our table . . . just the two of us."

"You'll hear no complaints from me," Mam told her.

"I was out to see Riley yesterday," Mr. Hammond announced.

"Oh?" Mam looked surprised at the mention of a visit to Dad. "Was something wrong?"

"No, not at all. I go out to visit him every couple of weeks or so. But yesterday, I must say, he looked fit as a fiddle. Almost back to his old self. He sends his best wishes to everyone."

"He's really better?" Mam visibly perked up. "That's so good to hear. I suppose I should go visit him tomorrow since it's Sunday. I've written to him a few times this month, but I haven't been out there for about three weeks. I'm overdue."

"And he told me he'll probably get released later this summer."

"Are you serious?" Mam's voice cracked with emotion. "You wouldn't just say that, would you, Jack? Just to cheer me up?"

"No, it's the honest truth. Riley told me it could be as soon as August."

"So he's really beaten this horrible disease?" Margaret asked.

"It sure sounds like it. Anyway, the doctors wouldn't release him if he hadn't, would they?"

The dining room got noisy as they all talked about this good news, excitedly discussing the happy possibility of Dad coming home. Molly couldn't even remember the last time her home felt this much alive. Perhaps life for the Mulligans was about to get better.

"So Dad will be home this fall," Margaret said wistfully as Molly and Colleen cleared the table. "He'll be here to see his first grandbaby."

"Won't that be wonderful!" Mrs. Hammond clapped her hands. "Speaking of grandbabies, I wanted to request the privilege of giving you a baby shower, Margaret. Unless someone has already spoken up."

Margaret's eyes lit up. "I'd love that!"

"Oh, good! You look at your calendar and

let me know what dates would work for you. I thought perhaps a Sunday would be best since the store is closed. Or else in the evening." Mrs. Hammond went over to get the big cherry pie that she'd set on the sideboard. "I wish we had some ice cream for this," she said as she carried it to the table. "But with rationing—"

"I'll get us some cream." Mam got up, hurrying into the kitchen. "And I'll put on some coffee too."

"Your pies are so yummy, they taste good with or without ice cream." Molly lowered her voice as she handed her a dessert plate. "Don't tell Mam, but someday I want you to give me pie baking lessons."

Mrs. Hammond laughed as she cut into the pie. "Any time, Molly."

"How's your victory garden coming?" Mr. Hammond asked Molly as she handed him a piece of pie.

"Oh, you should go look at it," Margaret told him. "Molly's got cucumbers that are ready to eat. And little green tomatoes. And peppers and all sorts of things coming on. She definitely has a green thumb."

"Maybe you could give me gardening lessons in exchange for baking lessons," Mrs. Hammond told Molly.

"We don't have a lot of room in our yard," Mr. Hammond said. "But I think the side-yard, which faces south, may be a good spot for a victory garden. Not until next summer though."

"Do you think the war will still be going by next summer?" Margaret asked timidly.

"Well . . ." He frowned. "The great war only lasted a couple of years after the United States got involved. But from what I've heard, this war could last longer."

"That's what my social studies teacher says." Molly set a piece of pie in front of Margaret. "He said that—"

"Oh, no." Margaret groaned. *"Please,* not another lesson from Mr. Alder."

"I'd like to hear what Mr. Alder said," Mr. Hammond told Molly.

"Well, he said this war will probably last longer because the battle zones are far more widespread than in the previous war. Also, the military technology has greatly improved—on both sides. And finally, because the leaders of the Axis are more determined than their predecessors simply because we beat them so soundly in the previous war."

Mr. Hammond let out a loud sigh. "And that was supposed to be the war to end all wars."

"Enough talk of war," Margaret declared. "I am sorry I asked now." She pointed to Molly. "Don't you have letters to read?"

"That's right," Mam said. "Where are today's letters?"

"Do the Hammonds want to hear too?" Molly asked.

"Of course we do!" Mrs. Hammond firmly nodded.

So Molly extracted her three letters from her skirt pocket. She'd barely had time to quickly skim them and was eager to read them more carefully. "Which one first?"

"Bridget," Mam insisted.

"Okay." Molly opened the one from Bridget. "Here goes."

Dear Molly and family,

It's now the rainy season here and everyone and everything seems to be coated in mud. So please excuse the smudges on this letter. But I have good news! Virginia arrived here last week. She's part of my unit. I cannot even describe how happy I was to see her climbing off the transport truck. And now she and I are tentmates. We have a whole three-person tent all to ourselves. Very luxurious. Poor Virginia is still getting used to the daily deprivations here. I find it amusing since she was the one who originally came up with the idea of the two of us joining the ANC. And here I've been all these months, and now I'm showing her the ropes.

I've made a good friend in a doctor from Portland, Oregon. We first became friends because we are both from the West Coast. Most of the doctors and nurses are from the East Coast. His name is Dr. Cliff Stafford, and you can tell Colleen that Virginia thinks Dr. Cliff looks just like George Brent. Although Dr. Cliff is straight out of medical school, he's very good at caring for the wounded, and I admire him very much. Now, because I know Colleen will ask—no, he is not married. And, no, he is not my beau. I just happen to like him.

One of the nurses had to be sent home because she got a very bad case of malaria. A good reminder to Virginia and me to keep taking our anti-malarial medication and use our mosquito nets at night. I don't want to scare you, but we did find a very large snake in our tent the other day. According to a local, it wasn't poisonous. Just scary looking. Now it's time for my shift to begin, so I will say good-bye. I miss you all.

Love,
Bridget

"Oh, my!" Mam clapped her hands. "Bridget has met a doctor."

"She said they are only friends," Molly pointed out.

"That might be what she said, but I don't think it's what she meant," Margaret said.

"And she said he looks like George Brent." Colleen chuckled. "And George Brent is dreamy."

"She said that Virginia said that," Molly defended her sister. "Besides, we all know that Bridget is supposed to marry Patrick."

Mrs. Hammond laughed. "Well, I don't think any of us here believe in arranged marriages, Molly."

"I know that." Molly pursed her lips. "But I thought Bridget and Patrick were sort of destined to be together." She held up Patrick's letter. "And I try to keep the two of them connected by writing to them. I share news back and forth."

"So you're a letter-writing cupid?" Mr. Hammond teased.

Molly smiled sheepishly. "Maybe . . . a little."

"That's sweet of you," Mrs. Hammond said gently. "But I'm afraid you'll have to let Patrick and Bridget decide for themselves."

"Speaking of Patrick, what about reading his letter?" Mam urged.

"Okay. It's not very long." Molly unfolded Patrick's letter. As usual, he was vague about where his aircraft carrier was located. Mostly he talked about his navy buddies and the weather

128

and, as usual, he complained about the food, finally reassuring her that he was doing just fine and reminding her to keep being a good girl and to keep writing to him. "There." She refolded the letter, slipping it back into her pocket.

"I wish they fed our boys better," Mrs. Hammond said sadly. "When Patrick and Brian get home, I plan to cook all their favorite foods for at least a week."

"Sounds good to me." Mr. Hammond smacked his lips.

"Now for the third letter." Colleen winked at Molly. "Or maybe you prefer to keep that one private . . . since it's from your sweetheart."

"Sweetheart?" Mrs. Hammond's brows arched.

"Tommy is not my sweetheart," Molly declared.

"Says you," Colleen teased.

"Molly has a sweetheart?" Mr. Hammond scowled. "Not sure I like the sound of this."

"Tommy is not Molly's sweetheart," Mam clarified.

"He's just a lonely soldier boy she met at the USO," Margaret explained.

"I don't like the idea of our young Molly going to the USO," Mr. Hammond said. "I don't think your dad would approve either."

"The USO isn't a bad place," Margaret clarified. "I saw that for myself when Colleen took us there."

And now Colleen briefly told the Hammonds

about the USO rules. "It's very well chaperoned and a nice way to help our military men to feel welcome when they're away from home. It's meant to be a wholesome club. And if Brian or Patrick were in a strange city, I'm sure you'd both be glad to know they could go to the USO for a social evening."

"You're probably right." Mrs. Hammond pointed to Molly. "Now, are you going to read that last letter or not?"

"You really want to hear it?" Molly asked.

Of course, they all said they did.

Molly cleared her throat and started to read.

Dear Molly,
Thank you for your last letter. It's always a happy day when I get a letter from my favorite girl. I bragged to my buddies that my Molly is a famous movie star now. Of course, I eventually told them the truth— that you were only in a promotional film. I think they were impressed just the same. And since they've already seen your photograph (which is securely taped inside my locker, so I can see you every morning and every night) they weren't too surprised to imagine you as a real film star. I do hope I get to see your movie someday. I'm sure you look beautiful in it. How could you not?

I am so grateful for your friendship, Molly. I must admit that I think about you a lot. Sometimes it's what gets me through a hard day. And there are plenty of hard days. But I don't want to complain. I just thank God that I got the chance to meet you at the USO that night. I will never forget the pretty blonde girl in the gorgeous blue gown. But it was your brilliant smile that won me over. The whole thing felt like a fairy tale—the poor orphan boy befriended by the beautiful princess. Anyway, I look forward to meeting up with you again someday . . . when this war is over. Pray that it ends soon, Molly. Tell everyone back home to pray that it ends soon. Already it has cost our country and this world too much.

Sincerely yours,
Tommy Foster

"Oh, my." Mrs. Hammond was actually wiping her eyes. "He sounds like a sweet young man."

"And it sounds like he is sweet on Molly," Colleen added.

"He's just lonely," Molly said defensively as she returned the letter to her pocket. "He has no family. As far as I know, I'm the only one who writes to him.

"Sounds like he is in love," Mr. Hammond said. "Like he wants to be your beau."

"Molly is too young for a beau," Mam declared.

"He's not my beau." Molly's cheeks grew warm.

"Well, he may not see it like that," Colleen told her.

"Maybe I should straighten him out," Molly said. "I could write and tell him that I'm not—"

"No, don't do that," Margaret insisted. "Even if Tommy imagines there's more to your relationship than you intended, really, what can it hurt? Like he said in his letter, his memories of you are helping him through some hard days. What is wrong with that?"

Molly wasn't sure.

"I don't think there's a thing wrong with that," Mrs. Hammond said kindly. "If Molly is helping a young soldier—a poor boy with no family— to feel valued and loved while he's risking life and limb for his country, well, who could fault her for that?"

That seemed to be the general consensus. Everyone agreed that Molly should continue encouraging Tommy. Even Mam felt it was best. "It would be a shame to break the poor boy's heart while he's out there in harm's way. You can sort it all out with him after the war ends. When he comes home." She smiled. "And who knows, perhaps your feelings toward him will have warmed up by then."

# Eleven

*July 1942*

As the Mulligans walked home from church on Sunday, Molly felt seriously worried about Colleen. She'd been so down that Molly had even offered to go with her to the USO last night, but Colleen had declined. Then after mass, while Molly had waited for Colleen to light a candle, which she knew was for Geoff, she felt like crying at the sadness in Colleen's eyes.

"Are you okay?" Molly asked quietly as she and Colleen trailed after Mam and Margaret.

"I'm fine," Colleen said solemnly.

"I know you're worried about Geoff," Molly told her. "And I have an idea."

Colleen peered dubiously at Molly. "Really? What sort of idea?"

"Well, Margaret is driving Mam to visit Dad. What if we use Peter's car and take a little drive in the country?"

"In the country?" Colleen frowned. "Whatever for?"

"Sort of a field trip."

"A field trip?" Colleen looked at Molly like she was crazy.

"You know how I'm interested in gardening now. What if we were to visit a farm?"

"Whose farm?" Colleen looked suspicious.

"The Conrads' farm." Molly smiled nervously. "You said that Geoff's family has a beautiful farm, Colleen. I've always wanted to see it."

"Wh–what?" Colleen narrowed her eyes. "What are you suggesting?"

"Well, I'm certain that you want to know how Geoff is doing. What better way to find out than to talk to his family? I know you said his mom isn't so friendly. But you did like his grandparents, didn't you?"

"Well, yes . . . ."

"And you are Geoff's fiancée, aren't you?"

Colleen held up her hand, making the diamond to sparkle in the sunlight. "Yes, I am."

"So why not pay the grandparents a visit and find out how your fiancé is doing?"

Colleen tipped her head to one side. "You know what, for a baby sister, sometimes you're the smartest one of the bunch."

Molly laughed. "So, you want to go?"

It turned out to be a perfect day for a drive through the country. And Colleen didn't even mind that Molly wanted to drive. With the windows wide open and the wind blowing their hair, Molly and Colleen sang along to the Hit Parade songs playing on the radio. But Colleen turned off the radio after she told Molly where to turn. And as they drove down the long tree-lined driveway, Colleen got very quiet.

"Wow, this is a beautiful farm." Molly looked all around in wonder. "If you marry Geoff, will you two live out here? Will you be a farmer's wife?"

"I, uh, I don't know. I mean, Geoff is more interested in flying than farming." Colleen was smoothing her windblown hair now, reaching for her compact and lipstick.

"Don't be nervous," Molly said as she pulled up to the big white house with its tall columns. It was so elegant and pristine, reminding her of the plantation homes in *Gone with the Wind*. "Just remember that Geoff is your fiancé. You have every right to pay his family a nice social visit." She turned off the engine, then smiled. "Good luck."

"Aren't you coming up there with me?" Colleen frowned.

"Well, since we're not exactly invited or expected, maybe you should go up alone. Sort of test the waters, so to speak. If the coast is clear, you can wave for me to come join you."

"Yes, that's probably wise. I would hate it if Geoff's mom yelled at you."

"You think she's going to yell at you?" Molly suddenly questioned her plan. What if it back-fired?

"Probably not." Colleen produced a stiff smile. "Okay, here I go."

• • •

Colleen took in a long slow breath as she strolled up to the house. She nervously tugged at a white glove, squaring her shoulders and holding her head high. She still had on her church clothes—a sky blue linen skirt and fitted peplum jacket along with a wide-brimmed hat. She knew she looked stylish but not overdone. Geoff would be proud to see her like this—strong and pretty and confident as she faced his family.

The front porch looked similar to how it had looked at Christmastime. Except that there were a few more wicker chairs and some colorful flower pots. But all in all, it seemed very inviting in a country sort of way. Well, inviting for *someone*. Probably not her. She braced herself as she approached the front door.

As Colleen reached up to ring the doorbell, she hoped that one of Geoff's grandparents would answer. That would make this meeting so much easier. But before she pressed the bell, she noticed something hanging in the window. Something she didn't recall from Christmastime. Unless she had missed it somehow. Colleen stared at the small handmade banner, similar to the one Molly had made with royal blue stars for their loved ones in the military, and one lonely gold star for Peter . . . signifying his sacrifice. But this banner had only one star . . . and it was gold.

136

Colleen's hand covered her mouth as a shock-wave of horror surged through her. *No, no, it couldn't be!* That star could not possibly be for Geoff! Someone would've notified her. She tried to steady herself, thinking of another plausible explanation and suddenly remembering that Geoff's father had been killed in the Great War. That had to be it. This banner was to honor Geoff's fallen father. *Of course!*

"Colleen?"

She turned to see Geoff's grandmother, wearing a drab black dress, slowly rounding the corner of the wraparound porch with a puzzled expression. "Mrs. Conrad," Colleen said with shaky voice.

"Oh, my dear girl!" The old woman opened her arms. "So you know. You did hear the news. I was hoping you'd come to see us. I've been so—"

"Wh—what news?" A buzzing sound began to fill Colleen's ears.

"About Geoff." Mrs. Conrad embraced Colleen, patting her on the back. "I'm so sorry, honey. So sorry for all of us. Geoff was such a dear, dear boy. I'm still just heartbroken over—"

*"No!"* Colleen pulled away, wildly waving her arms in the air. "No—no! It's not true! It can't be true!" She pointed at the gold star with a shaking finger. "He's not—he can't be. Please, don't say it. Don't tell me he's dead. Please, don't!"

137

"Oh, Colleen. You didn't know?"

"Say it's not true. Please, I'm *begging* you!" Her ears were ringing and buzzing and the whole world seemed to be spinning sideways and getting blurry . . . and then it all went dark and silent.

Molly had been relieved to see the old woman on the porch. She must be the grandma. And the way she'd approached Colleen with open arms was encouraging. But then something went wrong. Colleen had stepped back and waved her arms and then crumpled to the ground like a rag doll. Molly's heart pounded in fear as she ran up to the house. "What's wrong?" Molly knelt beside Colleen. "Did she faint?" She looked up to the grandma.

"Oh, dear—oh, dear!" She wrung her hands.

"What happened?" Molly felt Colleen's forehead, then gently patted her cheek, trying to wake her up. "Colleen?"

"I'll get some help."

By the time Molly looked up, the grandma was gone.

"Colleen!" Molly said loudly. "Colleen, wake up!"

Just as Colleen's dark lashes began to flutter, the grandma, accompanied with what appeared to be the grandfather and Geoff's mother joined them.

"Are you okay?" Molly asked Colleen.

"I, uh, I don't know . . . I can't remember . . . what happened?" Colleen looked at everyone with a confused expression.

Molly wrapped an arm around Colleen's shoulders, helping her to sit up. She felt confused too. What had the grandmother said to upset Colleen like this? What kind of monstrous people lived in this beautiful house?

The grandfather pulled a wicker chair nearby. "Let's get her onto this," he said solemnly, helping to lift Colleen from the other side, and together they eased her onto the rocker.

"What happened?" Molly demanded of the grandmother. "Why is Colleen so—"

"He's dead," Colleen said in a flat voice. She pointed to a banner hanging in the window, a banner with a gold star stitched to it. "Geoff . . . is dead."

"Oh, no." Molly grasped the arm of the chair, feeling wobbly too. "No. It can't be."

Now Colleen began to sob—loud and hard and so uncontrollably that it reminded Molly of a wounded animal. And she didn't know what to do, what to say, how to comfort her sister, as her own eyes filled with tears. How could this be? Geoff was dead?

"Come in the house, girls," the grandmother said gently. "Edgar, get some water for these ladies."

"Yes," Geoff's mother said. "Let's go inside."

Before long they were all seated in a large and elegant living room. All the furnishings went so perfectly together that it reminded Molly of the house and garden magazine carried in the store. Edgar, the grandpa, had set a crystal pitcher of water and matching goblets on the glass-topped table. Molly tried to get Colleen to take a sip of water, but she simply shook her head. At least her crying quieted some, but she still had tears streaming down her face, and other than an occasional sob, the only other sound was the ticking of the big grandfather clock.

"I thought you'd already told her," the grandmother was saying to Geoff's mother. "You said you were going to tell her, Ellen."

"I planned to," Ellen said stiffly. "But I hadn't gotten around to it yet."

"But Geoff left you all of Colleen's information, he specifically asked you to contact her . . . should anything happen to him. You promised him you would do that, Ellen. I heard it with my own ears."

"I am still grieving," Ellen said defensively. "I haven't recovered from the shock myself."

"Well, this is a *shocking* way for Colleen to hear this news." Mr. Conrad sounded disgusted. "I don't know what to say."

"I am sorry." Ellen stared down at her hands in her lap, twisting a gold wedding band.

"When did it happen?" Colleen asked in a raspy voice. "How did it happen? What exactly did happen?"

Mr. Conrad moved over to the couch and, sitting next to Colleen, he put his arm around her shoulders. "Geoff's plane was shot down by the Japanese. It happened on the twenty-fourth of May," he explained in a gentle tone. "Somewhere near the Philippines."

"The twenty-fourth of May," she repeated woodenly. "No survivors."

"That's right," he told her. "Sadly so."

"How do they know there were no survivors?" Colleen asked with new energy. "Geoff assured me he always flew with a parachute. He said even if his plane was disabled, he and his crew would simply bail out. He told me not to worry—that he would survive." She looked at the grandpa with hopeful eyes. "Is it possible that—"

"I wondered the same thing, Colleen." He sighed. "I immediately wrote to the War Office to make an inquiry."

"Did you hear back?"

He nodded. "Just a few days ago. I was sent a detailed letter. It seems he was flying in a small squadron of only six planes somewhere near the Philippines. The letter wasn't specific about the exact location. They were attacked from the north by a large squadron of Japanese Zeros. Geoff's plane was leading the squadron and one of the first ones to be hit. But it was reported by the one surviving plane—the one flying in the rear of the formation—that Geoff's plane exploded in the air. They believed the entire crew died instantly. This was in their report they made after getting back to the aircraft carrier."

"They were certain?" Colleen's voice sounded shaky again.

He just nodded. "There had been hopes that one of the other planes had survivors, but none were found when they did a search."

Colleen let out a choked sob. "I just can't believe it."

"That's how we felt too," the grandpa said sadly. "Such a shock when the telegram arrived."

"When did you receive it?" Colleen asked.

He glanced at Geoff's mother. "About two weeks ago?"

She just nodded, still staring down at her hands.

Colleen looked at him and then over at Geoff's mother and grandmother. "I'm so sorry for your loss," she said quietly. "So very sorry." And now she removed her engagement ring, attempting to hand it to Geoff's grandfather. "I should return this since I'm no—"

"No!" He held up his hand. "That's yours, Colleen. Geoff gave it to you. He would want you to keep it."

"That's right," the grandmother agreed.

Geoff's mother said nothing but continued looking down.

"We need to go." Colleen started to stand, then wavered as if she were about to fall down again. Leaping to her feet, Molly wrapped a supportive arm around her sister's waist.

"Yes," Molly told them. "We need to go now." She looked back at them. "And I, uh, I am very sorry for your loss too. Very sorry." Helping Colleen to walk, Molly navigated their way through the fancy house and down the wide porch steps until she finally got Colleen safely into the passenger side of the car. As she closed the door, she looked back to see all three of them clustered together on the porch, just watching. But it seemed the big white house— previously so bright and cheery—was now draped in a heavy blanket of dark gloom.

"Go ahead and cry," Molly told Colleen as she drove them back down the long driveway. "Cry as hard and loud as you want. Get it out, if you can. I can take it."

But Colleen simply sat very still and straight, sobbing quietly. As Molly drove them back to San Francisco, she fought back her own tears. Her job right now was to keep the car on the road, to get them safely home.

# Twelve

For the next few weeks, Molly tried to help her sister through what appeared to be the greatest trial of her life, but it seemed Colleen was truly inconsolable. Oh, she went to work every day, but in her "uniform" of an old black shirt and dungarees, Colleen appeared to have given up on fashion. She didn't even bother with makeup anymore. And most of the time her hair, wrapped in a faded blue bandana, looked lifeless and dirty. Molly suspected that her roots had grown out, something that Colleen had always religiously guarded against. But now she no longer cared—about anything.

Even when Molly took the time to replace one of the blue stars on their banner with a gleaming gold one, Colleen said nothing. It was as if she weren't even there. All Colleen ever did was go to work or hide in her room. They weren't even sure if she was eating much, but whenever Mam questioned this, Colleen would snap back at her and tell her to mind her own business.

Despite being extra busy with the store—especially without Colleen's help on Saturdays—Mam and Margaret had tried to be supportive and understanding. But Molly knew their patience was wearing thin. After all, they'd experienced their own various forms of grief when Peter had been killed. They knew Colleen felt miserable, but they also knew she needed to pull herself together and move forward. But the harder everyone tried to cheer her, the more Colleen tugged away from them, going more and more inward.

When they planned a party for her nineteenth birthday, combining their ration coupons for enough sugar to bake a chocolate cake and inviting the Hammonds, Colleen barely touched the dinner, then excused herself to bed, refusing to taste the cake.

Mrs. Hammond had wisely decided to postpone Margaret's baby shower "until Colleen got better." But no one knew when that would be. And no one knew what to do to get Colleen out of her dark place. Perhaps there was nothing to be done besides wait and hope that eventually time would heal her wounds. Even the good news that Dad would be coming home at the end of the month didn't faze Colleen in the least. Sometimes Molly thought that her sister wished she were dead too, just like Geoff. And it scared her.

Fortunately, Molly had more than enough to keep her busy these days. Between helping at the store, tending her garden, canning with

Mrs. Bartley, and life in general, she had plenty to distract herself from her sister's pain. Just the same, she made sure to keep Colleen in her prayers. And she would light a candle for her whenever she got the chance. As well as for Bridget and Brian and Patrick. Bridget's latest news had been a little concerning. It sounded as if her hospital unit were going to be moved. Molly suspected the relocation was to get them out of harm's way, but Bridget couldn't let them know where she was going or even where she had been. Her biggest concern seemed to be whether Dr. Cliff would be relocated with them. Although Bridget tried to make it sound like her interest in the doctor's whereabouts was purely professional, Molly suspected otherwise.

"Come help in my garden," Molly urged Colleen one warm Saturday evening. "I've got everything coming on, and Mam and Margaret are too worn out to help."

"I'm worn out too," Colleen complained.

"We're all worn out," Molly declared. "But you're the only one who got a day off today."

"I work my fingers to the bone all week." Colleen glowered at Molly. "In that smelly old airplane factory." She held up her hands—as if the dark stains of grease were proof in point.

"That's exactly why you need some fresh air." Refusing to be intimidated, Molly grabbed

Colleen's hand. "Come on. Help me harvest."

Not surprisingly, Colleen complained all the way to the garden. And when Molly handed her a tin pail, pointing her to the tomatoes in need of picking and explaining, as if Colleen were a child, which ones to pick and how to do it, Colleen continued to grumble.

"Mrs. Bartley is going to help me put them up," Molly cheerfully told Colleen as she began to pick cucumbers. "On Monday morning we'll make tomato sauce and pickles and relish and all sorts of things."

"Good for you," Colleen said dourly.

Molly continued to chatter cheerfully. She didn't even care that she was aggravating her sister. Maybe Colleen needed to be aggravated. "I got a letter from Patrick today," Molly said absently, trying to think of ways to fill the void. "I think he's feeling down. I'm not sure why exactly, but his letter sounded a little glum." She waited for a response, but getting none, continued. "I suspect that Mrs. Hammond must've written to him about Bridget's doctor friend—and now Patrick probably feels jilted."

"How can he feel jilted?" Colleen said sharply. "It's not like they were engaged or anything."

Molly looked up from the cucumbers, thinking perhaps she'd hit a nerve. "Well, everyone always thought they would get married. And Patrick is off on that aircraft carrier out in the middle of the Pacific Ocean. Maybe he was dreaming—"

"My fiancé is lying at the bottom of that same ocean right now!" Colleen screamed at her. "Patrick is lucky to be alive! I don't care whether he wants to marry Bridget or the man on the moon, Molly Irene! Quit going on and on about him!"

"Sorry to—"

"And stop apologizing all the time!" Colleen stood, shaking her fist with a large tomato in it.

Molly didn't know what to say.

"I hate this!" She held up the tomato.

"You hate the tomato?" Molly asked.

"I hate this horrid war! I hate that it's taken Peter. I hate that it's taken Geoff. I hate what it's done to our world. I hate it! I hate it! *I hate it!*"

"I hate it too," Molly said calmly. "Anyway, I hate the killing and dying part of it. But I sort of like the way it brings people together. I like the way we've worked together as a family and—" Molly's words were stopped by a tomato that splattered right in the center of her forehead. She blinked, staring at Colleen in shock.

Colleen's expression was a mixture of horror and amusement. "I, uh, sorry, Molly."

Molly used her sleeve to wipe the drips of runny tomato off her face then, seeing an overly ripe tomato on a nearby plant, went over and plucked it off, then held it in the palm of her hand, bouncing it up and down in a threatening sort of way.

"Go ahead," Colleen said in a challenging way. "I bet you can't even hit me. I dare you."

And so Molly let it go, hitting Colleen smack in the face. "Oh, no." Molly ran over. "I'm sorry, I shouldn't have—" Once again her words were cut off by Colleen smashing a tomato right on top of Molly's head.

The fight was on. Several more overly ripe tomatoes were exchanged until both of them were dripping in red goop and giggling uncontrollably. "Stop, stop!" Molly was crying as Colleen held up one last tomato. "I want to can these and—" It was too late . . . Colleen let her have it.

"What is going on?" Mam demanded as she came out to the back porch, staring in shock at Molly and Colleen. "What on earth?"

"It's nothing." Colleen came over to put her arm around Molly.

"Are you bleeding?" Margaret cried out she emerged from the house with a dishtowel in hand.

"Just a little tomato war," Molly explained as she reached for the towel, handing it to Colleen. "We're fine."

"But your beautiful tomatoes." Mam frowned at Molly. "You worked so—"

"They were mostly the rotten ones." Colleen used the towel to wipe her face, then returned it to Molly.

"And it was worth it," Molly assured her as she cleaned her own face.

"You girls are a mess," Mam said with a puzzled expression.

Molly reached for the soggy blue bandana still tied around Colleen's head, snatching it off. "Besides you are way overdue for a shampoo."

Colleen just nodded.

"You can have the first bath," Molly offered. "I want to pick the rest of these cucumbers anyway."

"Let me get the rest of the ripe tomatoes first." Colleen went back to work.

Mam and Margaret still looked slightly stunned as they returned to the house. But Colleen and Molly worked peacefully together in the garden.

"Colleen?" Molly said quietly.

"Yeah?" Colleen didn't look up from picking tomatoes.

"I know I don't really know how you feel—about losing Geoff. I know it's not the same as losing a brother. But I can sort of imagine how badly it must hurt. Sometimes I think about you and my heart just aches, almost like I can feel your pain. And, well, if you ever want to talk about it, I'm willing to listen."

150

Colleen looked up with tear-filled eyes. "Thanks, Molly. I'll keep that in mind."

Colleen felt something snap in her that evening in the garden. Although it was painful, it was a good sort of snap. Perhaps it was like setting a broken bone. Bridget would probably know about that sort of thing. But later that night, Colleen took a long bath. And she even touched up her darkened roots with peroxide before shampooing her filthy hair. Oh, she still ached deep inside, and she doubted she'd ever be really happy again, but somehow she knew she was going to survive this. Not so much for herself . . . but for her family. She knew they needed her. And they needed her to be strong.

Audrey gave Colleen a second look on Monday at break time. "Looks like you're feeling better." She shook out a cigarette, holding the box toward Colleen.

"Thanks." Colleen took one. She still felt a bit guilty for her return to smoking, but under the circumstances . . . Well, she felt both Peter and Geoff would understand. Besides, she was only smoking a few cigarettes a day.

"So . . . Bernice has been bragging to everyone that the movie is going to be showing in theaters in a few weeks."

"Oh?" Colleen feigned interest.

"Yeah. Apparently it will be out in mid-September."

"That's nice." Colleen let out a long puff of smoke.

"I know it's been hard on you," Audrey said tentatively. "But I'm glad to see you're making a comeback, Colleen." She smiled. "I've missed you."

Colleen just nodded. "Thanks."

Each day seemed to get a little bit easier for Colleen, but she still didn't feel like her old self. She suspected that person was gone for good. And perhaps it was for the best. But at least she was able to talk and participate in a somewhat civilized manner. And if she felt the tears coming, she would simply slip away and wait for the sadness to pass.

But about a week after the tomato war, Colleen decided to take Molly up on her offer. Her reason was twofold. For one thing, Dad would be home in a few days and Colleen didn't want to be a big wet blanket for his homecoming. But the bigger reason was that she really needed to talk to someone. And although Molly was only sixteen, she was mature for her age. Somehow Colleen just didn't feel that Margaret or Mam would really understand.

As the two of them strolled down toward the waterfront, Colleen confided her biggest regret to Molly. "I keep wondering if Geoff got my letter," she said. "You know, the one Margaret gave me such a bad time for. I worry that Geoff might've gotten that letter and he might've been distracted by it and, as a result . . ." She paused to take in a deep breath. "As a result of being distracted because of my stupid letter, Geoff was shot down and killed—and it is entirely my fault." She choked back a sob. "Do you know what I mean?"

Molly didn't respond, but Colleen could tell by her furrowed brow that she was thinking about this.

"It's hard enough losing Geoff," she continued, "but if I'm responsible, well, I just can't live with that." Now she was crying.

Molly put her arm around Colleen's shoulders. "First of all, Geoff's plane was shot down by the Japanese and—"

"But what if Geoff was distracted and—"

"Geoff, from what I've heard, was an excellent pilot, Colleen. I really doubt he would've let a letter distract him. Besides, you don't even know if he'd gotten your letter by then. I've tried to remember back to when that happened, and I have a feeling your letter hadn't reached him. He certainly didn't have time to respond to it. But even if he had received it, you don't know that it would've troubled him. Margaret put that thought into your head. Didn't you tell us Geoff thought you'd make a beautiful movie star?"

"That's what he said. Even to his family."

"So why would he say something like that if he didn't mean it? Geoff struck me as a very modern man. The sort of guy who would have been proud to have a movie star wife."

"Yes!" Colleen said eagerly. "That is exactly what I felt like when I first met him. That's what drew me to him. He was fun and lively. He liked to have a good time. And even when I told him I was the black sheep of the family, he just laughed. He never judged me, Molly. He simply loved me for who I am—or who I was." She used her handkerchief to dab at her tears.

"I really think you're worrying about something that never happened."

Colleen blew her nose. "You really think so?"

"Don't you?"

Colleen nodded. "Yeah, I do." She threw her arms around Molly. "For a kid, you're pretty sensible, you know?"

Molly just laughed. "So I've been told."

As they walked home, Colleen asked Molly about Patrick. "I remember you were concerned about him last week. But I was in such a bad place, I couldn't really listen. I know I wasn't much help. Tell me again what worried you."

"It was his last letter," Molly said quietly. "It didn't sound at all like the old Patrick. I realize this war is taking its toll on everyone. And we have no idea what our servicemen are actually facing out there on the battlefield. But Patrick's letters are usually pretty cheerful. But this last one sounded sad. So I got to wondering if Mrs. Hammond might've written to him about Bridget's doctor friend."

"Dr. Cliff?"

Molly nodded. "Patrick may think Dr. Cliff is Bridget's beau. That he's lost his chance with her."

"You know what I think?"

"What?"

"I think Patrick has never been interested in Bridget like that. If he had, he would've stepped up long ago. He's certainly had plenty of opportunity over the years. I bet Patrick sees Bridget as a sister. And I seriously doubt that even if his mom did write to him about Bridget's Dr. Cliff that he would care."

Molly seemed to consider this. "Then maybe it's something else."

"Why don't you write and ask him?"

"I guess I could do that. But I usually try to keep my letters light and uplifting. You know?"

"And that's fine. But maybe he needs something more. You're such a good letter writer, and you've been a good listener for me. You could offer to listen to him too. Maybe he needs someone to talk to like that."

Molly nodded. "Okay, that's what I'll do."

Colleen felt a tiny wave of guilt now. "I know

155

you're only sixteen, Molly. But you've always seemed older. And I suspect this stupid war is forcing you to grow up even faster than you should. But I hope you still take time to enjoy being a kid. I mean, you'll have your whole life to be a grown-up."

Molly just shrugged. "I'm not worried about growing up too fast—or too slow either. I suppose I used to worry about being the baby of the family. But I really don't care anymore. I mean, I'm just me. And I'm in no big hurry to grow up. It'll happen quickly enough."

"Yeah, I guess. Unless you're Peter Pan, growing up is unavoidable." Colleen sighed deeply, wishing it weren't true.

# Thirteen

*Late August 1942*

It was Molly's idea to have a "welcome home" party for Dad. Mam had reservations, worried that he'd be too worn out to celebrate. And Margaret, weary after a long week at the store, couldn't provide much help. Colleen's contribution was to drive to the sanatorium to pick up Dad. It would also be her opportunity to tell him about Geoff, since so far, no one had wanted to share that sad news.

In the meantime, Molly had promised to take care of the rest of the details. And with Mrs. Hammond's help, as well as Mrs. Bartley's and Mam's, she'd managed to put together a fairly nice Sunday dinner to welcome their patriarch home.

Molly felt a sense of satisfaction to see their dining room table nearly filled with family and friends as she and Mam carried in Dad's favorite meal of roast beef and mashed potatoes. Along with some of the fresh produce from her own garden and an apple pie made by Mrs. Hammond. And contrary to Mam's predictions, Dad was energetic and animated—and very glad to reunite with his loved ones. So much so that, after dinner,

Mr. Hammond good-naturedly accused him of having been off on a vacation.

"You go and spend some time at a sanatorium and tell me if you think it's a vacation," Dad shot back at him. "I haven't had a good night's sleep since last winter and, let me assure you, I'm looking forward to sleeping in my own bed tonight." He reached for Mam's hand. "With my one true love by my side."

She chuckled with an embarrassed smile.

"So," Mr. Hammond said loudly. "Who's heard from the battlefront lately?"

"Molly got a letter today," Margaret announced.

"I did?" Molly was surprised. "I was too busy to even check. Who's it from?"

"Patrick," Margaret told her. "It's on the entry table."

"Well, then, you better read it to everyone," Mrs. Hammond told her. "That boy hasn't written to us in a couple of weeks."

"No one gets as many letters as Molly," Margaret said as Molly went to fetch her letter.

"That's because nobody writes as many letters as she does," Colleen added.

"She's our foreign correspondent," Dad said proudly.

"Go ahead, Molly," Mam told her, "read it."

Molly slit open the V-mail, unfolding the letter and getting ready to read. The only problem was that she'd invited Patrick to share more openly with her. What if he confessed his heart was broken because he was worried Bridget had fallen for Dr. Cliff? Molly couldn't bear to read his personal message to all these people.

"Go on," Dad urged. "Read it. I haven't heard how Patrick is doing since this war began."

"Okay." She took in a deep breath, preparing to read.

Dear Molly,

Thank you for your last letter. You were correct in assuming that all was not well with me when I last wrote to you. I was troubled about something. But don't worry, it has nothing to do with Bridget. She is like a sweet sister to me, and if she finds love with an army doctor, I can only wish her the very best.

My concerns, Molly, were for you. In her last letter, my mother shared how you are writing to a soldier. My mother feels it's very kind and generous of you to befriend this lonely young man, but I must say that it troubled me. I worry that you are too young to be involved with a young army man. I feel very protective of you and—

Molly stopped reading. This was getting far too personal—not to mention embarrassing.

"Keep reading," Dad insisted in a sharp tone.

"Yes," Mrs. Hammond agreed. "Please, finish it, dear. I'm worried I said too much to Patrick in my last letter."

Molly cleared her throat and, with trepidation, continued to read Patrick's letter:

—I'm concerned about a girl your age going to the USO dances and socializing with strange servicemen. I wasn't sure how to communicate my concerns with you, Molly, but because you asked, I feel it's my responsibility to answer. You are an intelligent and beautiful young girl, but like I warned you—and Peter did too— you are just the sort of girl that some boys would take unfair advantage of.

You are very pretty and you have such a kind and gentle and trusting heart, it worries me that some "lonely" soldier might try to swoop in and carry you away. Some men would have no regard for your youth. Believe me, I know such men!

So, as your friend and stand-in brother, I beg you to go carefully. Watch yourself, Molly. I've seen so much more of human nature since I joined the navy—I mean male human nature—that I feel much more protective of you now. So there you go. You asked me what was wrong, and now I've told you. I hope you will still consider me your friend and "brother." Please, take care!

Sincerely,
Patrick

"What?" Dad's voice was raised. "You've been going to USO dances while I'm gone, Molly Irene?"

"Not exactly." She grimaced. "I only went with Colleen and—"

"You're just fifteen and you are going to—"

"She's sixteen, Dad." Colleen went over to place a hand on his shoulder. "And Margaret and I took her there for her birthday." Now she quickly explained what a safe place the USO was and how Molly had been a perfect lady.

"Even so," he blustered. "Molly is a *child*. And Patrick has good reason to feel concerned for her welfare." He turned to Mam. "Why was I not informed of these goings on?"

"We didn't want to trouble you, dear. And I really wasn't—"

"I am the man of this house," he barked at her. "From now on, I will be informed of such things." He looked around the room with wide, angry eyes. "What else has transpired during my absence? What else have I missed out on?"

Everyone grew silent, and Molly stifled the urge to crawl under the coffee table. How had such a happy occasion suddenly unraveled like this?

Mrs. Bartley stood up to face him. "You have missed out on seeing your youngest daughter working hard to create the most beautiful victory garden in San Francisco," she said. "You have missed seeing your wife and daughters pulling together to get by while you recovered from your life-threatening illness. You have missed seeing Colleen going to the airplane factory every morning—come rain or shine or heart-break. You've missed watching Molly studying for and earning her driver's license. And you've missed Margaret managing the grocery store with brains and admirable diplomacy skills." She shook a crooked finger at him. "You have missed feeling the pride and joy that any father, having raised such a fine and upstanding family, may experience."

Mrs. Hammond started to clap, Mr. Hammond joined her, and soon everyone, including Dad, was clapping as well.

"Well said," Mr. Hammond told Mrs. Bartley.

"I'm sorry," Dad told everyone. "You are right, Mrs. Bartley, I have missed a lot during the last eight months. But the biggest thing I seemed to be missing today was my manners. Please, forgive me."

Molly refolded her letter from Patrick. Her cheeks still felt flushed from having read what seemed a far too personal letter to everyone in this room, but fortunately it seemed that Dad's outburst had effectively erased it for them. At least she hoped so.

Everyone started to chatter again and, seeing her chance to slip away, Molly quietly went up to her room, where she opened up Patrick's letter to read it again. And although a part of her felt flattered to think Patrick had been worried for her welfare, another part of her felt offended. How dare he insinuate that she would not have good sense when it came to being involved with a serviceman? Did he really think she would run off and marry Tommy? Did he think so little of her?

"Molly?" Colleen poked her head in through the cracked door. "Are you okay?"

Molly cringed, shoving the letter under her pillow.

"Can I come in?"

"Sure," Molly said in a flat tone.

"I know Dad hurt your feelings," Colleen said as she sat on the chair by Molly's vanity table. "But you know he meant well."

"I know." Molly shrugged, hoping to appear indifferent.

"So you took my advice and asked Patrick to share what was bothering him . . . and he did. Well, you know what I think?"

Molly frowned. "Not really."

163

"I think our dear friend Patrick Hammond is in love with you."

Molly blinked. "No, no . . . that's impossible. And crazy."

Now Colleen shrugged. "Well, I might've been reading between the lines, but it sure sounded like it to me. Maybe you should read his letter again."

"I just did."

"And you don't think that—"

"No, I don't," Molly answered sharply. "Patrick is just doing what Peter asked. Peter was protective of me. And when he left for the navy, he asked Patrick to keep an eye on me. So when Peter died, Patrick really stepped up. He's just being a very protective—albeit aggravating— big brother."

"Aggravating?" Colleen tipped her head to one side.

"Because it feels like Patrick doesn't trust me—as if I'd do something stupid like go elope with Tommy Foster on his next leave." Molly couldn't help but laugh. "And here I am, just barely sixteen. That is so ridiculous."

Colleen pursed her lips. "It happens."

"Well, Patrick has nothing to worry about. It won't happen to me!"

"Maybe you should write him that."

"Maybe . . . ." Although Molly wasn't so sure. Her nose was still out of joint for feeling accused of being stupid and childish. She was not stupid and childish! Perhaps Patrick would just have to wait for her response. That would teach him!

The atmosphere of the Mulligan home definitely changed with Dad back in the house. Some for the better, Margaret thought, and some . . . well, not as much. On the bright side, Mam seemed less anxious and worried. But on the other side, the household of women, which had gotten quite relaxed during his absence, was suddenly thrust into a much higher gear. Dinner had to be served by 6:30 sharp, and household chores were no longer allowed to be neglected or postponed. Dad was king of his castle, and he wanted everyone to know it.

It might've been different if Dad were strong enough to carry his weight or to help out at the store, but his doctors insisted on at least six weeks of convalescence time at home. And after that, he was only supposed to work part-time at the store. Certainly that would help since it would be nearly Margaret's due date by then. But she still wasn't sure it was enough to keep them going. She was considering some of Molly's ideas, but other than stocking some canning supplies, she really hadn't made many changes to their inventory. Mostly she was trying to keep their family business in the black.

"Maybe you'd like to start keeping the books,"

Molly suggested one evening as they were finishing up dinner. Dad had just complained of boredom.

"I suppose maybe I could do that," he agreed with some hesitation.

"Unless you're not ready for that," she said apologetically. It was hard to know what Dad was capable of these days. He could really bluster sometimes, and other times he seemed weak as a kitten.

"Maybe it's too soon," Mam said from where she was lowering the blackout curtain nearby.

"Why are you putting those confounded drapes down already?" Dad demanded. "The sun won't set for half an hour yet."

"I start on them after dinner," Mam told him. "Just like I always do."

"But maybe I'd like to see the sunset," Dad protested.

"Fine." Mam stopped lowering the dark curtain. "I'll leave this one up for you, Riley. And you can put it down yourself—just don't forget."

"I'm not completely useless," he said in a slightly gentler tone. He turned back to Margaret. "And as for keeping the books, I'm glad to do it if it's not a problem to keep them at home. I'm just not sure how that would work for you."

"It's not that I can't keep doing them at the store." She picked up his dirty dinner plate. "But unless we hire another store clerk—which

166

doesn't seem financially prudent—I am already spreading myself too thin."

He patted her belly. "Not too thin here, Maggie Girl."

"Dad!" She slapped his hand with a scowl.

"How many babies do you have in there anyway?" he teased.

*"Dad!"* she said again.

"Stop tormenting her," Mam reprimanded him.

"Look how big she is," he said without mercy. "How long until your baby comes, Margaret? Any day now?"

"In about six weeks." She snapped indignantly. She carried the dirty plates to the kitchen where Colleen and Molly were washing. "Our father!" she growled as she set the dishes down.

"Are you praying?" Colleen said wryly. "Our father *in heaven?*"

"Ha! Hardly!"

"Don't mind Dad," Molly admonished. "He's just making up for all the lost time. Eight months is a long time to go without being able to tease your daughters." She chuckled.

"Why don't you go keep him company," Margaret suggested to Molly. "I'd rather dry dishes than listen to him ramble on about the war again."

Dad had become something of an expert on the war happenings during his time in the sanatorium. With little to do besides lie around and listen to his little radio and read all the newspapers, Dad could probably converse intelligently with the Secretary of War these days. Instead, he would subject his wife and daughters to his longwinded discourses.

Molly held out the dishtowel. "Are you sure?"

"Certain." Margaret untied Molly's apron strings, removing it and tying it around her own oversized waist. "And just see if you can get a word in edgewise this time."

Molly just laughed as she exited the kitchen. Soon Margaret could hear the sound of Dad's voice rising and falling. She felt a tiny bit sorry for Molly but knew her baby sister could handle Dad's rants and ramblings better than she could. Margaret was still trying to get one of Dad's horror stories out of her head. Just a few nights ago, he had told them about a kind-hearted Jewish doctor who ran an orphanage in Poland. Just a couple of weeks ago, the good doctor, along with all his employees and about two hundred orphans, were picked up by Nazis, escorted to an extermination camp, and killed. Probably with gas.

Margaret shuddered as she turned up the radio, tuning it to a musical program. Trying to block thoughts of war—and the fact that her beloved Brian would soon be in the thick of it—she dried the dishes that Colleen handed to her and hummed along with the music.

• • •

"I predict the next big battle will be in Guadalcanal," Dad told Molly with authority. "We've got US forces in the New Hebrides now. And we've started driving the Japanese out of the Solomons. It's really starting to heat up down there."

"I wish we knew exactly where Bridget's unit is stationed," Molly said quietly. This wasn't a topic she could freely discuss around Mam or Margaret, or even Colleen after her recent loss. But Dad never seemed too disturbed by war talk. And Mam had already retreated to the front room to listen to *Betty and Bob* on the radio. "If you're right about Guadalcanal, it worries me a little because I have a feeling Bridget's hospital is in that same region."

Dad frowned. "What do you mean? Where exactly do you think your sister is stationed?"

Molly hopped up to get the atlas that she always kept handy, opening it up to the map of the South Pacific. "I really don't know for sure." She pointed to the area. "But I have a feeling she's somewhere near New Guinea."

"What makes you think that?" Dad looked doubtful. "I suspect she's more over this way." He pointed to the Midway Islands, an area now dominated by American forces.

"Well, we know she's in the tropical area that gets monsoons. And in one letter, she mentioned a store owned by Australians," Molly told him. "And New Guinea is governed by Australia, so it—"

"No, no." Dad scowled darkly. "I do not like the idea of our Bridget being all the way over there. That is too close to Japan."

Molly knew she needed to backtrack now. "Well, I could be wrong about New Guinea. It was just a wild guess. Anyway, it sounds like she's in a very remote area. I doubt the Japanese have any interest in a spot like that. Besides, the Geneva Convention was created to protect military hospitals." Of course, Molly knew— and she knew that Dad knew—the Axis leaders had little respect for the rules of the Geneva Convention. She pointed to the window. "Looks like a pretty sunset tonight. Do you want to come watch it from my garden? I need to go pick some produce for the store."

"Fresh air would be good." He slowly stood, and Molly, sensing that he was feeling weak, took his arm.

"It's been fun selling my vegetables at the store," she said as they went out through the front door. "And it's a lot less work than canning." She chuckled. "It was fun at first, but I can see why so many people prefer to buy canned goods from grocery stores now."

"But you should feel proud to see those colorful jars of vegetables in our pantry," he told her.

"That is quite an accomplishment. In fact, I think we should keep the garden going even after the war ends."

"It's a lot of work," Molly confessed as they walked around the narrow side yard toward the back. "But I do enjoy seeing seeds growing into big, lovely plants. And then when the produce starts to show up, well, it feels almost miraculous." She led Dad to the wooden bench that Mrs. Bartley had set between their two gardens. "You just relax and enjoy the fresh air, and I'll gather a basket of produce." As Molly used her garden knife to cut the stem of a long yellow squash, she said a silent prayer for Bridget. Hopefully Molly was wrong about where her sister's hospital was located. Because if she really was anywhere near New Guinea, she would definitely be in harm's way. And after losing Peter . . . and then Geoff . . . Molly felt certain the Mulligan family couldn't take too much more.

# Fourteen

*Mid-September 1942*

Molly paused from sweeping in order to glance at the newspaper rack by the front door. It was Saturday evening, and she and Colleen were tidying the front part of the store. They were closing early in order to get to Margaret's baby shower tonight. "Don't tell Margaret," Molly said to Colleen.

"The baby shower?" Colleen paused from locking the front door. "Margaret already knows."

Molly tapped the newspaper rack with her broom handle. "I mean *this*." She pointed to the headline of the afternoon newspaper: *Japanese Incendiary Bombs Land in Oregon*.

"Oh, well, it's not like those bombs did any real damage." Colleen used the rag in her hand to give the finger smudges of the glass door a quick wipe. "The fire has already been put out."

"But it could've been worse. And Oregon is close to California." Molly swept a small pile of debris into the dustpan. "And it was all anyone talked about this afternoon. I was glad that Margaret was working in the office so she didn't have to hear it.

"Well, she shouldn't worry so much. After all, we have the Civil Defense watching our coastline for us. I'm sure there are dozens of old men out there with their binoculars right now."

"You're probably right." Molly dumped the dustpan contents in the trash. "Just the same, let's not mention it to Margaret. You know how she can get. We don't want her going into a tizzy right before her baby shower."

"That's true." Colleen gave the counter a swipe, then tossed her cleaning rag beneath the counter. "We'd better get going. I promised Mrs. Hammond we'd have her there by six."

As they went to get Margaret from the office, Molly felt somewhat relieved for Colleen's nonchalant attitude about this recent attack on American soil. However, Molly wasn't so sure it was nothing. If Japanese air balloons could drop incendiary bombs in Oregon, they could surely drop them over San Francisco as well. For all she knew, there could be balloons headed their way right now.

As a result of these concerns, as they went out to the car, Molly kept a close eye on the sky. But with the fog rolling in, it was hard to see much. Still, as Colleen drove, Molly tried to keep watchful eye . . . just in case.

Fortunately, Margaret was completely oblivious to what had happened in Oregon. Instead, she was happily chattering about the baby shower and the friends she hoped would be there tonight, and before long they were being welcomed into the Hammonds' home, which was decorated with streamers of pale pink and baby blue. And there on the center of the dining room table was the stork Molly had created a few days ago. Constructed from cardboard and tissue paper, it looked pretty good from a distance. Anyway, it was festive.

"There she is," Mrs. Hammond announced, hurrying over to embrace her daughter-in-law. By now Margaret was so wide through the middle that it wasn't easy to get one's arms around her, but Mrs. Hammond made a worthwhile effort. And Margaret looked sweet in her pink gingham maternity dress, with her cheeks glowing. A reminder to Molly to get out her camera. She had promised to take photographs that they could later send to father-to-be Brian, aunt-to-be Bridget, and uncle-to-be Patrick.

After Margaret got settled, Molly went into the kitchen to see if she could be of any help and, seeing Mam flush faced and weary looking, Molly insisted she go out and join the party. Taking over where Mam had been making little sandwiches with various deviled fillings, Molly didn't mind not being out with the others. They were mostly Margaret's friends from school, along with some of Mam's and Mrs. Hammond's older friends.

"Want some help?" Colleen came into the kitchen with a somewhat solemn expression.

"Sure." Molly handed her a knife. "You can do the egg salad if you want."

"Margaret seems to be enjoying herself," Colleen said glumly as she spread the yellow mixture onto a slice of bread.

"That's good." Molly glanced at Colleen. "Are you okay?"

Colleen just shrugged.

"Are you . . . Do you . . . I mean, is this about Geoff?"

Colleen barely nodded.

"Did something happen out there?"

"Just that Mrs. Hughes . . ."

Molly paused from sandwich making. "What did she say?"

"She saw my engagement ring." Colleen held up her hand, turning it so that the large diamond twinkled in the overhead kitchen light. "She assumed that I was engaged to someone new."

"Oh?"

"She said, '*My, my, now that was quick work.*' You know what I mean . . . . Just dripping with disapproval."

"Oh, dear." Molly shook her head. "That's a bit insensitive."

"So I explained this was the ring Geoff gave me."

"Uh huh."

"Then she suggested that I shouldn't still be wearing it." Colleen set down the knife with a clang. "She actually said, *'You of all girls should know that there are lots of other fish in the sea, Colleen.'* Can you believe that?"

Molly scowled. "That is hugely insensitive. But then, it's Mrs. Hughes. That woman wouldn't win any consideration awards, would she?"

"No." Colleen picked up the knife. "She most certainly would not."

"I'm sorry," Molly said quietly.

"You know what really gets me, though." Colleen looked at Molly. "I'll probably never have any of this. A baby shower, or a wedding, or any of the things Margaret has. And I hate feeling jealous, but the truth is I *am* jealous. Oh, don't worry, I won't tell her. I'm not going to rain on her parade." Colleen's eyes were tearing up. "Do you think I'm a horrible sister?"

"I think it's natural you feel unhappy," Molly said quietly.

"Really?" Colleen sounded surprised. "You don't think I'm selfish?"

"Not really. You've been through a lot, Colleen."

"What about this then?" Colleen lowered her voice. "The truth is that I'm jealous that Brian is still alive—and that Geoff is not. How's that for sisterly love?"

Molly didn't know what to say. That did sound bad.

"It's not that I wish Brian were dead," Colleen whispered. "I really don't."

"I know you don't. You just wish that Geoff was still alive. No one could fault you for that."

And now Colleen started to sob. Molly hugged her, trying to comfort, but it seemed to just make it worse. "You should probably go home," Molly finally told her. "At least until you feel better. I'll make an excuse. I'll tell Mam you're checking on Dad. She'll probably be relieved about that. And Margaret is so caught up in the shower, I doubt she'll even notice."

"Thanks," Colleen muttered. "I'll slip out the back."

After Colleen was gone, Molly continued making the sandwiches, but as she spread the chicken salad, she realized something deep inside of her was feeling angry—a low quiet rumbling like a volcano that wanted to erupt. She hated this war! She hated what it had cost her family—hated how evil leaders in far corners of the world could be so selfish and heartless! She hated how all of her family's lives had been disrupted by it. Even tonight, what should've been a happy celebration, the war had snuck in and stolen some of it from them. But most of all, she hated that this war was far from over—and that her loved ones were still in the midst of it—and how it might cost them even more!

• • •

By the time Colleen got home, her tears had mostly subsided—and she felt foolish for letting her emotions get away with her like that. But since she was home, she decided to check on Dad. If all was well, she'd return to the Hammonds' and perhaps no one, besides Molly, would be the wiser.

"Colleen?" Dad looked up from his newspaper. "Why aren't you at Margaret's baby shower?" His brow creased with concern. "Have you been crying, darling?"

The lump returned to her throat and she just nodded, sitting on the footstool across from him. "Molly told me to come home until I can get control of myself."

"What's wrong?" he asked gently.

And so, for the second time, she told about her encounter with Mrs. Hughes. "I don't know why it got to me like that, but—"

"Viola Hughes is a big-mouthed busybody," Dad declared. "I don't even know why she was invited to the shower in the first place. No one can stand her."

"Because she's Mrs. Hammond's sister-in-law," Colleen reminded him. "She would've thrown a fit if she hadn't been invited."

He reached over, patting Colleen on the head. "I know you're still sad over Geoff, darling, but you've been handling it so well . . . . I

178

almost made myself believe you were over it."

She blinked. "Over it? Oh, Dad, I don't think I'll ever get over it."

He nodded sadly. "I never told you this before, Colleen, but I remember when you announced that you had a new young man. I could tell by the twinkle in your eye that he was someone special. But I was convinced the young man would be a complete cad. And I was all ready to put my foot down and tell him to shove off." Dad chuckled. "But then I met your young man— and I liked him so much, I could hardly believe it. Geoff Conrad was a good man, Colleen. You did well to find him. I couldn't have been more proud of you."

"Thanks, Dad." She felt fresh tears pushing up now. "That means a lot to me."

"I was as sad as I could be when I heard the news about him." Dad folded his newspaper, laying it down. "And later, I wanted to tell you something, but your mam said not to."

"Tell me something?" Colleen used her handkerchief to blot an escaped tear. "What do you mean?"

"Oh, your mam is probably right. I should just keep my thoughts to myself."

"What thoughts, Dad?"

"Well, I remembered how, in the Great War, I heard how some families were notified that their young men were killed in action. But it turned out the servicemen were still alive—in prison camps or unconscious in hospitals without any identification. And I'd read a few accounts of that same thing happening in this war. And I said this very thing to Mam. I wondered if this could've happened to Geoff."

"I had the same thoughts, Dad. And I wish it were possible. But I asked Geoff's family, and Geoff's grandfather told me that he'd contacted the war department with similar questions. Apparently they sent him a full report . . . accounts from the one surviving plane in the squadron."

"I see." Dad frowned. "Although I still wonder how anyone could have such certainty about these things. In the thick of an air battle? Wouldn't it be difficult to know exactly what transpired?"

She nodded. "I've had similar thoughts."

"And it's not that I want to give false hope, Colleen. I suppose it's simply that, like you, I'm not willing to let him go. Remember . . ." He sighed. "That's how I felt about Peter too."

Colleen hugged him. "Even so, it's encouraging to know that you really liked Geoff. I'm glad you shared that with me."

"He was a good man." Dad patted her cheek. "And it's reassuring to know you are a good judge of character, Colleen. For sure and for certain, you had found a good one in Geoff Conrad. And it's a shame he's gone."

"I know." She glanced up at the clock. "I should probably go back to Margaret's baby shower." She stood, smoothing her skirt. "I think I'll be okay now." She attempted a smile. "Thanks for talking to me, Dad. I feel better."

"Don't forget to bring me home some dessert." He winked.

"You got it." Colleen did a quick check of her face in the mirror, but since she hadn't bothered to put on much makeup this morning, there wasn't much need of repair work now. Although she did put on a bit of lipstick and run a comb through her hair. Then, as she hurried back to the Hammonds', she reminded herself that she had once been a fairly good actress. She might not feel happy and lighthearted, but perhaps she could pretend that she was. For Margaret's sake.

Colleen went in through the back door to discover Molly now helping to put dessert on the plates. "Need a hand?" Colleen offered.

"Yes!" Molly eagerly pointed to a loaded silver tray. "Take those out there."

Colleen carried the tray out and, smiling at everyone, acted as if nothing whatsoever had been wrong. And to her relief, no one seemed to be the least bit concerned that she'd been missing earlier. That probably proved the Eleanor

Roosevelt saying that Mam liked to quote from time to time. *"You wouldn't worry so much about what others think of you if you realized how seldom they do."*

After the desserts were served, Margaret's good friend Carol O'Rourke insisted it was time for Margaret to begin opening gifts. And to Colleen's surprise, she no longer felt envious as she watched her older sister opening all the various baby gifts. In fact, she became quite enthralled with all the tiny pieces of clothing and baby items. And when Margaret began to unwrap Colleen's gift, she watched with great interest. Mam had cut out the pieces for the christening gown, but due to her headaches, she'd quickly passed it on to Colleen. "Let this be from you," she'd insisted after Colleen showed her the finished gown. "I never could've done this fine of work."

And Colleen actually had felt proud of the garment, with all the tucks and inset lace and tiny pearl buttons. It really was beautiful. And no one needed to know that Colleen had sometimes imagined it was a part of her wedding gown while she'd been sewing it in the privacy of her room during some of the worst times of her grief. Or that the fabric had sometimes been splattered with her tears. By the time she was done, it looked perfect and beautiful. And as Margaret lifted it from the tissue paper, the whole room grew quiet, followed by oohs and ahhs.

"Did Colleen really sew that?" someone asked. "I had no idea she was so talented."

As the christening gown was passed around the room, Colleen felt glad that she'd returned to the baby shower. Not just for her own sake, but it was rewarding to see that look in Margaret's eyes just now. Almost as if she were proud Colleen was her sister. Wouldn't that be a welcome change!

# Fifteen

*Late September*

Colleen hadn't been to a movie in months. Not since hearing about Geoff. But word had gotten out that a short propaganda film about wartime women on the home front was currently playing with a new movie called *Across the Pacific*. And since everyone in her family was determined to attend the Sunday matinee, Colleen agreed to go along too. However, she tied a silk scarf around her hair and donned her dark glasses and hoped she didn't see anyone she knew there.

"You look like a film star," Molly told her as they waited in the ticket line.

"I don't want anyone to recognize me," Colleen whispered.

"But don't you think it would be exciting to be recognized?" Margaret asked.

"Not for this," Colleen hissed back at her. "This is going to be embarrassing." She wished she'd stayed home. Wasn't it bad enough that she'd had a grueling week at the airplane factory? Plus a long day at the grocery store just yesterday. She should be home getting some much needed rest. While the rest of her family chatted amongst themselves, Colleen feigned interest in the movie poster for one of the films they were about to see. Apparently it was starring Humphrey Bogart and Mary Astor. Then another poster caught her eye. It was a Bogart film too, but his costar was Ingrid Bergman, the young actress that Colleen had been following last year. For the first time since losing Geoff, she felt interested in seeing a film. But this movie wouldn't be out until November. Still, it was something to look forward to.

"Come on," Dad called out. "Let's get our seats."

Still wearing her dark glasses, Colleen followed her family into the theater. She'd already warned them that if the home front movie was too humiliating, she might quietly slip out of the theater and walk home. While Molly and Dad got in line for popcorn, she and Mam and Margaret found a row with five empty seats, and Colleen claimed the one on the aisle, determined to have an easy exit if needed. And it would probably be needed.

The smell of popcorn was giving her a headache, and she passed when Molly offered to share hers. Then after what seemed a long time, the theater darkened and Colleen held her breath for a long moment, waiting for the dreaded short film to begin. But, of course, there were the usual ads and movie trailers and finally, *WOMEN OF WAR, ON THE HOME FRONT* appeared on the screen. Colleen could feel her family's excitement, but she just cringed and shrank down into her seat, waiting for the horrible scenes of her in the kitchen, wearing a homely dress, her hair beneath a bandana, and no makeup, while pretending to cook. It would be so pathetic.

To her surprise, the narration for the movie was rather compelling. The way they made it seem that women "keeping the home fires burning" was so noble and strong was slightly heartwarming. She started to relax, hoping that perhaps her part in the movie had been cut—and then suddenly it was there before her, on the big screen! Even worse than she'd imagined. Could she possibly look less glamorous? Her mother and sisters looked lovely compared to her. Oh, why hadn't they just cut it?

Colleen resisted the urge to cover her eyes and scream bloody murder like she was seeing a horror movie. Instead she simply ducked out of her seat, then slunk out of the theater, hurrying up the hill toward home. The air was chilly and the wind was blowing, but interestingly, by the time she got home, she no longer felt so concerned about the silly movie. What did it matter who saw her looking like that, or what they thought of her? As she made herself a cup of tea, she realized she honestly did not care what anyone thought. *So there!*

As she sat down to sip her tea, she felt bad

that she'd run out like that. Really, it probably would've been fun to see the Bogart movie. And she didn't even know what the second feature was going to be. Not to mention she never got to see how Bernice looked in her film debut. "Oh, you silly goose," she told herself. "You should've just stayed."

Colleen had always known she was a shallow person. Appearance and image had always meant far too much to her, which her family often pointed out. But at the same time she'd always felt she couldn't help it. She was simply like that. Always had been for as long as she could remember. And her shallowness had caused her problems from time to time. Oh, nothing so serious that she couldn't get out of it. But she knew it wasn't an admirable quality. Sometimes she envied people like Molly—they seemed so guileless and unselfish. Truly good. But that would never be her.

Still, she thought as she rinsed her teacup, perhaps there was hope. Maybe she was on the verge of becoming just a bit less shallow. Wouldn't that be something? And, she told her-self as she up went to her room, maybe she would force herself to go back to that movie theater and sit through the whole thing. Not today. But maybe some evening this week. She'd force her-self to simply watch it—and to just get over herself. It would probably be like taking bitter medicine. It might taste nasty going down, but when she was done, she would be healthier for it.

By the time her family got home, Colleen had nearly forgotten her abrupt exit from the theater. Of course, her family, probably worried she was still upset, all acted like they were walking on eggshells.

"How was the movie?" she asked when they finally sat down together at the dinner table.

"Which movie?" Margaret asked.

"The women on the home front movie," Colleen clarified. "What did you think of it?"

"I thought it was well done." Dad forked a slice of meatloaf. "I was proud to see my women taking part in it." He chuckled. "And since I have the most beautiful women in my family, it's no surprise you were all picked to be in the movie."

"I don't know why you were so worried about it," Mam said to Colleen. "We all thought you looked just fine."

"You looked better than fine," Dad proclaimed. "I wish you looked like that every day, Colleen Maureen. I mean, the part where you were in the kitchen." He laughed. "Although I know you can't really cook. But you did look very natural."

"I thought you looked pretty too." Molly spooned out some peas. "I know you felt anxious about being filmed like that, but you're so photogenic. You looked just—"

"Speaking of photogenic," Colleen interrupted. "Did you see my coworker Bernice? She's a brunette and she was acting like a Rosie the Riveter."

"You mean that girl with all the makeup and the smirky smile?" Dad wrinkled his nose. "She wasn't nearly as pretty as *my* girls."

"I agree," Mam declared. "Not nearly as pretty as our girls."

Colleen couldn't help but laugh. After all, what else could her parents say?

"Well, I'm glad to see you're over it," Margaret said as she passed her the potatoes. "I know I am."

Molly laughed loudly. "Yes, but you should've heard Margaret complaining on the way home. Saying how she looked so fat and ugly."

"Which is total nonsense," Mam insisted. "Margaret looked perfectly lovely."

"And she wasn't nearly as fat then as she is now," Dad teased. "Are you certain you're not carrying twins, Maggie? They do run on my side of the family, you know."

Molly was surprised at how many of her classmates had seen the short home front film, and equally surprised by their positive reaction. It was as if they really thought she was a movie star now. And despite her efforts to convince them otherwise, they continued to believe it.

Some of the younger girls even asked her for her autograph.

"This is so silly," she told Dottie on Monday morning. "I hardly did anything in the movie."

"That's not true," Dottie told her. "You got more screen time than any of them. Even that brunette lady who worked on the airplanes wasn't on as much. And Colleen sure wasn't. If you ask me, you were the star, Molly."

Molly just laughed.

"Anyway, I think you should make the most of it. And, unless I'm imagining it, you've caught the eye of a certain fellow."

"Who?" Molly demanded.

"Charlie Stockton," Dottie declared.

"Charlie Stockton?" Molly was shocked. Charlie wasn't only the most popular boy in the senior class, he was also the star quarterback of their football team—and all the girls seemed to be in love with him.

"I think you are imagining things, Dottie." Molly closed her locker, then glanced around.

"I guess time will tell," Dottie said smugly. "But if Charlie asks you out, you have to promise to ask him if we can do a double-date. I've been dying to get to know Charlie's best friend Bill."

Molly chuckled. "Certainly, I can promise that. And I can assure you that it's a promise I won't have to keep. Because Charlie will not be asking me out. From what I hear, he's had his eye on Ginny Reynolds. Besides." She held her head high. "I'm not the least bit interested in Charlie."

"And if you think I'll buy that, Molly Mulligan, you should try to sell me that big red bridge over San Francisco Bay."

The home front propaganda film was a hot topic at Colleen's workplace too. It seemed like nearly everyone at the airplane factory had seen it over the weekend. And those who hadn't seen it planned to do so soon. Colleen wasn't too surprised that Bernice was strutting around the factory, acting like the big film star. And to her own relief, Colleen didn't really care. It was amusing, but that was about all.

"So did you see it?" Audrey asked her during lunch break.

Colleen quickly confessed her need to leave the theater. "It's embarrassing to admit, but I looked so awful in those opening scenes, I just couldn't stand it." She smiled sheepishly. "Of course, I regret now that I didn't have the backbone to watch it. I plan to go again sometime this week." She lowered her voice. "How did Bernice do? How did she look?"

Audrey wrinkled her nose. "Not that great. If you ask me, you looked much better—even without your hair and makeup done."

Colleen smiled. "Thanks. You're sweet."

Audrey just shrugged. "It's the truth, Holly-wood."

Colleen couldn't help but chuckle. It had been awhile since Audrey had called her by that nickname. And, for whatever reason, it felt kind of good. It almost felt like Colleen might eventually return to normal. Or perhaps it would simply be a new normal.

"You were sure great in that movie," Wallace Carlton told Colleen as she and Audrey were going out to the parking lot after work.

"Thanks," Colleen told him, controlling her-self from making excuses for why she wasn't looking her best that day. "I haven't really seen the whole thing yet."

"You haven't?" He squinted in the afternoon sunlight. "Why not?"

"Because she couldn't take it," Audrey teased. "She's one of those actresses who has a hard time seeing herself on the big screen."

"Really?" Wallace peered curiously at Colleen. "I think that's kind of admirable. It means you're not vain."

"Unless it means you're extremely vain." Colleen put on her dark glasses with a smirk.

Wallace grinned. "Well, I suppose that makes sense too." He patted her on the back. "Anyway, I like that you don't seem to take it too seriously." He glanced around the parking lot. "Not like some girls—although we won't mention names."

192

"I heard that Bernice brought publicity photos to work," Audrey said quietly. "That she was offering to sign them for coworkers in her division."

"It's true," Wallace confirmed. "She tried to push a glossy off on me." He laughed. "But I said no thanks." He pointed at Colleen. "So how about if you let me take you to see that movie? I wouldn't mind seeing *Across the Pacific* again myself. Bogart was really good in it."

Colleen didn't know what to say.

"How about it?"

"Uh, can I think about that? And get back to you later?"

He smiled brightly. "Sure. No problem." Then he gave them a mock salute and headed to the opposite side of the parking lot.

"Well, look at you," Audrey said cheerfully. "You were just asked out by the factory's most sought-after bachelor."

Colleen rolled her eyes as she slid into the driver's seat.

"It's true," Audrey continued. "All the single girls have been after that guy. Some of the married ones too."

"Well, I'll admit that Wallace is good looking." Colleen had actually thought Wallace resembled Errol Flynn when she'd first met him. Although now she wasn't so sure. "But I've wondered why he's not in the service."

"Haven't you heard?"

"Heard?"

"He was injured in a car accident. He ranked 4-F at the draft board."

"Really?" Colleen considered this. "So he'll never get sent overseas?"

"I don't think he could even get a desk job."

"Well, as interesting as that is, I'm not interested."

"So you're going to turn him down on the movie invitation?"

Colleen nodded. "I'm not ready to get involved with a guy. I doubt I'll ever be."

"I'm sure you believe that now, Colleen. But mark my word, you won't always feel that way."

"How can you possibly know that?" Colleen regretted the sharpness in her tone.

"Because I think about it sometimes. You know that I dearly love Bill. And if anything happens to him, I'll be devastated. But I believe—given enough time—I could find love again. I feel certain of it."

"Well, that's you. And I'm me. And I feel certain there was only one true love for me. And he is at the bottom of the South Pacific."

# Sixteen

When Colleen got home from work on Monday, Dad seemed agitated about something. "You're here," he said eagerly. "It's about time. I've been—"

"It's the same time I always come home. What are you so worked up over?" She reached to touch his forehead. "You're not sick again, are you?"

"No, I'm fine." He went over to the phone table. "But you need to look at this." He picked up the notepad they used for phone messages, waving it in the air.

"Okay." She hung her plaid wool jacket on the hall-tree by the front door, then came over to see what was on the notepad.

"It's urgent, Colleen. I promised this lady you would call her back as soon as you got home— she's called numerous times. I thought you got home sooner than—"

"Does this say *Georgina Knight?*" Colleen tried to decipher Dad's penmanship. "And who is Joanne Proctor? And *Rory?*" She looked up at Dad with disbelief. "No, no, it couldn't be."

He held up his hands like he was as confused as she felt.

"There's a talent agency in Hollywood,"

Colleen said slowly, "called the Knight Agency. It's owned by Rory and Georgina Knight and—"

"Yes—yes!" Dad exclaimed. "That's what this Joanne person claimed too. She said she works for the agency. And she wants to talk to you."

"Are you kidding me?" Colleen had to sit down. Still holding the pad in her hands, she stared down, trying to make sense of it. "Do you think someone is pulling my leg, Dad? Is this a practical joke? Maybe someone at work or—"

"This Joanne woman sounded like a real person to me. Very brisk and businesslike." He pointed to the paper. "And see, she gave me two phone numbers. One for *before* five o'clock. And one for *after*. And—look, Colleen—those are long-distance numbers. So it can't be someone in San Francisco playing a prank on you."

"Oh, my goodness!" Colleen stood up, walking around the front room in circles and trying to think. "What should I do? What should I do?"

"Well, to start with, you should call that Joanne lady. I promised her you would."

"Yes, yes." Colleen reached for the phone. "But I don't know what to say to her."

"Just say you're returning her call, darling. Let her do the talking."

"Will you stay right here?" Colleen asked. "Sort of listen in? In case I miss something." She smiled nervously. "Or faint."

"You bet. I don't want to miss this. Maybe you should sit down again."

With trembling fingers, Colleen dialed the second phone number and then sat down, waiting with high anxiety as it rang on the other end.

"Knight Talent Agency," a female voice said.

"I'm calling for Joanne Proctor." Colleen tried to keep her voice even.

"This is Joanne. How may I help you?"

Colleen identified herself and said that she was returning a call.

"Oh, Miss Mulligan, thank you for getting back to me so quickly. My boss, Mrs. Knight, saw you in a small propaganda film that is currently playing. She felt that you may have some potential. Tell me, do you have any acting experience?"

"Not really. Oh, I did act in some high school plays, and I've always had aspirations. But this past year I've been, well, helping my family, and then there's the war effort and so on . . ." She knew she was rambling as well as exaggerating her situation. But she couldn't explain everything. She didn't think this woman wanted to hear about Colleen's engagement and loss, or how it had nearly paralyzed her. "So . . . consequently I haven't pursued acting at all this past year."

"Perhaps acting is pursuing you," Joanne said cheerfully. "Tell me, how are you with singing and dancing?"

"I'm no Ginger Rogers, but I've been told I'm a pretty good dancer. And my voice is okay. I played the lead role in *Rosalie*."

"That's good. So, here's the deal, Miss Mulligan. My bosses would like to invite you down here for a screen test."

"A screen test." Colleen nearly dropped the telephone receiver, looking at Dad with wide eyes. "You want *me* to do a screen test?"

"Yes. We think you may be just what we're looking for—a fresh-faced, girl-next-door type. The role is for a blue-eyed, blonde coed, sort of a sidekick. And they're not interested in a big name since Darla Devon and Robert Miller are starring in this film. Of course, it's a musical. But it's also a war picture, which we expect to be a good combination. Patriotism, singing, dancing—the market will eat it up. And, don't worry, the part you might be considered for doesn't involve any solos."

Colleen was speechless.

"Well, how does it sound to you?" Joanne asked. "Are you interested in coming down here?"

Colleen swallowed hard. "Yes, yes . . . I do think I'm interested."

"Great! How soon can you come?"

"How soon do you need me?"

"Oh, like yesterday." Joanne laughed. "For some reason we've had difficulty finding just the right girl. And, don't get me wrong, we don't know that you're right either. Not without a screen test. And, of course, Pinnacle's approval."

"Pinnacle Pictures?" Colleen felt lightheaded.

"Yes, that's right."

"Well, I do have a job, but I could probably get some time off." What was she saying? She would quit her job if necessary. "In fact, I'm sure I can come whenever you think is best."

"Great. I'll make flight arrangements for you first thing tomorrow. Hopefully we can get you down here by Wednesday. Does that work?"

"Yes," Colleen said eagerly. "That's fine."

"Great. You don't by any chance have a portfolio, do you?"

"A portfolio," Colleen said with uncertainty. "I do have a few photos, but not what you'd call a proper portfolio."

"Yes, well, if all goes well, we will take care of that too. Anyway, I'll be in touch tomorrow. Is this the best number to reach you?"

"Yes. If I'm not home, I'm sure my father can take a message."

"Perfect. He seems like a real sweet guy."

Colleen looked at Dad, standing nearby with an expectant expression. "Oh, yes, he is."

After they said good-bye, Colleen turned to Dad. "Did you get the gist of that?"

"I think so. It sounded like they want you to be in a motion picture?" His pale blue eyes were big.

"Well, it's just a screen test. No guarantees."

"But it's still exciting." He grinned.

She nodded. "It feels like I'm dreaming."

Dad gently pinched her arm. "Feel that?"

She smiled. "Yes. Thank you." She sighed. "I know you and Mam have never been too excited about my movie-star dreams. But I hope you'll support me in this."

"Oh, Colleen, I think it's just grand. So much has happened this past year—trials and tribulations we never expected to face. And I know I can be a stubborn old cuss sometimes, but I am trying to change with the times. Remember how proud I was to see my girls up on the screen at the theater? Well, I doubt that would have happened just a year ago."

Colleen knew that was true.

He placed a hand on her shoulder. "Here's what I think, Colleen. This may be just what you need to help you get on with your life."

"What about Mam?"

"I think she'll agree with me. I have a feeling Mam will give you her blessing."

"It just seems so unreal." Colleen stared at the paper with the notes and phone numbers. "Too good to be true, that they would want to test me after I looked so terrible in that home front film."

"We all told you we thought you looked very pretty on the big screen," he reminded her. "I don't know why you couldn't see it for yourself,

Colleen. But it's probably like Margaret said—you believe film stars should be coated in makeup."

"Joanne—she's an assistant to the people who own the talent agency—anyway, she said they are looking for a fresh-faced, girl-next-door type."

"You can do that," he assured her.

They could hear Margaret, Molly, and Mam coming in through the backdoor, chattering happily as they walked into the kitchen. Colleen jumped to her feet, eagerly running out there to tell them her news.

"Are you serious?" Margaret frowned. "Hollywood is calling you? Are you sure it's not some of your goofy work friends pulling a practical joke?"

"It's no joke," Dad told her.

"Why shouldn't Hollywood call Colleen?" Molly defended. "You saw how gorgeous she looked on the big screen. She outshone us all."

"You looked pretty too," Margaret told Molly. "I don't see Hollywood calling you."

"I'm just a kid." Molly stuck out her tongue.

"And here you were so worried," Mam told Colleen, "saying how you didn't look pretty enough without all your makeup and doodads." She patted Colleen's cheek. "It's like I've always told you, Colleen, you're an attractive girl. You don't need all that other stuff. And it seems that Hollywood agrees."

"So you don't mind if I do this?" Colleen asked Mam in disbelief.

"I think it's meant to be," Mam told her. "I think it's just what you need."

"And if you get the movie role, maybe you'll make so much money that you can help your family out," Margaret added. "The store could use a financial boost about now."

"I'd love to help out more," Colleen assured them. "Of course, there are no promises I'll get the role. This is simply a chance to try."

"And won't you have fun going down there," Molly told her. "Imagine how exciting it will be—you in Hollywood! Having a real screen test!"

Colleen nodded. Yes, it was exciting. But not the way she'd imagined it would be back when she used to entertain dreams of becoming a film star. This was more of a subdued sort of excitement. As if something still weighted her down, making her wonder if she could ever be truly happy again. And she knew, deep within, that if she could trade this Hollywood dream to get Geoff back, she would gladly do so.

# Seventeen

*Early October*

It felt dreamlike to walk across the tarmac to the waiting airplane. Colleen paused at the bottom of the plane steps, turning to wave at Molly. Mam had written an excuse for Molly to be late to school so that she could drive Colleen to the airport. And Molly, in true photographer fashion, had her camera ready to document Colleen's first flight. "Be sure and turn to wave," Molly had told her. "Just like a real starlet."

So Colleen blew Molly a dramatic kiss and, smiling broadly, waved again, then turned to board the plane. Colleen knew she looked very stylish in her pale-gray fitted jacket and matching skirt, along with her wide-brimmed hat and gloves, black patent-leather handbag, and matching pumps. This suit was one of her splurges before her film "debut" in June, but she'd never worn it. And after the past several months, it felt very strange to be dressed so impeccably.

As she took her seat, Colleen tried to appear at ease, as if she flew all the time. It was good acting practice. She thought about her coworkers as she calmly flipped through a fashion magazine. Audrey was the only one she'd shared news of her screen test with—well, besides Mr. Perry, who'd generously offered her a whole week off. As the plane began to rumble down the runway, she glanced out the window, noticing the water all around. Colleen tried to appear nonchalant, as if she weren't really worried that the plane would end up in the bay.

As the plane took off, soaring up into the air, Colleen kept her eyes fixed on the glossy magazine, staring at the Evening in Paris perfume advertisement as if she couldn't peel her eyes off the midnight blue bottle, when in reality she was afraid to look out the window. She felt her heart racing wildly, but instead of showing her fear, she simply took in several deep breaths—an exercise she had utilized before performances in high school. She could do this . . . . She could do this. Besides, she reminded herself as the plane now flew over the coastline, if she were killed in a plane wreck, it would be like joining Geoff. And yet, she realized, she didn't really want to die. Not yet. And that surprised her.

She was met at the Los Angeles airport by a driver holding up a placard with MISS MULLIGAN written across it. Just like Joanne had told her would happen. The man collected her baggage for her and, after loading the two suitcases and makeup case onto a cart, led her out to a waiting limousine. It really did feel dreamlike as he drove her from the airport and eventually down palm-tree-lined streets. She guessed she must be in Beverly Hills or perhaps Hollywood. She wasn't sure and wanted to ask questions but knew that would probably sound unsophisticated. She simply watched and waited until finally he parked by a large office building.

"Miss Proctor will meet you in the lobby," he told her. "I will deliver your luggage to your hotel."

"Thank you." Colleen reached for her handbag, wondering if she was expected to tip him, but she quickly decided that was probably up to her hosts. She got out and, smoothing her skirt, took in another calming breath, then strolled up to the building, waiting as a doorman opened the door for her.

"There you are!" a tall brunette woman in a chic black-and-white suit rushed toward her. "Miss Mulligan, I would recognize you anywhere." She shook her hand. "I'm Joanne Proctor. Welcome to Beverly Hills. Did you have a good flight?"

"Yes, thank you." Colleen flashed her brightest smile. "It's a pleasure to meet you, Miss Proctor."

"Call me Joanne." She pointed to the elevator. "The Knight Agency is on the top floor. Mr. and Mrs. Knight are waiting to meet you."

Colleen felt a fresh wave of nerves as the elevator went up. She could think of nothing to say and hoped she wasn't about to lose the breakfast her family had insisted she eat this morning. Now *that* would be embarrassing.

"Are you nervous?" Joanne asked as the elevator slowly stopped.

Colleen slowly nodded. "Yes, I'm afraid so."

"Don't worry. That's perfectly normal."

Colleen smiled. "I guess it's a good acting opportunity, to pretend I'm as cool as a cucumber."

Joanne chuckled as the doors opened. "Exactly."

Standing even straighter, Colleen held her head high, emulating confidence—*she could do this!*

Although their office was spacious, modern, and gorgeous, Mr. and Mrs. Knight both seemed like surprisingly normal people. "Please, excuse our casual appearance," Mrs. Knight told Colleen after the three of them were seated in the sleek white leather chairs. She had on wide-legged orange pants, a creamy white silk blouse with flowing sleeves, and a large diamond-encrusted bangle around her wrist. Meanwhile, Mr. Knight wore a tan sports jacket and tweed trousers and wasn't even wearing a tie.

"This was supposed to be our day off," he explained as he picked up a silver cigarette box. "We only came in today to meet you."

"Thank you for giving up your free time for me." Colleen gracefully crossed one leg over the other, grateful she'd stocked up on nylons before the rationing began.

"Rory needed to be assured you passed muster before we got in too deep." Mrs. Knight's dark eyes twinkled as she took a cigarette. "What think ye?"

Mr. Knight gave an approving nod as he offered the open case to Colleen. "So far so good."

"Thanks." Colleen took a cigarette, then waited while Mr. Knight leaned over to light it for her.

"Turn your head to the right," he commanded as she took a slow drag from the cigarette. "Now to the left."

She did as he said, trying to act as if this was just another day in the life of Colleen Mulligan. Not!

"Are you engaged?" Mrs. Knight pointed to Colleen's left hand with highly arched brows.

"Oh . . ." Colleen had only meant to wear the engagement ring during her flight—for good luck. "I *was* engaged. My fiancé was a navy pilot . . . shot down last spring . . . in the South Pacific."

"Oh, dear, I'm so sorry." Mrs. Knight sighed. "This war."

"I'm sorry too." Mr. Knight sadly shook his head. "Although that story makes for good publicity. That is, if we get to that place, which still remains to be seen."

"Pinnacle has been very picky," Mrs. Knight

told Colleen. "We've sent over two dozen girls already. We started with experienced actresses until we heard the director was really hoping for someone new. A 'fresh face,' he keeps saying. Then I saw you in that propaganda film last weekend. And I thought you could be just what we need."

"She was interested in your younger sister too," he told her.

"But, according to the short film, she's only sixteen, correct?"

"That's right."

"Well, if Colleen makes it in Hollywood, there would probably be some opportunities for the little sister too." He leaned back in his chair and, rubbing his chin with a hard-to-read expression, his eyes locked on Colleen.

Suddenly Mrs. Knight leaned forward, as if closely studying Colleen too. "Have you lost weight since the propaganda movie was filmed?"

"A little," she confessed. "You see, I didn't find out about my fiancé's death until shortly after the filming and, as you can imagine, well, I took it pretty hard." She had no intention of telling them just how hard.

"Well, I think it looks good on you," Mrs. Knight told her. "And Pinnacle has been going for thinner girls lately."

"I can't believe I'm saying this," Mr. Knight said and snuffed out his cigarette, "but I can't seem to find a single thing that needs to be changed. Can you?" He looked at his wife.

She stood up now, slowly walking around Colleen, holding her cigarette between two fingers and studying Colleen like a science experiment in a petri dish. "The brows are just right. Not too thick, not too thin, nice arch. Good chin, not too sharp, not too soft. Nice mouth, full lips. Good eyes, nice color." She leaned forward to peer closely, tapping Colleen's nose. "And even though her nose isn't perfect, I think it has character."

"What's your natural hair color?" Mr. Knight asked.

"Dishwater blonde," she confessed.

"You carry off the platinum just fine," Mrs. Knight confirmed. "Not all girls can. And I'm glad it's not cropped. So many young actresses come in here with short hair. This way the hair stylist has something to work with."

"Stand up," Mr. Knight commanded, "and walk over to the windows and back."

Colleen did as instructed, using her best posture and stride as she slowly strolled over to the big windows. She paused to admire the skyline. "Nice view," she commented, trying to act as if every nerve wasn't standing on end.

"Nice figure," Mrs. Knight said. "Good legs."

"How tall are you?" Mr. Knight asked. "About five-foot-six?"

"Seven," she admitted.

"Weight?" Mrs. Knight asked. "About 115?"

Colleen turned around. "I haven't weighed myself lately, but that's probably close."

"And her voice tone is pleasant," Mrs. Knight said as Colleen walked back to her chair. "And she seems well spoken. Good manners."

Colleen knew it was silly to take offense at these comments. This was simply how Hollywood worked. She'd read and seen enough to understand it. An actress was like a commodity to these people. Similar to investing in a racehorse. They needed to feel confident that all the parts and pieces were there.

Mr. Knight reached for the phone, and soon he was asking Joanne to bring in the contract. He turned to Colleen as he hung up the receiver. "So, Miss Mulligan, are you ready to sign on with us? Want to become a Knight girl?"

"She'll want to read the contract first," Mrs. Knight pointed out.

"Of course. But if she's going to get to the photo shoot on time, we should keep this ball rolling." He looked up as Joanne came in with a folder. "Here we go."

And, just like that, they were going over the contract. Colleen asked a few questions and then, because she could find no reason not to, signed each copy.

"Welcome to the Knight Agency," Mrs. Knight

said as they both shook her hand. "Today will be a preliminary screen test. If Pinnacle likes what they see, we'll set up a more thorough screen test with costume changes and an actor to read lines with you. Probably by Friday or Saturday. But our work here is done, for now anyway." She stood.

"Thank you, Mrs. Knight." Colleen stood too.

"From now on, it's Georgina." She nodded to her husband. "And Rory."

"And Colleen." She beamed at them. "Thank you both for giving me this opportunity."

"Hopefully you'll be just what Pinnacle is looking for." Rory patted her on the back. "But don't take it too hard if you're not."

"Just do your best." Georgina opened the door. "And even if it doesn't work out at Pinnacle, we may have something else to offer."

"You have a look that appeals to Hollywood," Rory assured her. "If you can act, well, that'll be the icing on the cake." He winked at Georgina as if this was a private joke.

"Joanne is going to go with you for the screen test," Georgina said as Joanne met them in the reception area. "And then for a photo shoot. We need to put together a good portfolio ASAP."

Colleen nodded. "Okay."

"We'll get a package to Pinnacle, likely by the end of the week. And then we'll arrange to meet up with you early next week—hopefully with the good news that Pinnacle is offering a contract." Georgina turned to Rory. "And we better run. The Warners are probably already waiting for us at The Derby." And just like that, the glamorous couple hurried off on their way.

"Ready?" Joanne asked Colleen. "Need to powder your nose or anything?"

Colleen gratefully took the opportunity to visit the ladies' room, resisting the urge to pinch herself as she laid her copy of the Knight Talent Agency contract on the counter. Oh, she knew this was simply her foot in the door, but at least the door hadn't closed yet.

"We have a small filming studio in the basement," Joanne explained as they went down in the elevator. "Very simple setup, but useful. And the lighting isn't bad either. Marco will be the cameraman, but it will be up to you to sparkle and shine." She peered closely at Colleen. "I'll make sure your makeup is okay. We need to keep it light and youthful looking, but no shine. Anyway, we've got the basics down there." She pointed to Colleen's jacket. "And this should be just fine for this test. Simple yet classic. The color's not too light, but bright enough to reflect back on your face." She touched Colleen's hair. "We could pin it up, but I think Pinnacle may prefer seeing it down."

"I'll trust your judgment," Colleen said as they emerged into the dimly lit basement.

"It's kind of creepy down here," Joanne said as she led Colleen down a dark hallway. "One of our actresses refuses to come down. She says it's haunted." Joanne laughed. "And she could be right, but I've never been troubled by ghosts." She unlocked a door. "Here we are." She flicked on the lights, and they entered a little room with a small makeup table and clothing rack. "Take a seat and make sure you like what you see." She pointed to the table. "I'll see if Marco is set up."

Colleen sat down and stared at her image in the well-lit mirror, wondering how she might improve her appearance. She'd purposely kept her makeup relatively subdued today. She knew they were looking for the girl-next-door. Perhaps her lip color was a bit intense. She used a tissue to soften her lipstick and then some face powder to ensure there was no shine on her nose, chin or forehead. She decided to unbutton the top button of her jacket, making her appear a bit more casual. Finally, she took a brush through her shoulder-length hair, smoothing it neatly under, and then, not liking how tidy it looked, she gave it a gentle shake. More natural.

"Marco is all set," Joanne announced as she returned. "Looks like you are too."

Colleen smiled brightly as she stood. "I think so."

"Have you done this before?" Joanne asked as she opened the door to the filming studio.

"Only in my dreams."

Joanne laughed and then introduced Colleen to a dark-haired cameraman named Marco. "You'll sit there, Miss Mulligan." She pointed to the straight-backed chair.

"Please, call me Colleen." She gracefully sat, crossing and tucking her legs beneath the chair.

"Okay." Joanne smiled. "So I will ask you a series of questions designed to give you the opportunity to display various emotions. Don't worry about getting any of the answers right—that's not what this is about. We just need you to act and look natural and relaxed. Like you're perfectly comfortable. Just visiting with a friend. But don't be too relaxed. We don't want you to put people to sleep. Show us that you're vivacious and friendly and confident. And don't forget you're the girl next door." She smiled. "Okay?"

"Okay." Colleen folded her hands in her lap.

"Feel free to use your hands or shift your posture as needed." Joanne sat in the chair by the camera, opposite of Colleen. "Anything that adds animation or life—as long as it looks natural." Joanne turned to Marco. "Ready when you are."

Colleen took in a deep steadying breath as Marco said, "Rolling." And, just like that, they were off to the races. To Colleen's relief, she began to relax as she chatted with Joanne. Almost as if the camera weren't even there. In some ways, Colleen almost felt like her old self as she talked and laughed and joked with Joanne. And after about fifteen minutes, Marco said, "Cut."

"That was perfect," Joanne told Colleen.

"Really?" Colleen blinked in surprise. "Is that all we do?"

"Yes. That's a take. I don't see any reason to redo it. Do you?"

"Not if you don't."

Joanne turned to Marco. "Thanks for your work. You know what to do with the film."

"What will he do?" Colleen asked.

"He and his partner will edit it, cutting out my part. They'll make it about seven minutes."

"Oh . . . okay." Colleen stood.

"Don't worry, Miss Mulligan." Marco grinned. "You're going to look great. Nice work. I never know how long these short screen tests will actually take. Sometimes we're in here for hours and most of it gets cut."

"That's true." Joanne was leading Colleen out. "You really were a natural."

Colleen was tempted to confess about how badly she'd messed up in the home front movie, but she stopped herself. She didn't have to lay all her cards on the table. After all, these people seemed to believe in her. Maybe it was time she started to believe in herself again.

# Eighteen

"Your appointment at Bouchard's isn't until three." Joanne said as they stepped out of the building into the bright sunshine.

"Bouchard's?"

"Henri Bouchard. He's a fabulous photographer. Very much in demand. And, believe me, it wasn't easy getting him at such short notice. Henri owed Rory a favor we had to collect on." She led Colleen over to a shiny yellow convertible with its top down. "Here we are."

"Pretty car," Colleen said as she got inside.

"It belongs to the agency, but I'm allowed to use it when caring for clients. Anyway, I thought I'd take you to your room. You're staying at the Beverly Hills Hotel."

"Really?" Colleen tried to contain her excitement. She'd heard of this popular hotel before but never thought she'd be a guest there.

"Bouchard's studio is just a few blocks from the hotel. And since we'll have some time to kill, I thought maybe we should get some lunch. I'm guessing you might be hungry."

Colleen actually felt too keyed up to eat, but she agreed that was a sensible plan. As Joanne pulled up to the iconic hotel, she explained how Colleen would need to do some costume changes during her photo shoot. "You're welcome to use some of your own clothes if you like. Well, I'll have to approve them, of course. Don't worry if you don't have anything suitable. Henri keeps a rack of appropriate garments."

"Okay." Colleen stared up at the hotel sign in wonder as they got out of the car. *This was for real.* She was really here. For a brief instant, she imagined writing to Geoff about this amazing experience—and then she remembered. Still, she had a feeling he would be proud of her. He would probably be patting her on the back right now.

"How about the Polo Lounge for lunch?" Joanne handed her keys to the parking valet.

"Sure." Colleen nodded, trying hard to appear natural as they went into the lobby, acting as if she did things like this every day. The interior of the hotel was bright and cheerful, with tropical colors of coral pinks and palm greens. Exotic and exciting. She had to chuckle as she realized her coworkers had probably just returned to their work stations. Wouldn't it be wonderful if she never had to go back to work there? Oh, she would go in to tell everyone good-bye, but she would not miss the noisy place, or the smell of grease and metal.

As they ate a light lunch, which Colleen barely made a dent in, she told Joanne about some of the outfits she'd brought from home and, finally, Joanne suggested they should go up to Colleen's room and go through the outfits one by one.

With Joanne's help, they selected several garments that would work for the photo shoot, including a pink and white sundress, a pair of wide-legged black trousers and a periwinkle blue silk blouse, her hound's-tooth skirt and jacket, and the striped swimsuit, which Molly had insisted she bring in case there was a pool. Joanne selected shoes and accessories as well, neatly packing them into Colleen's smaller suitcase.

"You'll be glad to have your own swimsuit since they always need a swimsuit shot in the portfolio and a good fit is important." Joanne snapped the suitcase shut. She pointed to Colleen's cosmetics case. "Bring that too. We'll want to shoot you in various makeup looks, you know, for future use. Pinnacle Pictures isn't the only game in town."

Before long, they were at a very elegant photography studio, and Henri Bouchard's assistant was barking orders at Colleen. With Joanne's help, Colleen managed to change from outfit to outfit—everything from denim overalls and a red gingham shirt to a silver sequined evening gown and white fur wrap. Joanne and the assistant helped Colleen to make the appropriate adjustments to her hair and makeup. And then Colleen would return to the shooting area and do as Henri commanded, posing and smiling while his camera clicked and clicked.

• • •

As she waited for her obstetrician to see her, Margaret wondered what Colleen was doing right now. Probably something much more glamorous than this. She remembered how, just last night, Molly had insisted Colleen pack her black-and-white striped swimsuit. "Your hotel will probably have a swimming pool," Molly had pointed out. Margaret could just imagine Colleen now, lounging next to a gleaming blue pool, enjoying a luxurious and unexpected vacation.

It had been Dad's idea to call Dr. Groves this morning. Of course, that was after Mam had called him in alarm. They'd barely gotten to the store when she'd noticed Margaret's ankles looked puffy. Mam had insisted Margaret sit down and put her feet up, and while Margaret complied, Mam had called Dad. Naturally he had taken it upon himself to call Dr. Groves.

"Your appointment is for two o'clock," he'd informed Margaret after he showed up at the store within the hour. "You go home and rest until then. Meanwhile I'll take over here."

"But you—"

"Don't argue with your father." He'd sternly shook his finger at her. "Do as I say, young lady. Either you can take yourself to the doctor, and I will stay at the store to help your mother. Or else I will take you to the doctor and leave Mam here by herself."

So here she was, waiting for Dr. Groves and daydreaming about the exciting life her sister was leading. In fact, it seemed that all three of her sisters led more thrilling lives than she did. Even Molly, who had been nominated for her school's homecoming queen—probably a result of their "movie-making" fame—appeared to be having the time of her life right now. The high school's star quarterback had even called her up at the house to ask if he could be her escort at the dance. Molly had been beside herself.

And Bridget, they had just learned, had been transferred to a "more civilized" location. Apparently it was to get her unit out of harm's way from where they'd been stationed before. But to everyone's relief, Bridget had been allowed to disclose this information. She and her nurse friends were enjoying a leave in New Zealand, and the way she spoke of this enchanting British island made it sound as if it were the most delightful place in the world. Of course, this was probably because Bridget had grown understandably weary of the deprivations of dwelling in a soggy tent in the muddy jungle and being devoured by mosquitoes while caring for the wounded. Certainly, Margaret did not envy her that! Although she had felt a bit jealous when Molly had read Bridget's long and detailed letter last night. It sounded as if Bridget and her nurse friends, invited to spend a fortnight at a beautiful country estate owned by a millionaire, were enjoying a rather elegant vacation.

Then there was Colleen—down in Hollywood, being considered for a role in a real motion picture! Margaret could hardly bear to think about that. Just watching Colleen packing her bags last night had been painful. And then she'd flown out of San Francisco on an airplane this morning! When had Margaret ever been on a trip like that? And it was unlikely she ever would. Oh, she knew that after all Colleen had been through these past months, she should be glad for her sister.

Besides, she reminded herself, she still had Brian. And she would soon have a delightful little baby! But staring down at her swollen ankles, which seemed to ooze out of the sturdy oxford pumps Mam insisted she wear, it just didn't seem fair. It really felt like everyone—except her—was out there having a good time. Her life basically consisted of working at the store and planning for a baby. And sometimes, like right now, it just wasn't enough.

She reached down to her enormous midsection. Beneath her cotton maternity blouse, her belly was as tight and firm as a watermelon. A very big watermelon! She reminded herself that she would soon be holding a *bundle of joy* in her arms. Shouldn't that make her happy? Her due date was less than a month from now. And when the baby came, wouldn't it change everything? She could imagine herself wheeling the baby down the streets of San Francisco in the baby-buggy the Hammonds had presented to her on the night of her baby shower. Wouldn't that be fun?

Her long months of pregnancy would soon pay off—and her sweet baby would make up for everything. She thought about the adorable baby outfits she'd received at her shower. And the other ones that she and Mam and her sisters had sewn. And then there was that beautiful christening gown. It would be so exciting to take her new baby for the big christening day. Mam was already talking about the celebration they would have afterward.

Except that Brian would not be here. According to his last letter, he wouldn't have a leave for some time. Their baby might be walking by the time Brian came home. Still, she knew she should be thankful. At least Brian was still alive. So far, he hadn't been shipped off into active duty. Of course, he thought his military service was rather boring. Although he was an officer, stationed in England, his job seemed to consist of making sure that the US Army would have plenty of forks and spoons and army boots. Not exactly what he'd dreamed of when he'd enlisted.

To be fair, this wasn't exactly what she'd dreamed of either. Oh, she had desperately wanted to be married to Brian. And she'd definitely wanted to have children—four or five eventually. At least it was what she'd been hoping for just a year ago. The only thing was that this confounded war had messed everything up. Instead of playing house with her loving husband by her side, she was doing this alone. The war had disrupted her dreams.

"Mrs. Hammond?" A nurse, dressed in a sleek white uniform, stood in the doorway with a clipboard.

Margaret glanced around, then remembered *she* was Mrs. Hammond. "Yes?"

"The doctor will see you now."

Margaret clumsily pushed herself to her feet, grabbed up her purse, and followed the nurse into an examining room, where she put her through the usual drill and then the doctor came in. But instead of talking in his normal jovial way, he looked slightly concerned. "You appear to have developed toxemia," he said soberly.

"Toxemia?"

He pointed his pen toward her ankles. "That's what caused the swelling." Now he pointed to his clipboard. "And your high blood pressure."

"What does this mean? Is my baby in danger?"

"If you ignore your condition, it will likely get worse, and then you could both be in danger." He helped her to lie back and then, using his stethoscope, listened for the baby's heartbeat.

"Is the baby okay?" she asked as he stood up straight.

"Sounds just fine."

"Is there medicine for toxemia?"

"No. The only treatment is bed rest, Mrs. Hammond. Probably from now until your baby is safely delivered."

"Will the baby be safely delivered?" she asked with anxiety.

"As long as you follow your doctor's orders." Now he smiled, but there was still concern in his eyes.

"You mean to stay in bed?" She frowned. Mam and Dad would definitely have to hire someone else to help at the store now.

"That's right." He was writing on the clipboard. "I know your husband is in the army, but do you have family at home? Someone to help care for you?"

"I, uh, yes, I'm sure I can figure something out."

"Good." He pulled out his stethoscope, listening to her heart while she took some deep breaths. "Have you had headaches?" Now he poked and prodded her here and there.

"Sometimes," she admitted.

"If your headaches get worse or you experience dizziness or more swelling or any of the other symptoms I've written down here"—he handed her a slip of paper—"you be sure to give me a call."

"So the baby really is okay?" she asked again.

"The heartbeat was strong. But it's up to you, Mrs. Hammond. You must stay in bed. Fortunately, your due date isn't too far out."

"I drove myself here," she admitted. "Is it safe to drive myself home?"

"Yes. But go directly home. Go directly to bed. Understand?"

She nodded somberly.

"And let your family take care of you." He smiled. "Pretend you're on vacation."

"Vacation?" She sighed to remember how she'd just been longing for a vacation. But not like this.

After nearly two hours running back and forth between the changing room and photography studio, the photographer was finally done and Colleen felt exhausted. She had no idea a photo shoot could be so demanding. Oh, it had been fun posing in some of the elegant outfits, but all that changing and rushing and the pressure to look at ease and yet please the camera . . . well, it was harder than it looked.

But by the time Colleen and Joanne were back at the hotel, Colleen's energy had returned, and when Joanne invited her to join her for an early dinner, Colleen gladly accepted.

"Nothing fancy." Joanne touched up her lipstick as the elevator took them up. "So you won't need to dress up."

"That sounds good to me." Colleen sighed to think of how many times she'd changed her clothes these past two hours. "I think I'm actually hungry now."

"Great," Joanne said. "I'd hoped you'd be interested. I already made reservations at the Formosa."

Colleen felt a fresh wave of excitement as they dropped her bags in her room. The Formosa Café was a Hollywood hot spot. "I wonder if we'll see anyone famous."

"I'd be surprised if we didn't."

As it turned out, they saw several celebrities, but it was Katharine Hepburn who really captured Colleen's attention. "She's so beautiful," Colleen whispered as the movie star, dressed in pleated trousers, was led to a corner table, where she sat down and lit a cigarette. "Do you think she's meeting someone?"

"From what I've been hearing, I'd guess it could be Spencer Tracy."

"Spencer Tracy?" Colleen gasped to imagine what her family would say if she were able to get a glimpse of one of their favorite movie stars.

Joanne lowered her voice. "I hear Spencer and Kate are more than just costars now."

"Really?" Colleen was trying not to stare at Miss Hepburn, but it wasn't easy.

"Didn't you see *Woman of the Year*?"

"Yes, of course." She nodded eagerly.

"Rumor has it they fell in love while making that one."

"I heard that, but I figured it was just Hollywood gossip—you know, to sell magazines and get publicity for the movie."

"From what I hear, it's true." Joanne's brows arched. "And now it seems that my prediction is right. Don't stare, though."

Sure enough, Spencer Tracy, dressed very casually in a white knit shirt and tan trousers, was now joining Miss Hepburn.

"Of course, they will tell everyone that it's because they're working on another film together," Joanne said quietly, "but I'm pretty sure there are sparks flying between the two of them. Don't they make a handsome couple?"

Colleen nodded without even looking at them. "I thought they were great together in *Woman of the Year*. I loved that film."

"And I'm sure you know about what happens in Hollywood." Joanne smiled slyly. "The way that actors and actresses can fall in love when they costar together?"

"I do read the Hollywood magazines," she confessed.

"Some of those stories are nothing more than hype," Joanne told her. "But some stories—like Clark Gable and Carole Lombard—they were the real deal." She sighed sadly. "That poor man was totally shattered when she was killed in that plane wreck last winter."

"That was so heartbreaking." Colleen felt slightly teary to remember how Clark Gable had lost his beloved wife.

"She'd flown to her hometown for the war effort," Joanne said absently. "Selling war bonds. I think she made about two million dollars. Can you believe that?"

"I read about how Mr. Gable went out to the mountains to search for her, thinking perhaps she had survived."

"But she didn't. And everyone told Carole not to fly in the winter time."

"I read she was so eager to get home, to get back to Clark. They were so in love." Colleen reached for a handkerchief—the emotion getting the best of her—and let out a choked sob.

"I'm sorry," Joanne said suddenly. "I didn't mean to upset you."

Colleen felt embarrassed now, as if an explanation were needed. "It's just that I—I can relate to Clark Gable's pain." She quickly explained about Geoff going down in a plane too. "I'm trying to move forward, but I loved him so."

"Oh, my—I'm so sorry." Joanne reached over to grasp her hand. "I had no idea."

"I know you didn't. It's just that story about Gable and Lombard hits close to home." Colleen sniffed, trying to think of a way to change the subject. "I hear that Mr. Gable recently joined the military. I think he's in England right now. No one expected someone like him to join in the war effort. But he's really a remarkable man, isn't he?"

Joanne glanced toward the celebrity couple. "Spencer is going to miss Clark. Those two are very good friends."

"Well, at least Spencer has Miss Hepburn now." Colleen let her gaze pass over the glamorous pair. They were both smoking and laughing. Clearly they were delighted to be together, almost oblivious to the world around them. It reminded her of how it had been with Geoff. Just the two of them, and nothing else had mattered.

# Nineteen

*Mid-October 1942*

Colleen hadn't even been gone but a few days when Molly realized how much she missed her. For one thing, Molly needed advice on what to wear for the homecoming celebration. She didn't really expect to be elected homecoming queen. After all, she was only a junior. But because she was on the ballot, she was expected to participate in the court. And Charlie Stockton had already volunteered to be her escort. Those two factors alone demanded a pretty gown. She couldn't expect any help from Margaret. Not simply because Margaret needed to rest quietly until the baby arrived, but also because Margaret had never been much help in the fashion department.

Oh, Molly knew it was silly to be so enthralled over this shallow social event. Especially in light of what was going on, both in her family as well as the larger world these days. But, like Dad would remind her, she was still a kid—and she should enjoy some kid-like activities before she grew up and left all that behind.

Homecoming wasn't the only reason she missed Colleen. Ironic as it seemed, the two of them had actually become quite close these past few months. So much so that Molly wasn't sure how she'd react if Colleen was actually cast in the motion picture. Selfish as it was, she did not want Colleen to move away from home. She did not want to lose her. Not after losing Peter . . . and then having Bridget so far away. Was she supposed to give up Colleen too?

Molly wondered if was wrong to pray for Colleen to *not* get the movie role. Because, honestly, she believed deep down that Hollywood was not the best place for Colleen. Oh, sure, it might help her to forget Geoff—for a while anyway. But would it be worth it in the end? What if Colleen got involved with the wrong sort of fellow down there? Didn't that happen all the time with pretty young starlets? Weren't they often preyed upon by unscrupulous older men? And Colleen seemed very vulnerable right now. What if she settled for someone who was unworthy? Wasn't that just the sort of thing that Peter—and later Patrick—had often warned Molly about? Had anyone ever warned Colleen? Or had she been too strong-willed to listen back then? Perhaps she would listen now.

Margaret didn't like feeling like a burden to her family, especially when they were somewhat shorthanded. But at least Dad had hired another clerk for the store. Still, Margaret knew it was an expense her family could barely afford right now. And her bedridden condition and need of "supervision" was not helping a bit.

"We are not going to leave you alone," Mam had declared right after hearing Margaret's news. And despite Margaret's protests, Mam had implemented a plan where all her family members shared shifts. She'd even drawn up a schedule that she'd thumb-tacked to the wall by Margaret's dresser. At first it had been sort of fun to get all this extra attention, but by the sixth day of her confinement, Margaret was feeling like a caged animal. She desperately wanted some time to herself.

"I appreciate your help, Mrs. Hammond," Margaret said carefully. "But I really don't need someone by my side every minute of the day."

"First of all, I've told you not to call me Mrs. Hammond." She patted her hand with a patient expression. "Call me Mom or Louise, whichever suits you, dear. And second of all, you *do* need someone with you. Your doctor said so." She held up a V-mail letter. "And I almost forgot, I just got this in the morning's mail. Jack hasn't even seen it yet."

"From Brian?" Margaret's heart gave a happy lurch. "I haven't heard from him for nearly a week."

"I'm sure your letter must be on its way." Louise unfolded the letter and started to read.

The beginning held the usual pleasantries as well as a couple of highlights regarding his stay in England.

As you know, I've been spending most of my time at a desk, ordering supplies and provisions for the troops that will eventually be transported to the European front. However, that is not how I'd hoped to spend my time in the war effort. I'm relieved to say that will be changing before long. Although, as usual, I can't disclose where I will be transferred to or any specific timeframe, I am pleased to say it will be a leadership position in a more active assignment. I am looking forward to it . . .

Margaret's ears grew dull to the rest of the letter. All she could think was that Brian was about to be moved to the battlefront. From what little she'd heard, since she normally tried not to listen, this would be in North Africa. But was he saying he would be leading troops? How dangerous would that be?

"Are you all right, dear?" Louise was leaning over to peer at Margaret.

"Yes—I'm fine," Margaret said a bit sharply.

"You look pale." Louise reached over to feel of her forehead.

"Really, I'm fine." Margaret took in a deep breath. "It's just that I do get weary of this." She patted the bed. "And I really don't need to be baby-sat all the—"

"Well, I'm your baby's grandmother and I feel honored to share in this responsibility." She chuckled. "And it gives me an excuse not to go work at the shop with Jack for a few hours."

"Yes, I understand all that, but you don't have to sit by my bedside," Margaret smiled stiffly. "I'm grateful that you're here, Louise, but I can be on my own for a bit."

"But don't you get lonely, stuck up here in your little room, all by yourself all day?"

Margaret held up one of the novels that Molly had brought her from the library. "I'm content to quietly read for a bit." The truth was she was tired of visiting with everyone. They all seemed so determined to be cheerful and helpful, trying to lift her spirits. And then she felt the need to be cheerful and bright in return—even when she felt anything but, like right now. The truth was, it was getting quite aggravating. Margaret was tempted to imitate Greta Garbo and say, "I just vant to be alone," but wasn't sure her mother-in-law would see the humor in it.

Louise put the white baby booty she'd been knitting back into her bag, then pointed to the little brass bell that Mam had put on Margaret's bedside table—to be used in case Margaret needed assistance in the night. "Well, I suppose if you promise to ring that, I could go sit in the front room and knit in there. If you're sure, dear."

"Yes, I'm sure." She smiled gratefully. "Thank you."

Margaret sighed in relief as Louise took her leave and then, determined not to obsess over Brian's safety, she opened her novel and let it take her completely away. It was around eleven when she heard the telephone ring. Probably Mam checking in on her, although she usually called at noon. Hopefully Louise wouldn't drag the phone up the stairs, using the long cord that Dad had installed last weekend.

"Colleen?" Louise said eagerly. "Oh, how are you?"

Suddenly Margaret did want the phone in here. She wanted to hear Colleen's voice and find out what was going on down in Hollywood and when her sister was coming home. Hopefully she didn't get the movie part. Margaret wouldn't admit it to anyone—especially Colleen—but she was praying that it would all fall apart. And Colleen would come home and help her family. Either by working in the store or returning to her job in the airplane factory.

"It's your sister, dear. Long distance." Louise came into the room with the black telephone.

Margaret set aside her book, reaching for the

235

telephone receiver. "Colleen?" she said eagerly. "How are you?"

"I'm just fine," Colleen said cheerfully. "How are *you?* Mam told me about you being stuck in bed the last time I called. I'm so sorry. I hope it's not too serious."

"I'm all right. Just bored."

"And the baby is fine?"

"Yes. The doctor said the heartbeat is strong. I just need to take it easy until the baby arrives. Hopefully in about three weeks." Margaret grimaced. Three weeks in bed sounded like eternity. "But tell me about what you're doing. How is Hollywood?"

"Oh, Margaret. It's like a dream. The hotel I'm staying in is so beautiful. You would love it. And everyone has been so nice to me. But it's been hard work too. My first screen test wasn't terribly difficult. In fact, it was rather fun. Apparently, I did okay. Then I did a photo shoot so the agency representing me could put together a portfolio for the studio. We had to wait a few days to hear their response. But it was positive, and on Friday, I went into Pinnacle to meet the producer and director."

"Oh, my goodness. That must've been scary."

"I was pretty nervous. But my agent was with me. And I think I did okay in my interview."

"So what does this mean?" Margaret felt uneasy. "Did you get the role?"

"No, no, they haven't made their final decision yet. But they did decide to have me do my second screen test. That will be at the studio. Someone will pick me up at one and the screen test will take two or three hours. I was just sitting here in my hotel room and suddenly I felt so nervous, I just had to talk to someone at home."

"I'm so glad you called. It's so good to hear your voice." And it really was good. Except that Margaret wished Colleen was here instead of down in Hollywood. "When will you come home?"

"The agency booked me a flight for tomorrow afternoon. I'll arrive in San Francisco around four. Hopefully, Molly can come pick me up. Georgina—she's the co-owner of the Knight Agency—said it will probably take Pinnacle about a week to make their final decision. And I might as well wait at home to hear back."

"Do you think they'll pick you?"

"I hear they have it narrowed down to about three, including me. But if my final screen test doesn't please them . . . well, I'll be out of the running."

"Oh." Margaret frowned.

"So . . . I know I never used to put much stock in prayers—although that's been changing— but please pray for me, Margaret. Pray that my screen test isn't a flop."

"Oh . . . okay."

"Because I really *want* this. It's funny too, because when I came down here I didn't think I cared that much. In fact, I didn't really care about much of anything. But since I've been down here, working so hard for this, doing my best, doing everything they ask of me, well, it's like I've really started to care. *I want this.*"

Margaret didn't know what to say. She wanted to scream, *"No, no, no!"* but knew that would be wrong—and hurtful.

"I'm sorry," Colleen said suddenly. "I'm going on and on about myself. So, tell me, Margaret, how are you really feeling? Is it nice having some forced rest? Are you terribly sick?"

"I really don't feel that bad. I'm tired and I get headaches sometimes. But mostly it's about boredom now." She lowered her voice. "And it gets old having to be watched all the time."

"Watched?"

"Mam scheduled everyone to sit with me. I really don't think I need it, but no one seems to listen to me."

"Poor Margaret. Well, maybe I can help with your boredom. When I get home and it's my turn to sit with you, I'll entertain you with all my Hollywood stories. Did you hear that I saw Spencer Tracy and Katharine Hepburn at dinner my first night here?"

"No!" Suddenly Margaret felt a tiny bit more interested in her sister's possible film career.

"Well, I'll tell you about everything when I get home. You rest up and take care until then, Margaret."

Margaret agreed to this—as if she had a choice—then said good-bye and hung up. Lying in bed, she tried to imagine her sister rubbing elbows with people like Spencer Tracy and Katharine Hepburn. And even though Margaret had never been as star-struck as Colleen, she did have respect and admiration for certain celebrities, and it was staggering to think of Colleen actually down there with them. Even so, she wasn't sure she could pray for Colleen to do well on her screen test. Not with real sincerity anyway. Just the same, she reached for her rosary—hanging on the bedpost—and prayed three Hail Marys. And, really, that was the best she could do.

Molly was so excited to pick up Colleen from the airport. It felt as if her sister had been gone for a month, not just a week. And as she watched Colleen coming down the steps from the plane, it seemed that she had changed. Or maybe she was just more like her old self. But there was a confident spring in her step.

"Welcome home!" Molly exclaimed as she hugged her. "I missed you."

Colleen laughed. "I was only gone a week."

"It was a long week." Molly reached to

take her sister's cosmetics case. "I'll carry that."

"Oh, it's good to be home," Colleen said happily. "I missed you too. And everyone. But it really was fun to be down there."

"I want to hear all about it," Molly said as they walked across the tarmac. "First of all, was it exciting to fly?"

"The first flight was pretty scary," Colleen admitted. "But coming home wasn't so bad. In fact, it was actually kind of fun. The view from up there is so amazing. Everything looks so small—the cars and houses all look like tiny toys. And the ocean is so vast and blue and beautiful." She slowly shook her head in wonder. "And, of course, it made me think of Geoff. But it didn't hurt nearly as much this time." She looked at Molly. "Almost as if I'm getting over it—I mean the ache deep within me. I'll never get over losing him. But it really did feel like the pain was subsiding."

"That's wonderful, Colleen."

They collected her luggage and were soon in the car. As Molly drove, Colleen talked in the old animated way Molly remembered from before. It seemed that going to Hollywood really had been good medicine for her sister.

"And yesterday's screen test went extremely well," Colleen was saying as they got closer to home. "I wasn't so sure, but Georgina

Knight was with me, and afterward she said she didn't think it could've gone any better."

"That's so great, Colleen. I'm thrilled for you." And Molly was happy . . . but she was also worried. "So do you think Pinnacle will pick you?"

"I honestly don't know. I have no idea who my competition is. And, as you know, I don't have a big name. According to Georgina, that shouldn't matter. But she also mentioned that one of the actresses in the running does have a name. And you never know—names have a lot of value in Hollywood." She giggled. "Speaking of names, my agents have suggested I go by my middle name—for a screen name."

"Maureen Mulligan?" Molly tried it out as she parked in front of the house.

"It does have a nice ring to it, don't you think? *Miss Maureen Mulligan.*"

"Yes, it actually sounds like a real movie star."

"Do you think Mam and Dad will mind?"

"I don't see why. They gave you that middle name." Molly got Colleen's two suitcases out of the trunk. "How long will it be until you hear back from the studio?" she asked as they walked up to the house. "I mean about whether or not they picked you?"

"Georgina said it will take at least a week. Maybe two."

"Will you go back to work at the airplane factory?"

"I'm not sure." Colleen frowned. "I want to hear what Mam and Dad think before I make a decision. With Margaret being so sick and all, I wonder if I should quit the factory and go to work at the store and help out more at home. At least until I hear about the movie. And even if I am cast, filming won't begin until mid-November."

"Mid-November? That's not that far off." Molly cringed inwardly as she lugged the suitcases up the front steps. Was it possible that Colleen would be gone in less than a month? Molly didn't like the way her family kept shrinking. Well, at least they still had Margaret—and her baby would soon join their numbers. As long as nothing else went wrong . . . and Molly was praying that it wouldn't.

# Twenty

To Margaret's surprise, Colleen turned out to be the best medicine when it came to lifting her spirits. Even better than Molly—and that was saying a lot. Colleen seemed to be back to her old cheerful self—with a bit of sobriety beneath the surface. Still she was vivacious and interesting and, Margaret hated to admit it, *entertaining*.

Mam and Dad both felt Colleen should give up the airplane factory job until she heard back from Hollywood. "You can work part-time in the store and help out at home," Dad had told her. "And if your motion-picture dreams don't come true, I'm sure the airplane factory will be glad to take you back. I heard they'll soon be hiring again anyway."

"But not until Margaret has her baby," Mam had insisted. "We need extra help until then."

It was on Colleen's third day of sitting at home with Margaret that she got a phone call that seemed to take her back down to the dark place where she'd spent so much time after losing Geoff. Margaret could instantly tell that something was very wrong, but when she questioned Colleen, she simply brushed it off.

"I know something is troubling you," Margaret finally said. "Was it your agency from Hollywood? Did they call to say you weren't chosen for the part?"

"No, no . . . That's not it." Colleen gave what seemed a forced smile as she set a tray of lunch in front of Margaret.

"Tell me," Margaret demanded.

"I don't want to worry you," Colleen said. "You're not supposed to get anxious about—"

"Not knowing what's wrong is making me very anxious," Margaret declared. "And I won't be able to eat a bite of my lunch if you don't come clean with me."

"Oh." Colleen nodded. "Well, that was Geoff's mother on the phone."

"What did she want?"

"I don't really know. I mean, she wants me to come out to see her. But she didn't say why. And I was so uneasy—just hearing her voice out of the blue—that I didn't ask."

"But you'll go see her?"

"I promised to come out after Mam gets home this afternoon."

"By yourself?"

Colleen shrugged. "I guess so. Molly is scheduled to work at the store after school. And I don't really want to take Mam with me."

"No, that probably wouldn't be good. I'd go with you, Colleen, if I were in better shape."

Colleen smiled. "Thanks, Margaret. I know you would. But I'm a big girl. I can do this.

And, really, it wasn't as if she sounded angry or anything like that. Mostly she just sounded sad."

"Well, I'll be curious to hear all about it." Margaret dipped her spoon into the soup and, not for the first time, felt grateful for her lovely in-laws. The Hammonds, in her opinion, were just about perfect.

Colleen experienced a new wave of nerves as she walked up to the big white house. But, she reminded herself, if she could face Hollywood screen tests, she could surely face this. Besides, what could Geoff's mom possibly say or do to her that could be any worse than what she'd said or done before?

"Thank you for coming," Ellen Conrad said graciously as she opened the door. "Please, come in."

Colleen felt slightly off guard as she went into the foyer. She wasn't used to this kind of treatment from this woman. She cautiously began to unbutton her coat.

"Let me take that for you," Ellen offered. As she hung it in the closet, she invited Colleen to make herself comfortable in the living room. "I've got tea set up for us."

Feeling like she was playing a role in a movie—one where no one had given her a script—Colleen went into the living room and, taking off her gloves, sat down on the sofa, trying not to remember how a little less than a year ago, she'd sat in this very spot with Geoff by her side. Both of them so full of hope and love and dreams . . . oblivious to how it would all fall apart so quickly.

Ellen joined Colleen with a cardboard box in her hands. "The navy sent Geoff's things to me." She set it next to the tea tray. "I thought perhaps you'd want to go through it too. There may be a few mementoes you'd like to have."

"That's very kind of you." Colleen was stunned. Why was Ellen being so nice?

Ellen poured a cup of tea. "Do you take anything?"

"No, just black." Colleen's hand trembled slightly as she reached for the cup. "Thank you."

"I want to apologize for the way I handled things." Ellen spoke slowly as she stirred cream into her tea. "As Geoff's grandparents pointed out, I was wrong not to inform you straightaway about Geoff's death." She looked up with sad blue eyes, similar to her son's but not nearly as vibrant. "I don't think it was out of spite, although I'm not certain that it wasn't. But I was so devastated by the news . . . ." Her voice cracked. "I was barely functioning."

Colleen reached over to put her hand on Ellen's. "I understand completely. I was devastated too. I've only recently begun to feel that I'm out from under that heavy black cloud of sadness myself." She considered telling her about Hollywood but thought better of it. Geoff's mother would not approve.

"I also need to apologize for the way I treated you, Colleen, the first time we met. I know I was abhorrent. Geoff's grandparents reminded me of that as well. My only excuse is that Geoff is—was—my only son. After losing his father, I was always fiercely protective of him. And, as you know, I was upset that he wanted to be a navy pilot. And I suppose I attributed part of that to you. As if you had some control over my strong-willed son." She shook her head. "I know better."

"If it's any comfort to you, I wasn't a bit glad when Geoff told me he was joining the navy. My own brother had just been killed at Pearl Harbor—and I hadn't wanted him to go."

"I know." She nodded sadly. "These are things that have been troubling me, Colleen. The way I treated you so badly, holding you responsible for things you had no control over. I am truly sorry."

"I accept your apology. And I'm sorry for my actions too. I'm sure I was arrogant and full of myself when I met you."

"You were young. I can't fault you for that." She took a sip of tea.

"And if it's any consolation, I loved Geoff with my whole heart." She sighed. "I'm afraid I'll never love anyone like I loved him."

"I understand that." She set down her teacup,

looking at Colleen with misty eyes. "That's another thing I deeply regret, Colleen. I hope you can forgive me for this too. I'm so sorry—for Geoff and for you—that I was so obstinate about you two getting married before he went over-seas. If I'd had any idea—if I'd known how short his life was going to be—I'd have stepped back and given you both my blessing." And now she broke into full-blown tears.

Colleen set down her own teacup and, moving closer, put her arm around Ellen's shoulders. "All is forgiven. And I'm sure Geoff had already forgiven you."

Ellen looked at her with a puzzled expression. "Do you really think so?"

"Geoff was a very kind man," Colleen said with confidence. "I'm certain he would have forgiven you." She wanted to add that he would probably forgive his fiancée too—she still remembered the glib little letter she'd written, the one she could never be sure whether he had received or not.

"I hope you're right." Ellen slid the box closer to them, removing the lid. "It's not easy to see these things. But I felt you had the right. Much of this involves you." She lifted up a bundle of photographs. Mostly the ones Molly had taken. Some of them with Geoff and Colleen, smiling happily together. And several of just Colleen, sent after he'd been shipped overseas.

Colleen stared at one of the photos of her from

Christmastime. "That almost seems like someone else," she said absently. "Some carefree girl with no idea of what's around the next corner."

"And there are some letters here too," Geoff's mom held up a small bundle of pale pink envelopes. "Apparently some of these arrived after his plane was shot down . . . since they've never been opened." She sniffed one. "Perfume?"

"Chanel No. 5," Colleen admitted as she reached for the bundle, eagerly looking through to see that the letter she'd been so worried about was still unopened.

"If I had it all to do over again, I would do it differently," Ellen said.

"So would I," Colleen admitted as she slipped the letters into her handbag.

Together they sorted through the other things in the box. Although Colleen took a few of the photos, she left most of them for Ellen. "My sister Molly will have the negatives. We can get more made." She reached into the box to touch his officer's jacket, then pulled her hand back. "I don't think I can take anything else," she said in a choked voice. "It's just too hard."

"I understand." Ellen put the lid back on the box. "I feel the same, but this box will be stored in Geoff's old room, if you should ever change your mind."

Colleen knew she was on the verge of tears again and didn't really want to make a spectacle of herself. Especially since this encounter had gone surprisingly well. "Thank you for having me come out here," she said in a raspy voice. "You have no idea how much this means to me."

"Thank you for coming . . . and for your graciousness." Ellen glanced over her shoulder. "Geoff's grandparents will be relieved to hear it." She made a slight smile. "Perhaps they've been listening from the kitchen. Although they did promise to remain behind the scenes."

"Give them my best." Colleen reached for her handbag. "I should probably go. My dad will be worried if I don't get home before dark. He feels it's dangerous to drive too much at night because of blackout."

"Yes, yes, by all means, be on your way. And drive carefully." Ellen stood and, grasping Colleen's hand, looked into her eyes. "I believe you would've made a fine wife for my son, Colleen. I'm sorry I didn't see it then."

Colleen's heart gave a sharp twist, but all she could do was nod and say a gruff thank you and good-bye. But as soon as she got into the car, the tears started to trickle down. But these were bittersweet tears. Not nearly as painful as her last visit. As she drove down the tree-lined driveway, a blur of green and gold, she felt that perhaps these tears had healing powers. And by the time she entered the main highway, to her relief, her crying subsided. Somehow, she knew, she was going to be okay.

Molly was glad for Colleen's help in getting an evening gown together for the homecoming celebration, but she was not fond of Colleen's insinuations about Molly's relationship with Charlie Stockton. Why couldn't she understand that they were simply friends?

"But I thought Margaret told me you were dating him." Colleen pinned the remodeled neckline of the pale blue satin fabric. She was remaking one of her own gowns to resemble one that she'd worn down in Hollywood during a photo shoot.

"No, it's not like that," Molly insisted.

"But you went to a movie with him, didn't you?" Colleen removed a pin from her mouth, carefully inserting it into the bodice.

"Yes, with Bill and Dottie too."

"So it was a double date."

"I guess you could say that. But I didn't really think of it like a date."

"So he didn't even kiss you afterward?"

Molly giggled nervously. "Well, he tried to, but I shook his hand."

Colleen laughed, grabbing the pins from between her lips. "Don't make me choke on a pin, Molly." She nudged her shoulder. "Quarter turn."

Molly turned slightly. Now she could see her reflection in Colleen's full-length mirror. "That looks really pretty," she said. "You were right about changing it to cap sleeves. Very stylish. If you don't become a film star, maybe you could be a costume designer."

"That would be fun." Colleen nodded. "But not as exciting as being in a motion picture. Turn again."

Before long, Colleen was peeling the filmy gown off Molly. "You're going to be the prettiest girl in the court," she said as she laid the dress on her bed. "Even if you're right about not being elected queen." Her brow creased. "But don't be so sure. After all, you're a Mulligan. You should carry on the family tradition."

"I'm not you, Colleen." Molly tied the belt on her dressing gown. "And I'm sure I never would've been nominated if I hadn't been in your movie. For some reason, that seemed to change everything."

"You went from an egghead to a bombshell."

Molly laughed. "Well, I wouldn't go that far."

"Well, you turned the head of Charlie Stockton. And if he's anything like his older brother, I'm sure he must be quite a catch."

"Did you date Charlie's brother?"

"I wanted to. But he was a senior when I was a freshman." Colleen paused to thread a needle. "I don't think he even knew I was alive."

"Charlie is really popular with the girls." Molly sighed. "And I guess I'm flattered that he likes me . . . ."

"You *guess?*"

Molly shrugged. "I don't know. I mean, he's nice enough to me, but he sort of makes me nervous too. I'm not exactly sure about what he expects from me." She frowned. "And, to be honest, the idea of being Charlie Stockton's girlfriend is a bit intimidating."

Colleen snickered. "Oh, my. Baby sister is growing up."

Molly scowled. "I'm not a baby."

"I know you're not." Colleen smiled as she stitched. "But you are *my* baby sister. Even when you're fifty years old, you'll still be my baby sister."

Molly glanced at the clock by Colleen's bed. "Well, if I'm going to finish my letter to Patrick, I better get back to it."

"Did you tell him about being in the homecoming court? And Charlie Stockton?" Colleen's brows arched with interest.

"Sure. Why wouldn't I?"

Colleen chuckled as she looked back down at her stitching. "Well, you know Patrick. He's a lot like Peter. He may have some brotherly objections."

Molly folded her arms across her front. "You know, it can get pretty confusing for someone like me. Half the time my family—and friends—are encouraging me to grow up, and the other half of the time, they seem determined to keep me a little girl."

Colleen laughed. "It must be difficult being the baby of the family."

"It is." Molly put her hands on her hips dramatically.

"Then I must say, you're very good at it." Colleen grinned at her.

Now Molly threw her arms around Colleen's shoulders, giving her a hug. "Thanks for helping with the gown. I don't know what I'd do without you." She remembered the favor she was exchanging for the dress alterations. "I took the negatives you mentioned to the drug store. Your prints will be ready in about a week, and I even got a couple of them enlarged. I hope you don't mind."

"Not at all. Thanks!"

As Molly went to the kitchen to finish Patrick's letter, she felt comforted to see Dad sitting in the living room, reading his newspaper in the golden glow of the table lamp. And she could hear the muffled sound of the radio playing a soap opera in Margaret's room upstairs. Mam would be up there with her, probably crocheting something for the baby. Even with Peter and Bridget gone, they were still a family. And that felt good. She just wished it could always be like this.

# Twenty-One

*Mid-October 1942*

Margaret knew her due date was still two weeks away, but when she woke up early on Wednesday morning with what felt like stomach cramps, she grew so concerned that she began to ring the little brass bell by her bed. And suddenly every member of her family was standing in her bedroom, in various stages of dress, peering at her with anxious curiosity.

"What's wrong?" Dad demanded, his face white with shaving cream.

"I think I'm in labor," she said nervously.

"Oh, dear!" Mam fumbled with her dressing gown, mis-buttoning the front.

"I'll call the doctor," Colleen offered in a surprisingly calm tone. She was still in her pajamas with her hair pinned up.

"The number is by the phone," Dad told her. "I'll get dressed and bring the car around."

"I'll get dressed too!" Mam dashed from the room.

"And I'll help you get dressed," Molly told Margaret. "What do you want to wear?"

"That plaid maternity dress." Margaret pointed to the dress hanging on her closet door. "It's the biggest one I have, and I'm sure I'll need it."

With Molly's help, she struggled to get out of her nightgown. Molly was just slipping the dress over her head when Colleen returned. "Dr. Groves will meet you at Saint Luke's," she told her. "Is this the bag you're taking?"

Margaret looked over to where Colleen was pointing to Margaret's overnight bag. "Yes, that's it. But the baby things aren't in it yet. The layette is on the dresser," she explained. "And put my slippers in too, please."

Colleen packed the bag, snapping it closed. "I guess if you need anything else once you're at the hospital, you can just let us know and we'll bring it for you."

"Isn't this exciting?" Molly was brushing Margaret's hair now. "You're about to become a mommy, Margaret. Colleen and I will be aunties."

"Are you ready?" Dad called from downstairs. "I've got the car warming up in front."

"We just need to get her shoes on," Colleen yelled back.

"And her jacket," Molly added.

Margaret felt slightly lightheaded as she slipped her feet into her oxford shoes, waiting as Colleen tied them for her. "I haven't been out of bed for so long," she said meekly. "What if I can't walk?"

"We'll help you." Colleen slipped a supportive hand around Margaret.

"That's right." Molly did the same.

"Take your time," Colleen said. "Stand when you're ready."

Margaret took in a deep breath, bracing herself, then slowly stood. "I feel weak as a kitten," she said quietly.

"We'll support you." Colleen steadied her.

"Just try to take a step," Molly encouraged.

Margaret took a tentative step and then another. And feeling the strength of her sisters, one on each side, she slowly made it down the stairs. But halfway down, her stomach began to cramp up again. "Oh, dear." She cringed. "I think I need to sit." Her sisters eased her down onto a step, waiting while she doubled over, groaning in pain. When it stopped, they helped her to stand, slowly easing her down the rest of the stairs and to the center of the front room, where she suddenly felt too weak to continue.

"I'm going to fall!"

"Get a chair," Colleen yelled to Mam.

Mam grabbed a straight-backed chair, sliding it behind her just in time, but before Margaret could catch her breath another pain came upon her and she let out a frightened shriek.

"Maybe we should call for an ambulance," Mam said nervously.

"No, that's too expensive," Margaret said between clenched teeth. "I can do this. Just give me a minute."

Soon they were moving again, Margaret flanked by her sisters with Mam coaching from in front. They managed to get her out the front door, down the front steps, and finally—blessedly—into the back of Dad's car. Mam hopped in front and Colleen told them that she and Molly would follow in Peter's car. And suddenly Dad was driving—none too slowly—through the streets of San Francisco.

Fortunately, Saint Luke's was not too far away, and it wasn't long until a strong orderly and nurse were helping Margaret into a wheelchair and wheeling her into the hospital. Soon she was settled into the maternity ward. But after about twenty minutes, and to Margaret's surprise, her labor pains completely ceased.

"What's wrong?" she asked the doctor after he finished his exam.

"I'm afraid it was false labor," he told her.

"False labor?" She looked down at her enormous midsection. "But I'm pregnant. How can my labor be false?"

"It happens. Usually a few weeks before the due date. It's nature's way of preparing the body for giving birth."

"But what about the baby?"

"The baby is fine."

"So I'm not going to give birth today?" Margaret was blinking back tears.

"I'm afraid not." He frowned. "Although it's possible you could go into real labor, I don't expect you to. Not today anyway."

"So what does this mean?" She sniffed as the nurse handed her a tissue. "Do I have to go home?"

"You don't have to go home, Mrs. Hammond, but you need to remember your due date is still two weeks away. It may be that long before you go into real labor." He wrote something on her chart. "But considering your condition, with toxemia, you might prefer to remain in the hospital until your baby arrives."

She frowned. "But that would be very expensive."

He nodded grimly. "Your husband is in the army—we may be able to get you into Letterman. Although you said Saint Luke's was your preference."

Margaret grimaced. She'd already heard that the army hospital was overly full of injured soldiers who had been serving in the South Pacific. Besides the fact that she couldn't bear seeing those wounded soldiers, she'd heard a rumor that their obstetrics care wasn't as good as Saint Luke's. "I'll go home," she said glumly.

"You're certain?"

"Yes." She was determined to be strong. "I'm

259

sure you're right. The baby probably won't be here for two more weeks."

He turned to the maternity ward nurse. "Prepare the patient to be released."

It was difficult to explain to her family what had happened and, although Margaret tried to hold back her tears, she fell completely apart on the ride back home. Making the walk up the stairs with Colleen and Molly's help was torturous.

"I'm going to stay home with Margaret today," Mam announced after they'd all regrouped in Margaret's room like a miniature army. "Colleen, you go to work with Dad this morning."

"And I asked Jack to put a sign on the door," Dad said. "In case any early morning customers arrived to find us not there."

"Oh, dear!" Mam clapped a hand over her mouth. "I forgot to let the Hammonds know that it was a case of false labor."

"The hospital will tell them," Dad told her.

"Yes, of course." Mam pointed to Molly. "You go to school as usual. I'll write you a note for being late. But I want you to come straight home afterward. Just in case."

Margaret felt tears coming again. "I'm sorry to be such a bother to all of—"

"Not another word," Dad told her. "We're your family. It's our job to help you bring your baby into this world."

260

"That's right," Mam agreed. "We're as excited about this as you are."

"I don't even want to go to school now," Molly said. "I'd rather stay here with you, Margaret." She peered at Mam. "Will you call the school if Margaret goes into real labor?"

Mam nodded. "Yes, dear. Of course."

"If Margaret goes into real labor, I want you to call for an ambulance," Dad told Mam.

"But the expense," Margaret protested.

"Hang the expense," he told her. "You know your mam doesn't drive. And it will take too long for us to get back from the store."

"Maybe I should stay with her," Colleen offered. "Mam could go to—"

"No!" Mam insisted. "I will stay home with Margaret."

That settled it, and before long everyone went off in different directions and Margaret, feeling like nothing in her life ever went as planned, cried herself to sleep.

Several days passed and Margaret still did not go into real labor and everyone, slipping back into their usual routines, decided that she probably wouldn't deliver her baby until her real due date. The one bright side of Margaret's false labor was that it rattled Dad badly enough to make him go to his own doctor for a checkup and TB test. To everyone's relief, the results were good. His heart and lungs were fine and his TB test was negative. He would not have to avoid being around the newborn baby when it came.

Colleen was trying to be patient—she knew Margaret was devastated with disappointment—but after a couple of days of nursing her, she grew quite weary of her sister's almost constant complaining. The way Margaret talked at times, it was as if she believed she was the only woman to be confined with pregnancy difficulties. Colleen was getting fed up! Even so, when Friday came along, she insisted on remaining home as Margaret's companion for the upcoming evening.

"It's your anniversary," she reminded her parents on Friday morning. Everyone had gathered in Margaret's room to finalize their plans. "The Hammonds made reservations to take you to dinner," she told Dad. "You both need a night out. No arguments. Just go and have a good time."

"I can stay home with Margaret," Molly offered.

"No, you cannot," Colleen said sharply. "It's your big night. For all you know, you could be homecoming queen tonight, Molly. And I worked so hard to fix that dress for you. You are *going!*"

"Colleen and I will be perfectly fine." Margaret reassured them in a sweet tone that she never used for Colleen. "Please, don't change your plans for me."

"We'll tell the Hammonds we can't do the movie theater after dinner," Mam said.

"No," Margaret insisted. "Go to the movie as well. I'll just be sleeping by then anyway. I won't even know you're not home."

"Yes," Colleen agreed. "It's silly to change your plans. Go have some fun. Celebrate your anniversary, and that Dad got a good health report, and that in a couple of weeks you and the Hammonds will be grandparents."

So, with everyone convinced Margaret had no intention of going into labor, Mam and Dad left with the Hammonds and Molly went to the dance with her friends, and Colleen looked forward to a quiet evening at home. Hopefully without too much complaining from Margaret.

"Here you go." Colleen set the dinner tray on the bedside table since Margaret's lap was pretty much nonexistent these days. "And don't worry, Mam prepared this for you—not me."

Margaret's expression was hard to read, but it almost seemed as if she was turning up her nose at the homemade cream of tomato soup.

"What's wrong?" Colleen demanded.

"I'm *not* hungry."

Colleen frowned. "Well, I'll leave it here awhile, just in case you change your—"

*"I'm not hungry!"*

"Fine." Colleen picked up the tray. "I'll eat it."

"Fine," Margaret snapped back at her.

Colleen resisted the urge to give her grumpy sister a piece of her mind. Instead, she carried the tray back down the stairs, then sat in the kitchen, hoping to eat in peace. It was hard not to feel vexed at Margaret. After all, everyone had been bending over backward for her. It seemed she could at least show a gram of gratitude.

It wasn't as if everyone else was having a great time these days. Indeed, Colleen's life had been no bowl of cherries lately. She hadn't mentioned it to anyone, but she felt fairly certain that her screen test had struck a sour note at Pinnacle. No news had to equal bad news because nearly two weeks had passed without a word from the Knight Agency. She suspected it was because Pinnacle had gone with an established actress. And the Knights were so disappointed—especially after wasting so much time and money on her—that they hadn't even bothered to let her know the bad news. Even so, it wasn't as if she was going around moping and grouching at everyone.

"Colleen," Margaret called from her room.

Colleen laid down her soup spoon, slowly getting up to see what Margaret wanted. Hopefully not her dinner, which Colleen had nearly polished off.

*"Colleen!"* she screamed loudly.

Colleen ran up the stairs, poking her head in the door. "What?"

"It's happening."

Colleen frowned as she went into Margaret's room. "What's happening?"

"I'm in labor."

Colleen tilted her head to one side. "How do you know?"

Margaret's eyes were wide. "My water broke."

"Huh?" Colleen glanced at the water pitcher and glass still sitting on Margaret's side table. "No, your water's right here."

"Not *that* water!" Margaret pointed at her stomach. "The water—the fluid around the baby. When it breaks, the water comes out—that's how you *know* you're in labor." And now she held onto her midsection with a loud groan. "This is it, Colleen! This is the real thing. I'm in labor!"

Colleen knew she needed to remain calm, but her head was spinning as Margaret moaned in pain. "I'll call for an ambulance—"

"No!" Margaret, still moaning, was already trying to get out of bed. "Too expensive!"

"But I can't get you down the stairs and to the car by myself." Colleen remembered how weak Margaret had been earlier this week.

"Yes, you can. We can do this." Margaret seemed to have caught her breath. "I haven't told anyone, but I've been getting out of bed by myself. Just to strengthen my muscles. When no one's around to see, I've practiced walking. If you help me to the car, we can do this."

"But you—"

"We can *do* this!" she shouted.

"Okay." Colleen nodded. "Just give me a moment to think." She went for Margaret's plaid maternity dress and was about to help Margaret out of her nightgown.

"You go call Dr. Groves," Margaret insisted. "I can handle this."

Colleen did as directed, leaving a message with the doctor's answering service. "Tell him this is real labor," she finally said. "My sister says her water has broken." She felt slightly foolish relating this information, since she really didn't know what she was talking about.

Seeing the straight-backed chair by the phone, she carried it to the foot of the stairs, then hurried back up to Margaret's room, where she set another straight-backed chair by the bed.

"Sit here," she told Margaret as she helped her get on her shoes. "I'll walk with you down the hallway, pushing this chair along with my foot, just in case you get too weak and need to sit and rest. Another chair's at the foot of the stairs."

"Good idea."

To Colleen's relief, they made it all the way down the stairs before Margaret had another pain and needed to sit in the chair. "Stay here and rest." Colleen dashed back up to Margaret's room, grabbed the overnight bag, which was still packed from the last hospital visit, along with her pillow, a blanket, and Colleen's purse. With her arms loaded, she ran down the stairs to see Margaret still in the chair, looking pale and weak.

"Are you sure I shouldn't call for an ambulance?"

"No." Margaret glared at her. "Just hurry."

"I'll bring the car around in front, then come back for you."

"Yes." Margaret's voice sounded husky. "Hurry."

Colleen's legs were trembling as she ran out back to get the car. Was this crazy? Was she wrong not to call for an ambulance? It seemed miraculous that she'd gotten Margaret down the stairs, but what if they tumbled down the concrete steps outside? As she drove the car around to the front of the house, she felt a rush of anger running through her. She was caught in this frightening position all because of this stupid war!

Otherwise, Margaret's husband would be driving his pregnant wife to the hospital. Brian should be the one biting his nails right now. But Brian was halfway around the world. And if the war hadn't taken Peter from them, he would be here to help Margaret right now. Together they could carry Margaret to the car—and then Peter could drive while Colleen sat in back with her sister. And what about Bridget? If she wasn't off serving her country, she could probably deliver the baby at home all by herself! But, no . . . thanks to this horrible, useless war, Colleen was completely on her own tonight. And she was in way over her head!

# Twenty-Two

I thought you were never coming back."
Margaret looked up with wide eyes as Colleen
burst through the front door.

"Are you okay?" Colleen asked breathlessly.

Margaret's chin quivered. "Just scared."

"Well, the car's running and ready to go." She
helped her sister to her feet, once again pushing
the chair ahead of them and out the door. This
time they made it to the front porch before
Margaret needed to rest again. "Do you think
you can make it down the steps?" Colleen stared
at the concrete steps as if they were a rocky
mountainside. If only she'd called an ambulance.

"I'll hold the rail on this side, and you hold onto
me from the other—" Margaret sat back down in
the chair. "Wait until this pain goes away."

Colleen's heart pounded hard as she waited, but
when Margaret started to stand, Colleen jumped
into action and, using all her strength, she
wrapped both arms around her sister, helping her
navigate each step. Then at the bottom, when she
needed another break, Colleen eased her to sit
on the lowest step.

Finally, they were moving across the sidewalk

and Colleen was helping Margaret into the backseat. Breathing hard, Colleen reached over to arrange the pillow and blanket in an attempt to make Margaret comfortable. "Ready to go?"

"Beyond ready!"

Colleen jumped into the driver's seat but reminded herself to take it easy. This would be a very bad time to get into a car wreck. "How are you doing?" she asked as she paused at a stop sign. The only response was a loud groan of pain, and Colleen hoped this baby didn't want to be born in a car! "We'll be there in five minutes," she promised, stepping a little harder on the gas pedal. As the car sped down Market Street, Colleen prayed a silent, desperate prayer, begging for a safe trip to the hospital and a safe delivery of Margaret's baby.

"The hospital's just ahead," Colleen declared just as Margaret started to groan in pain again. "We're almost there!" She turned in the drive, parking in front. "I'll be right back!" she yelled. Colleen ran into the quiet lobby, feeling like a crazy woman. "My sister is having her baby— *right now!*" she yelled out, getting the attention of several hospital employees who followed her outside.

Colleen watched as they extracted a howling Margaret from the backseat. Before long they had her loaded onto a gurney and were wheeling her into the hospital.

"You're going to be okay," Colleen assured her as she walked beside the small entourage. "You're in good hands now."

Margaret grabbed Colleen's hand. "Please don't leave me!"

"I won't." As they rode up the elevator, Colleen held Margaret's hand, wondering about the car she'd left running down below. The hospital probably didn't have valet parking service. Hopefully, someone would move it for her.

Margaret let out a shriek of pain, clutching her middle with one hand and gripping Colleen's with her other one. So tightly that it hurt. But probably not as badly as Margaret seemed to be hurting. Colleen hadn't realized that childbirth was so painful. She hoped Margaret's labor wouldn't last too long.

"How far apart are the contractions?" the nurse asked Colleen.

"I, uh, I don't know." Colleen tried to think. "A few minutes maybe."

The nurse peppered Colleen for more information, writing the answers down on a clipboard. "If her doctor isn't here yet, we'll have a staff physician see to her. Just until Dr. Groves arrives."

"I left a message with his service," Colleen said as they exited the elevator.

"Let's get Mrs. Hammond straight to delivery," the nurse told the orderly. She turned back to

Colleen now. "I'm sorry, you can't come into the delivery room with her."

"I don't want Colleen to leave!" Margaret shrieked, holding more tightly to Colleen's hand.

"She'll be right outside the door," the nurse firmly told Colleen.

"Yes," Colleen reassured her. "I won't go."

"Come on," the nurse told Margaret as they stopped by a double door. "It's almost time for this baby to be born."

"You'll be okay." Colleen gently extracted her fingers from Margaret's grip. "I'll be right here. I promise. I won't leave you."

Margaret cried out in pain again—and in the same instant she was wheeled through the swinging double doors and into the delivery room. Colleen stood there, trying to grasp all that had just happened. She felt slightly dismissed now . . . and didn't know what to do. She felt too nervous to sit in one of the nearby chairs but knew she couldn't leave. Then, seeing a nurse passing by, she explained about her promise to Margaret and how she'd abandoned the car down below. "I left it running and—"

"I'm sure an orderly has moved it by now," the nurse assured her. "You can pick your keys up at the front desk."

"Thanks." Desperate for a cigarette, Colleen dug through her purse only to remember she'd left her cigarette case in her bedroom. She paced back and forth outside the delivery room. Then, seeing a vending machine down a long hallway, she was tempted to make a dash for it but remembered her promise to stay close by—and continued to pace.

She watched with relief as a gray-haired doctor dressed in white hurried into the delivery room. Hopefully that was Margaret's obstetrician here to save the day. Perhaps it was time to relax a bit. If only she had a cigarette!

Colleen had barely sat down when a nurse she hadn't met emerged from the delivery room. "Are you the sister? Here with Mrs. Hammond?"

"Yes!" Colleen eagerly stood. "Is she okay? Did she have her baby yet?"

"No, it's too soon for that. And her doctor hasn't arrived yet. But the staff doctor is here. And he's concerned. Do you know how long Mrs. Hammond has suffered from toxemia?"

"I'm not sure." Colleen tried to think. "A couple of weeks maybe."

"We've tried to contact Dr. Groves, but he hasn't returned our calls."

"Oh, dear." Colleen bit her lip. "Is she going to be okay?"

"Dr. Meyers will be out to speak to you soon." The nurse returned to the delivery room, and now Colleen was pacing again. She wished she'd asked where Mam and Dad were going to dinner—or what picture they planned to see. She checked her watch, thinking perhaps they'd be home. But it wasn't quite eight.

"Are you Mrs. Hammond's sister?"

She turned to see the elderly doctor again. "Yes. I'm Colleen Mulligan, Margaret's sister."

"I'm Dr. Meyers. Are you her only family member?"

"I'm the only one here, but she does have other family. Hopefully they'll be here before too long. Is Margaret okay?"

His brow creased slightly. "I'm concerned that Mrs. Hammond's blood pressure is quite high. Probably because of the toxemia. But it's also a concern that her baby seems to be good sized, which suggests a long, hard labor—and I'm afraid that could put both mother and baby at serious risk."

"Oh, dear." Colleen twisted the handle of her purse.

"If I were Mrs. Hammond's attending physician, I would insist on a caesarian section."

"Is that surgery?" Colleen didn't know much about pregnancy or childbirth, but she thought she'd heard that term before. Although it sounded extreme.

"That's right." He nodded grimly.

"Is it very dangerous?"

"In my opinion, it's a much safer option than natural childbirth—for Mrs. Hammond, anyway."

"What did Margaret say about it?"

274

"She was so distraught and her blood pressure was so elevated . . . I gave her something to help her relax." He rubbed his chin. "So you're the only relative here on behalf of Mrs. Hammond? No husband?"

"Her husband's in the army, somewhere in England or North Africa or God knows where."

"Because a decision must be made, and we need consent to operate."

"So this is very serious." Colleen felt close to tears now. "You really think that she needs that surgery? What did you call it again?"

"A caesarian section." He pursed his lips.

"And it's up to me to decide?"

"At this stage, it is. If it turns into a real emergency situation, I will be forced to proceed even without consent. It would be a life-saving procedure. But it could be too late by then."

"You mean she could die?"

He nodded grimly.

"So it's your professional opinion that she needs this."

"Yes. I definitely recommend it. I just wish her obstetrician were here to confer with me."

Colleen looked into his gray eyes. "Have you ever done this kind of surgery before?"

"Yes, yes. Many a time. And it is actually a rather simple operation. And a life-saver, when it's necessary. Plus, I will have a physician assisting me. As well as an anesthesiologist."

"And it's dangerous to wait?" Colleen wished that Mam and Dad were here.

"The clock is not our friend right now. As I mentioned, the more Mrs. Hammond's labor proceeds, the more difficult it will become for both of them."

"Then I say you should do it," Colleen declared. "I trust you, Dr. Meyers." And she did trust him. Something about his age and his serious expression . . . he seemed like a knowledgeable and caring person.

"You've made a wise decision." He nodded. "The nurse will bring a form for you to sign." Now he smiled. "And before long, you will be an aunt."

Colleen swallowed hard as she watched him returning to the delivery room. Did this mean that she would be responsible? What if something went wrong? What if Margaret died in surgery? Suddenly the double doors swung open again and this time Margaret, with her eyes closed and an intravenous bottle being carried by a nurse with her, was wheeled out on a gurney. Her face was so pale and she was so motionless that for a moment, Colleen thought she was dead. But then she remembered that Dr. Meyers had given her something.

"Where are you taking—"

"To surgery," the nurse told Colleen.

Feeling like a stray dog, Colleen trailed behind

them. And once again, she was instructed to wait outside another door, watching as other members of the hospital staff went in. How many people did it take to perform this sort of surgery? How dangerous was it really? Had Colleen made the right decision?

Questions pummeled her brain as she paced back and forth, craving a cigarette. She was just turning around when she nearly collided with a middle-aged man in a black tuxedo.

"I'm Dr. Groves," he said urgently. "Is Mrs. Hammond—"

"In there!" Colleen pointed to the double doors. She wanted to ask him where his white doctor's coat was, but he was already going in. He'd obviously been at some social event, but his answering service must've figured out how to reach him. She felt a tinge of pity for the doctor. An obstetrician must have an awfully disruptive social life. But if his profession was delivering babies, he should remain available twenty-four hours a day! She wondered if Dr. Groves would agree with Dr. Meyers's recommendation for a caesarian section. Or if he disagreed, would it be too late?

Colleen sat down for a couple of minutes, but she was too distraught to remain put. Once again, she paced—back and forth, back and forth. And now, because her praying skills were not too polished, she prayed Hail Marys for Margaret.

After all, who would know better about giving birth than the mother of their Lord?

"Is this your first baby?"

Colleen turned to see a man in a navy uniform watching her with amusement.

"Sorry." His dark eyes twinkled. "I couldn't resist. I noticed you and the other woman when you entered the hospital. Sounded like she was about to have her baby."

"That was my sister," she said defensively.

"Why aren't you in the maternity section?" He took out a pack of cigarettes, shaking one loose.

"She's having a caesarian section." She looked longingly at his cigarettes.

"Want one?" He held out the pack.

"Thank you!" Now she confessed how worried she was for Margaret.

"Well, I don't know much about caesarian births," he admitted. "Well, except that they are expensive."

"Expensive?" Colleen hadn't even considered this.

"My wife wanted to have our second baby with a caesarian section." He chuckled. "She didn't enjoy bringing our first baby into the world. But when the doc told her what it would cost, and how long she'd need to remain in the hospital, she changed her mind."

"Oh." Colleen blew out a nervous puff of smoke.

"Anyway, this is my wife's third go round," he continued. "We have a five-year-old girl and a three-year-old boy. And I must say Judy was quite relaxed about the whole thing this time." He shook his head. "But I remember our first time here. I was probably even more nervous than you."

"Did the navy give you leave for the baby's birth?"

"No. I just enlisted a couple months ago, with the understanding that I couldn't ship out until she had the baby."

"So you're going to abandon her with the baby and the other children?" She frowned at him. "Just ship out on your merry way?"

His smile faded. "I'm not abandoning anyone. And I really don't like leaving her and the kids. But she's got two sets of doting grandparents and several aunts all eager to help her out. To be honest, sometimes it feels like I'm in the way whenever a new baby comes. Besides, it was Judy's idea that I enlist in the navy. She was worried I'd get drafted into the army and become cannon fodder."

"My sister's husband is in the army." Colleen narrowed her eyes as she took a long drag.

"Oh?" He grimaced. "Sorry about the cannon fodder bit."

"Well, at least Brian's an officer."

"Yes, that should help." He glanced down the

hallway. "I suppose I should get back to the maternity section. Although it usually takes Judy several hours before the baby arrives. But you never know."

"Thanks for the cigarette." She rewarded him with a smile.

He started to pocket the cigarette box, then stopped. "Want another?"

She considered declining his offer, then thought better of it. This could be a long night. "Thanks." She slipped the cigarette into her purse. "In the crazy rush, I left my case at home."

"Good luck." He made a quick mock salute.

"You too," she called out as he hurried back toward the maternity section.

It was a little past nine when Dr. Meyers emerged from surgery. Colleen snuffed out her second cigarette, rushing over to talk to him. "Is Margaret okay? I mean Mrs. Hammond? Is she okay?"

"Mother and baby are doing fine. Dr. Groves is tending them now."

Colleen let out a big sigh. "What did she have?" she asked eagerly. "Boy or girl?"

"A boy," he told her. "And a big one too. Nine pounds, eleven ounces and twenty-two inches long."

Colleen just nodded. She didn't know the size of an average baby but would take his word that Margaret's was a "big one."

280

"Dr. Groves agreed that a C-section was the way to go. Even more so after the baby was measured and weighed." He folded his arms across his front. "You made the right decision for your sister."

"Thank you." She smiled. "But it was your recommendation, doctor."

"Anyway, your sister will be moved to the maternity ward after she recovers from the anesthesia. May take an hour or two. But you should be able to get a glimpse of your new nephew in the nursery. Probably in about an hour."

She thanked him again and then, hoping that Mam and Dad or Molly might've gotten home by now, although it was only nine-thirty, she used the pay phone to call. When no one answered, she tried the Hammonds only to discover they were still out too. She wished there was some way to let them know they'd become grandparents! Then, realizing that Margaret was still unconscious and that the baby wouldn't be available for viewing for an hour, she decided to make a quick trip home. She'd leave a note for her parents and come right back.

By ten o'clock, Colleen was back at the hospital. Although she felt a bit more relaxed now, she was still on pins and needles. But she had one more task to complete. Stopping by the front desk, she inquired about sending a telegram to an overseas servicemen. "To tell him he's a father."

"I can help you with that." The receptionist smiled.

Colleen handed her Brian's contact information that she'd gotten from the phone table at home and before long, she was dictating a message. "Dear Brian—stop—you are a daddy—stop—A big healthy boy—stop—Margaret is fine—stop—more specifics tomorrow—stop—Love Auntie Colleen—stop." She paid for the telegram and, anxious to see Margaret and the baby, Colleen returned to the maternity ward waiting area, which was now blue with cigarette smoke. Three anxious fathers, including the sailor she'd recently met, all nervously waited for updates on their wives and babies. She looked on with amusement, then strolled over to the nursery viewing window.

It hadn't been an hour yet, but she figured she could admire the other babies. There were four. Three baby girls in pink blankets and a boy swaddled in blue. They all looked very small and ruddy and slightly wrinkled. And the boy baby was not happy. His face was scrunched up and he appeared to be howling at the top of his lungs. Not that she could hear much through the thick glass window.

These infants looked nothing like the Gerber baby image that graced the baby food jars

Colleen had tediously stocked on their grocery store shelves so many times. But then, she'd never been one of those women who got all giddy over babies. For that reason, she decided it might be wise to rehearse some flattering lines she could recite when it came to praising her nephew. Because it probably wouldn't do to tell Margaret that her baby resembled a red shriveled prune.

Colleen was about to leave when a nurse came wheeling another bassinette to the window. This one contained a baby wrapped in a blue blanket and the placard read HAMMOND BABY BOY. Colleen stopped in her tracks, staring down at the peaceful looking baby. He was not red or wrinkled or even crying. She blinked in surprise. With his dark curly hair and big blue eyes—and so alert that it seemed he was actually gazing up at her—this baby really was surprisingly attractive. She leaned into the glass, waving at him and giggling. "Hello, baby boy! Hello, little angel!"

"Is that one your sister's?" The sailor had joined her, looking on with interest.

"Yes. The Hammond Baby Boy. Isn't he adorable?"

The sailor leaned forward, letting out a low whistle. "Don't tell my wife I said so—and I'll deny it if you do—but I think that is the best looking newborn I've ever seen."

"And I'm his auntie," she said proudly. "The truth is I've never been very interested in babies before, but I have a feeling that's about to change."

"Well, he's a good looking boy. I sure hope Judy has a boy."

"I think I'll go see if his mommy is awake yet."

"It's not visiting hours," the sailor warned her. "The head maternity nurse is a bear. She may throw you out."

"I'll chance it." She looked both ways, then strolled over to the maternity ward and, peeking inside, spotted Margaret. She appeared to be asleep, and Colleen didn't really want to disturb her, but she did want to make sure she was really okay.

She tiptoed to her bedside, and Margaret was so still and quiet that Colleen felt worried. She touched her sister's hand, relieved to feel that it was warm.

Margaret's eyes fluttered open, but she looked confused and groggy. "Colleen?" Her voice was raspy. "Are we there yet?"

"Where?" Colleen pushed a strand of auburn hair off of Margaret's forehead.

"The hospital. Are we there yet?"

"Oh, yes. We're here." Colleen smiled. "You have a beautiful baby boy, Margaret."

Margaret blinked. "Wh—what?"

"He's here. Your son. I just saw him. He is absolutely gorgeous. Like an angel."

"I must be dreaming." Margaret closed her eyes, sighing happily. "I like this dream."

Colleen chuckled. "Yes, dear, you rest up now. You can see your handsome baby tomorrow." She leaned down to kiss her cheek. "Sweet dreams, dear sister."

# Twenty-Three

Margaret's memory returned to her in the wee hours of the morning—along with a severe headache and some intense pain in her stomach. "You'll feel better soon," the nurse assured Margaret after helping her to swallow a little white pill with water. "Are you ready to see your son?" she quietly asked.

"So it's true," Margaret said. "I did have a boy."

"Your boy is the toast of the nursery. Everyone is in love with him." The nurse slipped the blood pressure cuff on her arm, pumping it up.

"Really?"

"Oh, yes. He's a beautiful boy." She paused to check the pressure, then released the cuff. "Caesarian babies are always better looking." She stuck a thermometer in Margaret's mouth. "Because they don't go through all that labor and delivery. But even besides that, he's a real doll."

Unable to talk with the thermometer in her mouth, Margaret just nodded, but she was full of questions. Finally the nurse removed the thermometer.

"I had a *caesarian section?*" Margaret demanded.

The nurse put a forefinger to her lips. "Other mommies are sleeping."

"But is it true?" Margaret whispered. "Did I have a caesarian section?"

"You did."

"But I never agreed to that."

"From what I heard, it was an emergency procedure. You had toxemia and your blood pressure was—"

"But it will be terribly expensive." Margaret massaged the temples of her forehead, trying to think. How did this all happen? And why did she not remember any of it?

"That operation probably saved your life." The nurse briskly straightened up the covers on her bed. "Maybe your baby's life too. But you can ask your doctor for the full details." She smiled. "Now, would you like to see your beautiful boy before the pill you just took knocks you out again?"

"Yes, of course." Margaret attempted to sit up.

"No, no." The nurse pushed her shoulders down. "Don't use your stomach muscles. Not for a while." She handed her a control. "Just push this button. Slowly elevate the bed. And I'll go get your baby."

Margaret pushed the button, but the upward motion made her feel slightly dizzy, so she stopped. Closing her eyes, she replayed what the nurse had said about the operation, trying to calculate what it might cost. She knew it wouldn't just be the additional cost of the surgery. She would also need to remain in the hospital for a longer period of time. She had budgeted for a three-day stay, which was considered short. But to recover from surgery would probably take much longer.

"Here he is." The nurse carried in a blue bundle, laying him next to Margaret. "Isn't he gorgeous?"

Margaret turned to see a cherub face with rosy cheeks, but it was those big blue eyes that captured her heart. "He *is* lovely." She spoke quietly. "Hello, little boy. Welcome to the world."

"I saw your family here last night. I was just starting my shift when I noticed a very merry little crowd clustered in front of the nursery window gaping at your baby."

"Oh, I'm so glad they were here." Margaret fingered a dark curl. "You've got your daddy's hair," she whispered. "And your mama's eyes."

"And since Nurse Fletcher's shift had just ended—she's a stickler for rules—your family actually got to hold him too. You should've seen all of them in their white sanitary gowns, taking turns with your baby. The grandfathers were handing out cigars and a cute young girl had a camera and was taking pictures. It was quite the celebration."

"That's nice to know." She yawned. "I'm afraid I'm getting sleepy." She looked up at the nurse. "I hate to let him go, but I don't want him to roll off the bed."

"I'll take him." She bent down to scoop up the bundle. "Because of your surgery and recovery, your doctor recommends that he be a bottle baby."

"Oh?" Margaret frowned. This had never been her plan—but then when had her life ever gone according to her plans?

"He's already on formula and has quite an appetite too."

Margaret wanted to question this, but the medicine had already created a heavy fog in her weary head. "Good night, baby boy," she whispered groggily.

Molly was eager to visit Margaret the next day. Thanks to Mrs. Bartley, she'd put together a gorgeous bouquet of October roses. "They're the last of the season," Mrs. Bartley had told her that morning, "but perhaps the prettiest."

"Can't we go now?" Molly pleaded with Dad.

"Visiting hours don't start until nine." Dad glanced at the kitchen clock, then took a sip of his coffee. He was obviously trying to act nonchalant, but Molly knew he was as eager to go as she was. "Besides that, your mother's not ready yet. She's wrapping a package for Margaret

289

and the baby. And you know there's no point in rushing her."

"I think I'll head over there anyway." Colleen put on her hat. "I'll be a little early, but I may try to sneak in. That way I can visit with her a bit, then get to the store that much sooner."

"And I'll go with you," Molly declared.

"Suit yourselves." Dad picked up his newspaper.

"It's going to be fun being an aunt," Molly said as Colleen drove them to the hospital. "I can't wait to take care of him. I wonder how long it'll be until he comes home."

"That's a good question."

"Mrs. Hammond said that Margaret will need lots of help. Her niece had a baby by caesarian section, and Mrs. Hammond said it took her several months to recover from it."

"That long?" Colleen frowned.

"I can help her with the baby, after school and on weekends."

"But then you won't be able to help Mam and Dad at the store," Colleen pointed out.

"That's true." Molly frowned. "Well, Mam will probably make some sort of schedule. Like the one she had for Margaret when she got sick."

"I'll help whenever I can—with the baby and the store." Colleen parked the car. "And since I haven't heard back from the Knights in

Hollywood, well, I'm guessing I'll have plenty of time to help out." She sighed sadly.

"Do you think the studio picked someone else?" Molly had been almost afraid to ask about this, but since Colleen had brought it up, the topic seemed fair game.

Colleen nodded glumly. "Seems like it."

Molly tried not to sound overly happy as she gathered up her camera bag and bouquet of roses. "Are you terribly sad about it?"

"I guess I'd be lying to say I'm not. I let myself get my hopes up, Molly. So, yeah, it's pretty disappointing. I mean, I realize my family needs me—and I was thankful to be around for Margaret last night. So, really, it's probably for the best."

But Molly could hear the sadness in her sister's voice. And she felt guilty for wanting to keep Colleen at home with them. Really, it was selfish.

As they went into the hospital, Colleen pointed to the gift shop. "I noticed a pretty box of chocolates in the window last night. If the shop is open, I'd like to get some for Margaret."

"She'll love that."

Before long, bearing roses and chocolates and a card, Molly and Colleen walked into the maternity ward at precisely nine o'clock. They'd attempted to get in sooner, but the head nurse stopped them. Not that they minded too much since they were able to admire their gorgeous nephew for several minutes while they waited.

"How are you?" Molly asked Margaret after presenting her with the roses and giving her a gentle hug. She suspected by the grimace that Margaret was in pain.

"I'm okay." Margaret smiled stiffly. "Pretty sore actually. But the nurse went to get me a pain pill. Thanks for the roses. They're really beautiful."

"Your baby is beautiful." Colleen kissed Margaret on the cheek. "And so are you."

"Oh, go on with you." Margaret reached up to her uncombed hair. "I'm a mess and I know it."

"Well, you have every right to be a mess." Colleen handed her the chocolates. "You've been through quite an ordeal. But even so, you're still the prettiest mommy in here."

"Thank you very much." Margaret opened the box. "And thank you for these. And for all you did last night." She plucked out a chocolate, then offered the box to them.

"I'm just glad it all turned out okay." Colleen popped a chocolate in her mouth. "It was pretty scary for a while."

"I wanted to ask you about that." Margaret lowered her voice. "I was pretty shocked to hear I'd had a caesarian operation. I guess I was knocked out when they decided to do that." Margaret frowned. "Did you give them permission?"

"I had to," Colleen told her. "The doctor said it could be a matter of life and death."

"*Could* be?"

"Well, I can't remember his exact words, but he insinuated you and the baby were in great danger."

"Dr. Groves said *that?*"

"It wasn't Dr. Groves. He hadn't arrived yet. Dr. Meyers was attending to you."

"And you gave him *permission?*" Margaret's voice had an accusing edge to it. Molly hoped it was a result of her pain—not because she was truly mad at Colleen—but it was hard to tell.

"I didn't know what else to do," Colleen said simply.

"Do you realize how expensive my hospital bill is going to be now?"

"I'm sorry, Margaret. But I was the only one here. It felt like I had no choice but to agree. You could've died. What else could I have done?"

"I guess we'll never know." Margaret looked away.

"Has your doctor spoken to you about it yet? Dr. Meyers said that he'd be in to explain everything to you today."

"I haven't seen him yet." Margaret folded her arms across her front with an unhappy expression. "It's just that I never budgeted for anything like this, Colleen. Do you realize that I will be in the hospital for about two weeks? I can't even imagine what that is going to cost."

"I'll help you with it," Colleen offered.

"You don't even have a job."

"Can I fix your hair?" Molly offered, eager to change the course of this conversation. "I see your overnight bag—your hairbrush is probably in it."

"Sure, if you want."

Molly carried the bag over, digging through until she found the brush set as well as a small cosmetics bag. "I'll do your hair and Colleen can do your face."

Colleen frowned. "She may not want her—"

"Go ahead," Margaret commanded. "Make me beautiful if you can. Then Molly can take a photo of me with the baby to send to Brian."

"Speaking of Brian." Colleen took the cosmetics bag from Molly. "I sent him a brief telegram last night. Just to let him know he's a daddy. But I figured you'd want to send him the specifics today."

"Thank you."

As the two of them worked on Margaret, Molly chattered cheerfully, hoping to keep the conversation lighthearted. She told them some of the details of her previous evening. "I wasn't surprised that Gloria Zimmerman won homecoming queen. After all, she's a senior. And I was just honored to be part of it."

"How was the dance?" Colleen asked as she rubbed a bit of rouge into Margaret's pale cheeks.

"It was fun. All the girls loved my gown. I told them you designed it, Colleen. They were very impressed." Molly removed Margaret's pink bed jacket from her bag. "Let's put this on you. It'll look pretty in the photo."

"And how was Charlie Stockton?" Colleen's voice was laced with curiosity as she twisted the lipstick tube up.

"He did very well in the football game," Molly said carefully. "We won by a touchdown." And before Colleen could question her more about Charlie, Molly started in on a blow-by-blow report of the game. She had no intention of discussing Charlie Stockton right now—not in front of Margaret. She wouldn't mind confiding in Colleen later—when they were alone in her room. But, really, if she never heard the name *Charlie Stockton* again, it would be too soon!

"Hello to the new mommy!" Dad came into the maternity ward, carrying a potted plant Molly recognized from the gift shop downstairs. He kissed Margaret on the cheek. "Don't you look pretty!"

As greetings were exchanged, Molly got out her camera. Then as Margaret opened the package from Mom, Molly took a couple of photos. Before long, the baby was brought in and Molly took more photos. Some with just mother and baby. Some with Mam and Dad and the baby.

"I hate to break up the party." Colleen held up her watch. "But I should get to the store. You all know how busy it can get on Saturday mornings."

Molly was slightly relieved that Colleen was gone. It seemed Margaret had been unfairly harsh with her. But then again, Molly knew that Margaret was in pain and worried about finances. Before long, the Hammonds came and Molly took more photographs. It was obvious Margaret was getting sleepy and by ten o'clock, the head nurse was shooing them all out.

On the way home, Molly considered mentioning Margaret's concerns over the hospital bill to her parents. But they both seemed so happy, so she decided not to worry them. They would hear about it soon enough.

"We will all take turns visiting Margaret at the hospital," Mam declared as Dad dropped them off at the house before heading back to the store. "I'll make a schedule. That way she'll always have someone there during visiting hours, but we will still have plenty of hands at the store. And the Hammonds will be able to be at their shop as well."

"That's a sensible plan," Dad told her. "When will you and Molly be coming to the store?"

"By noon," Mam told him. "I'll bring lunch for everyone."

Mam and Molly were just going into the house when they heard the phone ringing. "I'll get it," Molly yelled, running for the phone. But as she reached for the receiver, a bolt of panic rushed through her. *What if it was Charlie Stockton?* Maybe she would simply say "wrong number" and hang up. But what if he recognized her voice? And so she disguised it, answering with a deep throaty *"Hello?"*

"Hello. I'm calling for Colleen Mulligan," a woman said in a crisp businesslike tone.

"Colleen's working at the store today," Molly answered in her normal voice.

"Oh, I see. Could you give me the number of the store?"

"I, uh, I don't know." Molly was unsure about giving the number to a stranger.

"I'm sorry, I forgot to say that I'm Joanne Proctor from the Knight Talent Agency. Miss Mulligan was down here—"

"Oh, yes, I know who you are," Molly told her. "I can give you the store phone number." She rattled it off.

"Thank you."

"Is it good news?" Molly asked eagerly.

The woman on the other end laughed. "Well, I'll have to tell Miss Mulligan about it first. But it isn't bad news."

Molly thanked her and hung up. "Mam!" She ran through the house, finally finding Mam just emerging from her bedroom. "I think Colleen is going to get the movie part."

"What?" Mam frowned. "Was that the phone call? They told you?"

"Not exactly." She followed Mam to the kitchen. "But I asked her and she hinted at it. She's going to call Colleen at the store."

"You gave her the store's number?"

"Why not? She could find it in the phone book if she wanted."

"Well, that's true." Mam tied on her apron.

"I wouldn't tell Colleen this," Molly said quietly, "but I really didn't want her to get the part. I was happy because it seemed like she wasn't going to. But then I saw how sad she was about it. And then with Margaret picking on her this morning—"

"What? Margaret was picking on Colleen?" Mam scowled. "Are you imagining things?"

"Margaret is worried about how much her hospital bill will be. You know, because of the caesarian operation and having to be in the hospital for two weeks."

"Two weeks?" Mam's brows arched. "That will be expensive."

"Anyway, Margaret was sort of acting like it was Colleen's fault. Like Colleen had been wrong to give the doctor permission to do the operation."

"Well, that's nonsense. Colleen simply did what

298

any of us would've done. When a loved one's life is in danger, you don't worry about the cost. The good Lord will provide for that."

Molly felt relieved. She'd been worried that Mam would be fretful over the money too.

"And we can all be thankful that both mother and child are just fine." Mam began to slice the bread, perhaps more thinly than usual. "Somehow we will make ends meet. We always do."

As Molly helped Mam make Spam and cheese sandwiches for lunch, she knew that was true. The good Lord always did provide . . . and somehow they always did make ends meet. But that hadn't prevented their family from shrinking this past year. And hearing that woman's voice on the phone a few moments ago convinced Molly that Colleen would soon depart them too. But at least they would have a new baby to welcome into the house. And, of course, it was grand to have Dad back home as well. And even with Peter, Bridget, and maybe Colleen gone, they could still be a family. At least she hoped so.

# Twenty-Four

Colleen was flying high after the phone call from Joanne. But her extra bright cheerfulness didn't stand out much since everyone at the store was in good spirits today thanks to the arrival of the new baby. Oh, certainly, they were busy enough. Dad, in the backroom, merrily whistled "Oh, Danny Boy" while he cut meat. Molly chimed in with him while she cleaned and trimmed a load of produce that arrived yesterday. Dirk, the guy that Dad recently hired, was back there too, unpacking and pricing cans. And Jimmy was out on deliveries.

Although Colleen was alone out front, she knew she could ring the bell to get more help if needed. And right now she was so energized, she didn't even want help.

"Good afternoon," she chirped to Mrs. Spencer as the elderly woman unloaded her basket onto the counter. "Isn't it a beautiful autumn day?"

"Oh, my yes." Mrs. Spencer opened her coin purse. "You seem in bright spirits."

As she rang up the groceries, Colleen told her about Margaret's baby. So far she'd told nearly all the customers—at least the friendly ones. And everyone had been pleased and excited to hear about it.

"Wonderful news! What did Margaret name the little fellow?" Mrs. Spencer asked.

"Peter Brian Hammond." Colleen totaled the purchase.

"Oh, that is sweet." Mrs. Spencer laid her money on the counter. "Peter for your brother and Brian for the baby's father. Very nice."

"And Peter is our dad's middle name too," Colleen informed her as she counted out her change.

"Even better. And I will be sure to bring a pair of blue baby booties with me the next time I come to the store."

Colleen smiled to herself as she bagged the groceries. She wouldn't tell Mrs. Spencer that Baby Peter already had a couple dozen baby booties. Why spoil the sweet lady's fun? She waved as Mrs. Spencer left and, since there was no one else out here at the moment, she did a happy spin around the counter.

"Practicing your dance moves?" Molly emerged from the backroom with a box of neatly trimmed lettuce heads.

Colleen grinned. "Not exactly. I'm just happy."

Molly set the box on the counter. "So . . . when will you go back to Hollywood?"

"I'm not sure," Colleen admitted. "But maybe as soon as next week. The studio scheduled the movie to begin filming the second week of November. And Joanne said they'll want me down there sooner, to get settled and to give me time to learn my lines. Sounds like they may even get me an acting coach."

"Do you need one?"

"It probably wouldn't hurt."

Molly's brow creased as she removed a wilted lettuce leaf that must've been overlooked.

"What's wrong?" Colleen asked her.

Molly let out a long sigh. "Well . . . for one thing . . . I'm going to miss you."

Colleen hugged her. "How about if you come down and visit me? Maybe for a weekend. Or on Christmas break. How would you like that?"

"Really?" Molly's eyes grew wide. "That would be fabulous. Me with you in Hollywood! Dottie will be pea green with jealousy."

"What's the other thing?" Colleen asked.

"Okay, ladies." Dad pushed the rolling cart stacked with the rest of the produce out of the backroom. "Let's get these veggies out before quitting time."

Just then the bell on the door jingled and Mrs. Jones and her daughter entered the store.

"I'll take care of these." Molly quickly took charge of the cart. "You take care of them."

"Okay." Colleen lowered her voice. "But you got the best part of that deal."

Dad chuckled as he ducked into the backroom. No one liked dealing with the persnickety Mrs. Jones. Particularly Margaret, who often amused her family with humorous stories. Besides the fact that this woman had little regard for rationing, which Margaret guarded judiciously, she was often just plain rude. However, Colleen felt she could handle the old biddy and her daughter today. Velma was the same age as Bridget and fitted the old adage that "the apple doesn't fall far from the tree."

"Good afternoon." She smiled brightly. "Can I help you ladies find anything?"

"I think we know where everything is," Mrs. Jones said.

"Oh, good." Colleen picked up the feather duster and proceeded to freshen up the home-canning supplies section, although the items there had hardly had time to gather dust. It had been Molly's idea to stock these preserving jars and lids and, according to Dad, they'd had to reorder twice.

"I haven't seen Margaret in the store recently," Mrs. Jones said as she browsed the baking section. "I hope she's not unwell."

"As a matter of fact, she just had her baby," Colleen said cheerfully. "A beautiful baby boy. Mother and child are both doing well."

"Margaret has had a baby? *Already?*" Velma made a suspicious frown. "I thought she'd only married recently. Did the baby come prematurely?"

Colleen knew exactly what this insinuation

was about—and she did not like it. "Margaret got married last December," she said. She didn't bother to mention it was the *end* of December. Why give Velma fuel for her silly fire?

"Yes. But this is only October." Velma had removed her glove and was actually counting on her fingers.

"October is the *tenth* month of the year," Colleen clarified. "In case you were wondering."

Velma slowly lowered her hand. "Oh, even so, that *was* still quick, wasn't it?"

Colleen shrugged. "A lot of servicemen's wives are having babies."

"I thought I heard *you* were engaged." Velma stared down at Colleen's ring finger. "Is he a serviceman too?"

"My fiancé was a navy pilot. His plane was shot down last spring. No survivors."

"Oh . . . I am sorry." Velma actually looked slightly contrite. "You probably wish you'd gotten married before he left. I've heard the military provides fairly good compensation for war widows."

Colleen laid down the duster, trying very hard not to be vexed by Velma's thoughtless words. "You're right. I do wish we'd gotten married before he left. But only because I dearly loved him." She glanced at Velma's left hand—no ring. "I suppose some women may marry for other reasons . . . ."

"Some young ladies have more patience than others when it comes to marriage," Mrs. Jones said as she carried her items to the counter. "For instance, I married late in life. I have no regrets over waiting. And Velma isn't the sort of girl who would settle for the first man that comes along. Even if he was going into the military."

Colleen had to bite her tongue, but she felt certain that the line of men waiting at Velma's door would not be long.

"Did you tell them the news?" Molly asked cheerfully as she came up front, still holding a bell pepper in her hand and a mischievous twinkle in her eyes.

"What news?" Mrs. Jones asked with arched brows.

"I already told them about Margaret's baby," Colleen told Molly.

"Not *that* news." Molly winked at Colleen. "I mean the news about you going to Hollywood." She turned to the Jones women. "Colleen's being cast in a major motion picture. It's a musical romance about the war, starring Darla Devon and Robert Miller. Don't you think Robert Miller is just about the dreamiest—"

"You're making that up," Velma said sharply to Molly. "My mother used to wash my mouth out with soap for telling falsehoods."

Molly's blue eyes grew big. "I'm telling the truth. Colleen *will* be in the movie. She'll play a debutante—Darla Devon's sidekick. She's probably going down there as early as next week. And they'll begin shooting in a couple of weeks."

Colleen nodded with satisfaction. Molly, as usual, had been paying close attention.

"I don't believe you." Velma pulled her glove back on. "Both of you are just saying that."

"Believe what you like," Colleen said nonchalantly.

"Just wait, someday you'll see the picture for yourself," Molly retorted.

Mrs. Jones leaned forward on the counter, glaring at Colleen. "You truly expect us to believe you are going to be in a motion picture with Darla Devon and Robert Miller? *Really?*"

"That's right." Dad came from the backroom. Still wearing his blood-splattered butcher's apron and welding a meat cleaver, he presented an intimidating figure. "Colleen's talent agency called just this morning. Long distance from Hollywood." He nodded to Colleen. "And her family is very proud and very supportive of her."

"Except that we'll miss her," Molly said a bit glumly.

"But you're going to come down there to visit me," Colleen reminded her. She turned to Mrs. Jones. "Is this all for you today? Just flour, salt and baking soda? What, no sugar?"

Molly looked like she was about to burst

into giggles as she hurried back to the produce section. Without saying another word, Colleen rang up the minimal purchase. She wouldn't have bragged like that to Velma and Mrs. Jones, but she didn't mind that Molly and Dad had done so. In fact, it was rather nice to see that gleam of pride in Dad's eyes. It filled her with hope and confidence.

Margaret wasn't sure if it was possible to feel one's own blood pressure rising, but as she mentally calculated the estimated cost of her unexpectedly long hospital stay, she found herself getting more and more anxious. Surely that wasn't good for her blood pressure. But, really, what could she do?

"Good morning." Colleen said cheerfully as she made her way to Margaret's bedside. Colleen, as usual, looked impossibly glamorous. Today she had on a chic gray suit that showed off her perfect figure and a wide-brimmed hat that perfectly framed her face. Margaret fought back feelings of envy as she waved a halfhearted hello.

"I brought you some reading material." In one hand Colleen held up a copy of *House Beautiful*. "For you to plan the dream home you and Brian will have someday." And in the other was a copy of *Vogue*. "And this is to remind you that, even though you're a mommy, fashion is still important." She laid them on Margaret's bedside table. "How are you feeling today?"

Margaret forced a shaky smile. "Okay . . . I guess."

"Mam and Dad and Molly are at mass. I told them I'd sacrifice mass to come sit with you." She grinned impishly as she scooted the chair closer to Margaret's bed.

"Such a sacrifice." Margaret knew that Colleen wasn't exactly devoted to church attendance. "But I'm glad you came. I missed seeing you yesterday."

"Well, since Mam and the Hammonds were here most of the day, and Molly and Dad last night, well, I decided to wait until you weren't in such demand. You're a popular girl these days. You and that beautiful boy of yours. I just ogled Baby Peter in the nursery. One of the nurses was giving him a bottle but sitting so close to the window it was almost as if she wanted to show him off." Colleen laughed. "And I couldn't help but notice a few other people admiring him as well. I'm sure they're secretly jealous their babies are not nearly so handsome." She set her gloves and handbag aside, then sat down. "I tried not to gloat."

"Well, as I pointed out to another new mommy," Margaret lowered her voice, "caesarian babies have the advantage of not going through a hard delivery and, according to my nurse, that improves their appearance. Of course, it comes with a cost. Not just financially either. It includes a much slower recovery time for the mother."

"Are you still in a lot of pain?"

"They give me pain medication. It helps. But it also makes me sleepy."

"Do you get to spend much time with Baby Peter?" Colleen picked up the comb and brush set and began to work on Margaret's hair.

"He was just in here with me. But then it was his feeding time, so they took him back to the nursery." Margaret frowned. "It's hard to really feel like a mother when they keep taking him from me. And they won't let me out of bed. I see other mothers moving about, keeping their babies by their beds. But it's not like that for me." Her chin quivered. "None of this has gone like I'd hoped it would." For some reason it was always easier to be bluntly honest with Colleen. Perhaps because Colleen never seemed to judge her. "But what's new about that?"

"I know it's been hard, Margaret. But it'll get better. Just give it time."

Margaret sighed. "I'm sure you're right. But I guess I'm not the most patient person in the world."

"You're far more patient than me. You always have been." Colleen continued to gently comb out the tangles, then began to smooth her hair with the brush.

Margaret knew that was true. Colleen had been born impatient. Despite being younger than Margaret, Colleen was always the one to run ahead, and she could find trouble in places her older siblings never thought to look. Meanwhile, Margaret had always been the one to lag cautiously behind, testing the way and planning the safest route. And where had that gotten her? In the meantime, Colleen's impulsiveness had never seemed to ruin her life—not like others predicted it would. Her sister always seemed to land on her feet. Well, for the most part anyway.

"There." Colleen laid down the brush set. "Beautiful."

"Thanks." Margaret knew who the real beauty was here, but it was sweet for Colleen to say that. "So Mam told me about your agent calling— about the motion-picture deal." She stared at Colleen in wonder. "I can hardly believe it—my little sister is going to be a real motion-picture star. Congratulations."

"Thanks. I'm still pinching myself."

"When do you go to Hollywood?"

"Probably later this week."

"Oh." Margaret wasn't even sure why this made her so sad, but it did.

"Hollywood's not that far from San Francisco. It's only about a five-hour drive. I told Dad he should drive you all down there sometime. If my place is big enough, you can stay with me. Or in a hotel. And if I'm not busy, I can show you the sights."

Margaret just nodded. For some reason, she felt on the verge of tears. She'd heard that new mothers could be overly emotional . . . perhaps that was it. "Colleen," she said in a choked voice. "I—I need to tell you something."

"What?" Colleen removed a silver tube of lipstick from her pretty gray handbag.

"I need to apologize for what I said to you yesterday. It was wrong for me to blame you—for me needing a caesarian operation. Dr. Groves stopped by to see me yesterday afternoon. He explained that it really was life-saving surgery. He said you and Dr. Meyers made the right decision." She blinked back tears. "I should've been thanking you instead of accusing you. I'm really sorry."

"Oh, sweetie." Colleen leaned over to gently hug her. "It's okay. I understand. You were upset."

Margaret sniffed. "It's just that I was so worried about the hospital bill."

Colleen handed her a tissue. "I know."

"I had it all budgeted. I'd be in and out of here in just a few days. And I thought I'd saved enough to cover everything." She blew her nose. "I probably should've gone to the military hospital. If I'd known I'd need a—"

"Margaret." Colleen held up a hand to stop her. "I don't want you to worry about the expenses. I've decided I'll cover whatever the extra amount is."

Margaret blinked. "What do you—"

"I'm not sure how much I'll make in my film, but I feel certain it'll be enough to pay your hospital bill."

"I can't let—"

"I *want* to."

Margaret started to cry harder now.

"Hey, that was supposed to make you feel better." Colleen grabbed another tissue, using it to blot Margaret's tears.

"It does. But it also makes me feel selfish for feeling so sorry for myself." She sniffed. "And maybe the bill won't be as bad as I keep imagining. And the Hammonds have offered to help too. But I know their leather shop is suffering, thanks to the war shortages. Have you heard the government is going to start rationing shoes? Mr. Hammond says it's due to shortages in rubber and leather and—"

"Shoes will be scarce?" Colleen looked genuinely alarmed. "Maybe we should stock up while we can. I saw the prettiest pair of tomato-red pumps in the City of Paris window last week. Suede with high wedged heels and the most delicate little ankle straps. Very chic."

Margaret couldn't help but smile. Leave it to Colleen to plan ahead for fashionable feet even in the midst of a shoe shortage.

Colleen held up the opened lipstick tube like a torch. "This is called Tropical Coral," she declared. "But the color's really not right for me. I thought it might look good on you though." She leaned over to apply it to Margaret's lips, giving her a blotting tissue. "Yes, it's perfect with your creamy complexion and auburn hair." She stood back and, holding her fingers like a picture frame, studied Margaret's face. "You really do resemble Maureen O'Hara." She set the lipstick on the bedside table. "Did I tell you that my agents want to use my middle name for my screen name? So I'll be Maureen Mulligan. Do you think anyone will confuse me with Maureen O'Hara?"

Margaret chuckled. "I doubt it. You don't look anything like her. But you could get confused with Veronica Lake. Especially with your hair like that."

Colleen patted her platinum locks. "I hadn't really meant to grow it out like this—it just happened during my dark period . . . after losing Geoff. But my agents seem to like the style."

Margaret took in a deep breath, preparing to say something that she'd been thinking about since yesterday. "There's something else I need to ask you, Colleen. And I want you to feel free to say no, okay? No pressure."

"You know how stubborn I am, Margaret. I never agree to something if I don't want to."

"Well, I wanted to get something figured out before you head off to your fame and fortune in Hollywood."

"What is it?"

"Well, I know you don't consider yourself a very religious person. You don't go to confession like you should. And you miss mass every chance you get."

Colleen grinned. "Like today?"

Margaret nodded. "But you do believe in God?"

"Of course." Colleen's mouth twisted to one side. "Although I do have questions for Him."

"Who doesn't?"

"So, what is it? What are you getting at?"

"I'd like you to be Peter Brian's godmother."

Colleen's blue eyes grew large. "Are you kidding?"

"No, I'm not."

"You would pick *me* to be your baby's godmother?"

"Colleen, you were here with me with the baby was born. Your decision helped save my life. And you've even offered to help with my hospital expense. On top of all that, you actually sewed Peter Brian's beautiful christening outfit. Why wouldn't I want you?"

"I'm speechless." Colleen shook her head.

"Will you?"

"Are you certain, Margaret? I mean you could have Bridget—she's so responsible. And

I'm sure most people would even think Molly is a better choice."

"Are you saying you don't want—"

"No. I'd love to be Peter Brian's godmother. I fell in love with him the moment I saw him. I'm very honored."

"And I'll understand if you can't make it back for his christening."

"I'll make it," Colleen insisted. "Well, if we can pick a day that works with my filming schedule. I'll really try to make it." She leaned over to hug Margaret. "Thanks for believing in me." As she stood back up, she reached into her purse again, this time removing a compact. "We need to get rid of that shine," she said as she opened it. "I'm sure you'll have lots of visitors again. You want to look your best."

Margaret closed her eyes as Colleen gently patted her nose and cheeks with the puff. The powder felt cool and comforting . . . kind of like Colleen had been this morning. Margaret sighed happily. Despite the fact that they'd gone through a lot of tumultuous ups and downs of sisterhood over the years, Margaret had to admit Colleen was almost always good medicine for her. Oh, sometimes it wasn't easy-to-take medicine, but in the end, it was usually for the best. The only downside was Colleen would soon be leaving home. And if Hollywood got a firm grasp on her, who knew when she'd return?

# Twenty-Five

Mam fixed a special dinner for Colleen's last night at home and even invited the Hammonds to join them. It was meant to be a celebratory time, but as the evening progressed, Colleen had to fight back melancholy. Was she really about to leave everyone and everything she'd known for her whole life?

It was ironic since Colleen had always hungered for more independence. She'd dreamt of having a glamorous life on her own, but now that it was about to happen, she wasn't so sure. Just the same, and for the sake of her family, she put on her best actress face—playing the merry life of the party and acting as if she had no doubts or regrets or fears. But by the time they'd finished dessert and the Hammonds had gone home, Colleen was tired of smiling.

"I'd really like to buy Peter's car from you," she told Dad after Mam and Molly had gone to bed. "I know you've been considering selling it to help with Margaret's hospital bill."

"Yes, although Margaret really doesn't want me to sell it." He frowned. "I'm not sure if it's because it belonged to Peter . . . or because it had been her main transportation. But she won't be working at the store now. Not for a long while anyway. And we don't need two cars in our family, especially since the government plans to start rationing gas before long."

"Well, think about it," she said. "I don't know what my movie contract looks like yet, but I think I can afford it."

"You already offered to help Margaret with the hospital bill," he reminded her. "Better be careful not to spend your money before you get it, Colleen. And make sure you save some . . . just in case you only get one motion picture." He smiled with sad eyes. "Although I have a feeling, once they get to know you, they won't want to let go of you so easily."

"Oh, Dad." She hugged him.

"But I mean it, Colleen. You better be wise about managing your money. Don't forget there's a war going on. You don't know what's around the next corner. Don't be wasteful like we hear some of those silly movie stars can be. Don't forget where you came from."

She smiled. "Is this my farewell speech, Dad? You didn't say any of this at dinner tonight."

He shrugged. "I was saving it up."

"Well, I promise you, I will try to be careful about managing my money."

"And something else." He looked intently into her eyes. "Be careful with the men down there, Colleen."

She suppressed the urge to roll her eyes. How

317

many times had she heard this kind of advice. "Yes, Dad, I know."

He shook a finger under her nose. "You do not know, Colleen. You're a pretty young lady, and you are smart. But there are crafty older men down in Hollywood. They will come at you like wolves in sheep's clothing. They will flatter you and promise anything. But don't be fooled by them. Don't let them pull you into their snares." He kissed her cheek. "Don't make your old dad have to come down there and straighten them out, because I will."

"I was just imagining you—the way you came out of the backroom when the Jones ladies were giving me a bad time—your bloody apron and meat cleaver in the air." Colleen laughed. "Very intimidating."

"Keep that image in mind whenever a fellow tries to take advantage of you."

She kissed him on the cheek. "I will do that, Dad. Now I must go finish packing. Good night."

Colleen was still chuckling to herself as she finished packing her bags to take on the plane, as well as the boxes of personal items her family would ship to her later. She didn't doubt that Dad would show up—and shake up—any man who tried to take advantage of her. She just hoped and prayed that never happened! Although it would probably make for good publicity.

• • •

Margaret had barely begun her second week in the maternity ward but desperately wanted to go home. Not only was it impossible to get a good night's sleep, but the food was lousy, and she barely got to see her baby.

"When do I get out of here?" she asked the doctor after he examined her on Monday.

"Have you been doing what I said?"

"I've followed your instructions to a T." She described how she'd inflated her little blue balloon—to keep her lungs cleared—and how she'd been slowly walking up and down the hallway. "And I don't even need much pain medication."

"Good." He put away his stethoscope. "How does tomorrow sound?"

"I get to go home tomorrow?" She resisted the urge to leap out of bed and dance.

"Only if you can promise me you'll have someone to help you. I mean 'round-the-clock care, Mrs. Hammond. You're not ready to tend your baby or return to any sort of housekeeping. Not for another two weeks. Maybe longer if we don't get your blood pressure issues resolved. Even at home, you'll need to rest and recover."

"Yes, I understand."

"But I don't see why you can't continue to recover at home—as long as you have someone there to help."

"Yes, I can do that," she said eagerly.

"Then I'll sign you out tomorrow afternoon."

It wasn't until the doctor left that Margaret had second thoughts. Had she jumped the gun in guaranteeing she'd have help at home? Mam and Dad had the store. Even with Dirk and Jimmy to help out part-time, and Molly after school, they were running short-handed. For a moment, she was vexed Colleen had abandoned her family for Hollywood. Then she remembered that Colleen was going to help her with the hospital bill. Well, somehow—even if she had to hire a babysitter—Margaret would have to make this work.

"Good morning." Louise Hammond came into the maternity ward with her usual smile. "I just saw my adorable grandson. Is it just my imagination or is he getting bigger?"

"The nurse said he's gained six ounces."

"Oh, my!" Louise sat down next to Margaret's bedside. "He's going to be a big boy, isn't he? I wonder if he'll get to be as tall as his daddy." She chuckled. "You look at Jack and me and you'd never have dreamt our boy would grow up to be six-foot-two-inches tall. But then, my father was nearly six feet tall. And don't forget Patrick is only an inch shorter than Brian."

Margaret sighed. "How I miss Brian."

"I just got a letter from him this morning." She opened her purse, extracting a V-mail letter. "I haven't even read it yet. Would you like me to read it to you?"

"I'd love that!"

Louise put on her reading glasses and opened the V-mail, slowly reading:

Dear Mother and Father,

This is the second letter I've written today. The first was to my lovely bride and mother of my son, congratulating them! I was so happy to get Colleen's telegram this morning. Of course, I don't have many details about my son as of yet, but I am over the moon to know both mother and child are doing well. I didn't want to admit it to anyone, but I was awfully worried about them. I could tell by Margaret's letters that she was concerned too, but I'm sure she was trying to protect me from knowing too much. So I am just very relieved to know they are both fine.

I am very concerned that Margaret doesn't return to working at the store. I know she plans to do this eventually. I wish I was making a larger salary so she wouldn't have to worry about money, but Uncle Sam's pockets seem to be as tight as ours. Anyway, I know Margaret is in good hands with both of you and her family around. I hope you will all encourage her not to be in a hurry to return to work. Or maybe not to return to work at all.

I believe there is no job more important, for a mother, than to be home with her children. The way that you were home with Patrick and me until we started school, Mom. And even then, you only worked part-time with Dad in the leather shop. Of course, I hope this war will be over long before our son is old enough for school.

Colleen didn't tell me the baby's name, but Margaret and I discussed this in our letters. So in my mind, our baby's name is Peter Brian. I hope that someone (probably Molly) is taking photographs. I would love to see him.

Now for my last bit of news. I didn't write to Margaret about this, because I don't want to worry her.

Louise abruptly stopped and, looking at Margaret above her reading glasses with a worried expression, she quickly refolded the V-mail.

"What is it?" Margaret pleaded. "For heaven's sake, don't stop now."

"Well, I, well . . . Brian doesn't seem to want—"

"Please," Margaret demanded. "Read it to me."

Louise slowly reopened the V-mail. "If you're sure."

"I'm positive." Margaret forced a smile. "I'm not a shrinking violet, Louise. I can take it. Really, I can. After all, I'm a mother now, I've been through a lot this past week."

"Yes, that's true. You have been through a lot."

Margaret nodded, trying to remain calm and composed as Louise read how Brian, unsatisfied with his desk job ordering and overseeing army supplies, had wanted to make a bigger contribution to the war effort. As a result, he'd requested active duty and had just learned he would soon be shipped to an "undisclosed location."

"Oh my." Margaret grimaced, trying to keep her voice even. "Well, Molly and my dad had predicted Brian may be sent to North Africa. I'd just hoped that perhaps he'd get to stay in England for a while longer. But I suppose that wasn't meant to be." She tried not to show how upsetting this truly was—nor would she admit she'd fervently prayed and lit candles at church, begging the Blessed Virgin to spare Brian from active duty.

"I hope Brian will forgive me for reading that to you." Louise removed her reading glasses and returned the letter to her purse. "I hope you're not disturbed by this news. And I know Brian won't want you to worry. It's not good for you or the baby."

Margaret didn't know what to say, but she felt angry . . . and slightly betrayed that Brian would share that with his parents but not with her.

"And I hope you're not upset that Brian didn't want to tell you—"

"I am upset," she said sharply.

Louise's brows arched. "Oh, dear."

"I'm Brian's wife. He should be honest with me about what's going on over there."

Louise got a thoughtful expression. "How about you, Margaret? Did you tell Brian about your toxemia? That you had high blood pressure? Did you write to him about that?"

"Well . . . no. I didn't want to trouble him with—"

"You see." Louise shook a finger in the air. "It works both ways, dear."

Margaret let out a long sigh. "I suppose that's true."

"I suspect Brian knows you're a bit of a worrier, dear."

"Really?" Margaret frowned. "Do you think I'm like that? A worrier?"

Louise laughed. "I'm afraid you come by it honestly. Goodness, I've been friends with your mother since long before you were born, Margaret. She's always been a worrier too."

Margaret considered this. "You're right. I can't

even count how many times I've told Mam not to worry so much—and I never wanted to be like that."

Louise patted Margaret's hand. "Well, you're still young. Perhaps you can nip this in the bud, dear."

Margaret nodded. "Speaking of Mam and worrying . . ." Now she explained about her promise to Dr. Groves, that she would have help when she was released from the hospital. "But with Molly in school and Colleen in Hollywood and me incapacitated, well, I know Dad needs Mam at the store and—"

"I will take care of you and the baby," Louise declared.

"Really?"

"Yes. I was just telling Jack this morning, business is slowing down so much at the leather store—what with the war shortages and belt tightening—that I really don't feel very necessary there."

"So you can help me?"

"I'd be delighted to. When do you expect to be released?"

"Tomorrow afternoon."

"Oh?" Louise reached for her purse and gloves. "Then I should probably get busy."

"Thank you so much." Margaret beamed at her mother-in-law. "That takes such a load off my mind."

"Don't you worry about a single thing." Louise stood. "And I'll let your parents know what's going on too. We'll take care of everything."

Margaret thanked her again, and Louise hurried on her way. She let out a relieved sigh, leaning back into her pillow. She was going home!

Colleen felt like she was living out a dream as Joanne showed her the tiny furnished apartment the agency had rented for her. "I'm sorry it's so small," Joanne apologized again. "It's called an *efficiency* apartment." She laughed. "But that might be because you can reach the kitchenette from the bed."

"Don't worry. I love it," Colleen assured her. "I really do."

"Well, it was the best we could do on short notice. We may find something else in time."

"I really think it's charming." Colleen ran her hand over the plastic topped kitchen counter. "And so modern too." She opened the tiny oven. "This is much newer than the one my mother cooks on." She chuckled. "Not that I expect to do much cooking."

"You are conveniently located near several good restaurants." Joanne smiled. "And only a few miles from the studio. Will you have a car?"

"Maybe." Colleen set one of her bags next to the bed.

"I've stocked you with some basic provisions."

Joanne opened the fridge and cupboards to reveal enough food to keep Colleen going for at least a week. Then she went over a few more details, reminding Colleen that she was expected at the agency tomorrow. "Georgina wants to go over the Pinnacle contract and some other things. I'll pick you up around ten."

"Great." Colleen felt like a character in a movie now, the ingénue just starting out her career, her first apartment, signing her first real motion-picture contract—it really seemed too good to be true. Hopefully it wasn't.

"So unless you need anything else, I'll see you in the morning." Joanne handed Colleen a packet of information about the neighborhood and maps and whatnot, then told her good-bye.

Colleen was glad to be in her little apartment by herself. She explored every nook and cranny, marveling at how truly efficient the small space had been used. From the Murphy bed that folded into the wall, to the fully equipped kitchenette and its diminutive but modern appliances, to the dinette table built into another wall. It was all as snug as a bug in a rug. And, sure, the time might come when she would feel the walls closing in on her, but for now it was perfect.

She changed out of her traveling clothes and began to unpack her bags. For such a small apartment, the closet was a good size—bigger than her closet at home. And the bathroom was a good size too. But as she unpacked her cosmetics bag in there, she realized she must've left her bag with toothpaste, soap, and other personal items at home. But since she'd noticed a corner drugstore right nearby, she decided to go gather some necessities.

It was surprisingly hot outside, but Colleen didn't mind as she strolled down the street. She was on her own, getting to know her new neighborhood, and she loved it. She took her time selecting just the right products and even paused to get a cherry-flavored Coke from the soda fountain. Then, as she walked back to her new apartment, she realized she had not felt this happy in ages—not since losing Geoff.

She took her time putting away her drugstore purchases as well as the rest of her clothes and shoes, and finally it was nearly six o'clock and, feeling tired but satisfied, Colleen sat down on the small sofa in the living room area. A sleek white phone rested on a small table next to it. She picked up the receiver, considering a phone call to home. She could tell her family she'd gotten settled and was doing fine, but stopped from placing the call. She wasn't a child anymore. She didn't need to check in. Besides, just getting home from the store, they'd all be busy right now.

She would wait and call them in a day or two, after she'd read and signed her movie contract and had more information to share with them. Still she wondered . . . What were they doing right now? Margaret and the baby came home from the hospital today. That alone probably made the Mulligan household a busy place tonight. Perhaps the Hammonds had stopped by.

Colleen could imagine all the females clustered around sweet little Peter. And, of course, the grandpas would be nearby, congratulating each other on having such a fine grandson. It was strange to imagine a baby in the house. A part of her was sad not to be there with them and she suddenly reached for the phone again—then stopped. No, they would be too distracted to chat right now. They'd be helping Margaret get settled, tending to the baby. And then Molly and Mam would start dinner. Really, they were too busy to even miss her.

# Twenty-Six

M argaret had mistakenly assumed that "going home" meant just that—that she would be at home in her own room tonight. Instead, after she was picked up by Brian's dad from the hospital, with Molly along to manage the baby, she was transported to the Hammonds' house. As Mr. Hammond parked in front of the house, she questioned this, but he patiently explained he was simply following his wife's orders.

"Since Louise will be caring for you and Baby Peter, she felt it would be simpler for everyone to have you both here."

"Dad and I brought all of your baby things over last night," Molly said as she got out with Baby Peter in her arms. "We helped Mrs. Hammond set it all up in Patrick's room."

"In Patrick's room?" Margaret felt thoroughly confused as Mr. Hammond gave her his arm, helping her out of the car.

"It's so sweet," Molly chirped. "It looks just like a real nursery."

"You got all the baby things from my room?" Margaret remembered how she'd taken such time and care to prepare her room for the baby, getting everything just perfect. The bassinette was next to her bed, and she'd filled several of her drawers with carefully laundered and folded baby clothes. She'd even transformed her dressing table into a diaper-changing table with a waterproof pad on top.

"I think we got everything." Molly waited for them on the sidewalk, rocking the baby back and forth. "Anyway, if we forgot something, we can bring it over tomorrow." She turned to go up the front steps.

"I just thought . . . I was going home," Margaret said meekly as Mr. Hammond slowly helped her up the steps to the house.

"But you did know Mrs. Hammond was going to care for you, didn't you?" Molly paused by the front door.

"Yes . . . but . . ." Margaret felt slightly breathless from the stairs. "I didn't know it would be here."

"Well, it would be rather inconvenient to have Louise stay at your house while she tends to you and the baby." Mr. Hammond set down Margaret's overnight bag to reach for the door-knob. "Everyone agreed this was the best plan, Margaret."

"Welcome, welcome!" Louise Hammond spread her arms wide. "Molly, you know where to take the baby, and I'll see Margaret to her room. Right this way, dear."

The only word Margaret could think of to describe her state of mind as Louise led her to

Brian's old bedroom was *discombobulated*. It wasn't a word she'd used much, but it seemed to fit. And as she was helped into her nightgown and settled into a twin bed, she wondered why she even felt surprised—since nothing in her life ever went as expected. Why should her homecoming be any different? But still . . .

"Now you just rest," Louise told her. "I'm sure the trip home from the hospital wore you out. Have a little nap before dinner." She tucked the faded blue checkered coverlet around Margaret, then, as she checked to see that the blackout shade was secured, she let out a little chuckle, running a finger over the dusty top of a chest of drawers. "My apologies for not getting this room cleaned up better, but we were so busy moving baby things here and setting up the nursery. But the sheets on the bed are clean."

Margaret was afraid to say anything, lest she insult her mother-in-law.

"And don't worry about a thing, dear. We'll take good care of that baby. You just get some sleep."

Margaret mumbled a halfhearted thank you. She wanted to fall asleep . . . if only to escape the garish school pennants adorning the dark paneled walls. Could this room be any gloomier? Her gaze wandered the room, taking in a shelf where a couple of sports trophies and a model clipper ship were coated in dust. She knew

Brian's mother had never been much into housekeeping. Louise blamed it on the fact that she worked with her husband in the leather shop, but Margaret suspected she simply didn't enjoy cleaning.

She closed her eyes and wished that she were in her own room in her parents' home. Was there any way to undo all this? Or did she have no say in the matter? She could hear the sound of Molly's and Louise's voices as they cared for the baby next door. It bothered her to hear her baby fussing. But the nurse had told her Peter would probably be hungry by the time they got home. Hopefully, Molly had informed Louise of this.

Eventually, she could hear Louise was preparing a bottle for him. She was explaining to Molly how it was done, and how to check the temperature of the formula. Meanwhile, the baby's cries were getting more intense—and Margaret wasn't sure she would be able to remain in bed much longer. Yet she knew she'd probably get scolded for getting up.

With frustration rising within her, she closed her eyes and began to count to ten. And then to twenty. Finally, after much counting, it got quiet and Margaret suspected they were feeding her poor baby. So far, Margaret had only been allowed to give him a bottle a couple of times—and only with nurse supervision. And even then, she'd felt rather incompetent. And now she felt jealous . . . and thoroughly discombobulated.

Margaret must've slipped off to sleep because it didn't seem long before Louise was helping her to sit up in bed and setting a food tray in front of her. "I wasn't sure what you'd like to eat, but Jack suggested my homemade chicken noodle soup." She smiled as she laid a napkin, like a bib, over Margaret's chest. "Good for what ails you."

"Thanks." Margaret attempted a smile.

Louise pointed to the brass bell Margaret recognized from home. "It was Molly's idea to bring that over. You just give it a jingle if you need anything. Jack and I will be in the kitchen having our soup."

"Is Molly still here?"

"No, she left a while ago." Louise lingered in the doorway. "She said to tell you good night and that she'll see you tomorrow after school."

Margaret sighed deeply as she dipped her spoon into the generous bowl of steaming soup. She knew that Louise's homemade soup was an improvement over the hospital's boring menu, but she had no real appetite. She tasted the soup and was surprised to discover that it tasted bland. Had Louise forgotten to add salt? If so, she would be back to remedy the situation.

However, Louise did not return with a salt shaker, and after a while the soup grew cold. Margaret tried another small spoonful, thinking perhaps she hadn't given it a real chance. But once again, the soup was flat and tasteless. Had something happened to her taste buds? She removed the bib napkin and pushed the tray away. With everyone treating her like a child, she felt like she might as well throw a tantrum like a child. She wanted to kick and scream and demand to go home!

"Aren't you hungry, dear?" Louise asked when she finally returned to check on Margaret.

"I guess not."

"I suppose all the excitement of coming home is a bit much." Louise smiled wearily. "Are you feeling all right, Margaret? Jack said that the doctor sent pain pills home with you."

Margaret considered the sleepy effect the pain pills had on her. She hadn't liked the drowsy feeling at first, but it did provide a good escape. "That's a good idea. I think I could use a pill."

Molly tried to hide her dismay as she started to clear the table. It had been hard enough to tell Colleen good-bye this morning, but not having Margaret and the baby coming home today had been a real blow. Oh, certainly, she'd tried to hide her real feelings for Margaret's sake. But it was all rather disturbing. In just one year, the Mulligan household had shrunk from seven to three.

"Do you want help?" Mam asked as Molly reached for her plate.

"No, there's not much to clean up with just us." Molly tried to sound cheerful, as if this were a good thing.

"Then I'll say good night," Mam told them. "I've got a fierce headache."

Dad helped her from her chair, kissing her on the cheek. "Rest up, dear. I won't even turn on the radio in the front room tonight."

So Molly didn't turn on the kitchen radio either. But washing the dishes, alone and in silence with the dark blackout curtains swallowing up part of the light, she suddenly began to feel exceedingly sad and lonely. The Mulligans did not feel like Mulligans anymore. And, for all she knew, they never would again.

By the time she hung up the damp dishtowel, she was thoroughly blue. She hated to feel sorry for herself, but it seemed unfair. All of her other siblings had grown up in a house full of noise and energy . . . and she was stuck with this? She flicked off the light with a slight moan, then went into the front room where Dad's face was screened by the newspaper.

"Good night, Dad," she said quietly.

He lowered his paper with a furrowed brow. "Are you okay, Molly girl?"

She attempted a bright smile. "Sure."

"Come over here." He patted the arm of his chair. "Let me see you up close."

She went over, perching on the chair arm. "Yeah?"

He held her chin between his thumb and forefinger, then shook his head. "Something is troubling you, child. You better tell your old dad what it is."

Molly bit her lip, trying to think of a good response.

"How about a game of chess?" he asked.

"Okay." She slid off the arm and quickly arranged the chess table and ottoman for a match. "I haven't played chess since Peter left home." She sat on the ottoman.

"I was just thinking of Peter," Dad confessed as he started setting up the black pieces. "It was about a year ago that he enlisted in the navy."

She nodded as she set up her pieces. "I was just thinking about how our family has shrunk."

"Just you and me and Mam now." Dad sighed.

"Yeah." She moved a white pawn.

"But maybe this is our opportunity, Molly." He moved a pawn.

"Opportunity for what?"

"For me to get better acquainted with my youngest daughter."

"Oh?" She brightened slightly as she slid her bishop out.

"So, tell me, how is school these days?"

"It's okay." She had no intention of telling Dad everything. It had been a week and a half since her incident with Charlie. And she felt the more time she put between them, the better it would be. Except that some of the kids were talking about her now. And she suspected that Charlie was spreading false rumors.

"Are you working on the school newspaper this year?" He moved a knight out.

"Yes." She nodded eagerly. "I was picked to be editor last week. I meant to tell you, but we were so distracted with Margaret and the baby, and Colleen going to Hollywood, I completely forgot."

"Congratulations!" He grinned as he took her pawn with his knight. "I'm proud of you, darling."

"Thanks. Well, not for that." She laughed as she took his pawn with her bishop. "It's not the first time, but it is kind of unusual for a junior to be an editor."

"Well, you're a smart girl, Molly. They obviously recognize that."

"I've also asked if I can be a photographer for the yearbook," she told him.

"You would be perfect for that."

As they played chess, chatting comfortably in the quiet front room, Molly realized that being part of a small family could have its benefits too. Sure, it would take some getting used to, but spending time like this with Dad was a pretty nice reward. Even when he beat her at the chess game, she didn't really mind.

"I guess I've gotten a little rusty." She stood and stretched.

"All the more reason for us to play regularly."

"Well, I better get started on my homework." She put the chess set away. "Algebra is waiting."

He reached for his reading glasses. "Did Mam tell you there was a letter for you?"

"No." She hurried over to the table by the front door where they set the mail.

"From Patrick." He picked up his newspaper again.

She picked up the V-mail and considered offering to read it to Dad, then stopped. After her last letter from Patrick, which had been a bit embarrassing, she'd decided to read his letters privately first—then share them later with editing, as needed. She told Dad good night then went to her room, where instead of doing her algebra, she opened the V-mail and was pleased to see it was a relatively long letter.

Dear Molly,
Thank you for your last letter. I was concerned to hear that Margaret was having difficulties in her pregnancy, but I'm sure you and your family must've taken excellent care of her. Especially since I just received the telegram from

339

my parents, announcing the good news about my nephew Peter Brian. That must be very exciting for everyone. I wish I were there to celebrate with all of you. But I'm hoping that you'll send me some photographs, Molly. And give the little tyke a hug for me. He and Margaret will probably be home by the time this letter reaches you. Your house must be as busy and loud as I remember it.

I was also glad to hear Colleen is doing better. It's hard for me to imagine our effervescent Colleen in a state of such sadness, but I know from your letters that losing Geoff really took a toll on her. However, it sounds like you have been good for her. I still chuckle when I think about the tomato fight in the garden. And I understand your reservation about Colleen going to Hollywood, but like you asked, I won't mention it to anyone. But I agree with you. It's probably best that Hollywood hasn't come calling.

I cannot believe it's October already. Especially since it's still hot and humid here in the Pacific. Fortunately, we get a nice ocean breeze to cool us off sometimes. But it's nothing like the crisp clean air in San Francisco this time of year.

And, strangely enough, when we have fog, it's never very cool or refreshing. Do I sound like I miss home? Well, I must admit that I do.

But more than I miss San Francisco, I miss my family and friends. At the same time, I'm thankful to have them. There are a few sailors who never get letters or packages from home. My heart aches for them. So I try to share bits and pieces of mine. And they do enjoy your photographs, Molly. One fellow blows you a kiss every time he passes my opened locker. I warned him that you're not yet seventeen and he better watch himself!

I want to congratulate you on being a candidate for homecoming queen. I must admit I was surprised since you never seemed very interested in such things. But I can't blame your classmates for choosing you. Although I'm a bit concerned over your choice of an escort because I'm sure that Charlie Stockton is Walt Stockton's younger brother. We used to call him "Wild Walt" because of his reputation with the girls. It wasn't good, Molly. I hope the younger brother is nothing like him, but as your "big brother" I feel I should warn you. Please, don't let any young man disrespect you, Molly. Stand up for yourself.

Okay, enough lecturing from me. I suspect (based on your last letter) that you don't appreciate it. I just hope that you know it's only because I care about you. Peter did too. You're a dear girl and we just want to protect you. But, yes, I do understand you're growing up, Molly. You made that quite clear in your last letter. I suppose it's just hard for us to let go of our bright shining girl in pigtails. I'll sign off now since I hear taps playing. Keep praying for me and my shipmates. We need God's protection more than ever these days.

Yours truly,
Patrick

# Twenty-Seven

*Early November 1942*

Margaret had never been so happy to come home before. Not as a child after a long day at school, not as an adult after a trying day at the store. But after two long weeks of being cooped up in Brian's boyhood bedroom at the Hammonds', she'd been tempted to climb those pennant-covered paneled walls. Oh, she was grateful to her in-laws for letting her stay with them during her recovery. Even if she had insisted it was too long, not that anyone was listening to her. But as Margaret walked through her parents' front door with Baby Peter in her arms, she had to control herself from jumping up and down for joy.

"Welcome home," Mam said happily.

"Thanks." Margaret looked around the familiar room with teary ears.

"We've got everything all set for both of you upstairs." Mam reached for the baby. "Why don't you let me carry him?"

"I can manage."

"But the stairs," Louise said. "You're not used to going up stairs, Margaret."

Margaret relinquished Peter to her mother.

"Molly helped me put Peter's things away this morning before she went to school. It was so kind of Jack to deliver everything." Mam smiled at Louise. "I told him we'll have you both for dinner on Friday to say thank you."

"Oh, that's not necessary." Louise chuckled. "Although we'd be pleased to accept."

Still carrying the baby, Mam led the way up the stairs. "The nursery is in Colleen's old room. Right next to you, Margaret."

"Peter gets his own room?" Margaret grasped the handrail, slowly going up the stairs and realizing how weak she still felt.

"That way you can have your own room to yourself. We thought you could rest better that way."

"But what about Colleen? What if she comes home?"

"Colleen assured me that her movie won't be done for a few more months," Mam said from the top of the stairs. "And she may stay down there even longer than that."

"How is Colleen doing?" Louise came behind Margaret, carrying her overnight case and the diaper bag.

"She sounded just fine." Mam smiled happily, swaying the drowsy baby in her arms as she waited for Margaret to make it up the stairs.

"Colleen really doesn't mind?" Margaret felt slightly breathless.

"That's what she said." Mam led them into

Colleen's old room. "Here we are, Baby Peter." She used baby-talk. "What do we think of our new nursery?"

"You painted it!" Margaret looked in amazement at the powder blue walls. Colleen had always complained about the previous color, calling it "dead salmon." "It's so pretty."

"That was Molly's doing," Mam explained as she laid Peter in the bassinette. "Mrs. Bartley gave her a gallon of paint."

"Where did this come from?" Margaret ran her hand over the rail of the white crib. It was topped with the blue and yellow baby quilt from her baby shower.

"Dad found it in the attic," Mam told her. "I thought we'd given it away. But he brought it down and painted it."

"And these adorable little pictures." Margaret stared at the framed nursery rhyme scenes hanging over the crib.

"Molly did those herself. She used an old picture book to draw the figures then restored her old box of watercolors to paint them."

Now Margaret noticed the padded rocking chair by the window. "Oh, Mam, that's the rocker from your bedroom. You didn't have to—"

"I wanted to," Mam said. "My mother gave me that rocker when Peter was born. And I rocked all my babies in it. It's only fitting that it should rock my grandbabies too."

Now Margaret really did start to cry. "It's all so sweet—so incredibly sweet."

"Oh, darling." Mam hugged her. "We just wanted you and Baby Peter to feel at home."

"I *do* feel at home," Margaret said tearfully. "Thank you."

"Well, I should probably go," Louise said quietly. "I told Jack I'd come to the shop today. It's time to go over the books."

Margaret turned to her with damp eyes. "Thank you again," she told Louise. "For everything. I really appreciate all you did for me—and for Peter." She hugged her tightly, hoping that this homecoming hadn't felt like a slap in the face to her. "Thank you so much. I don't know what I'd have done without you these past two weeks."

Louise smiled. "I was happy to help, dear. Now, you remember what your doctor said. You still need to take it easy. Don't push yourself too hard. Your only job is to take care of yourself and the baby for now. No other housework. No going to the store to work."

"Don't you worry about that," Mam told Louise. "We plan to make sure Margaret follows her doctor's orders. We want her to make a full recovery."

After Louise left, Margaret noticed that Baby Peter was just dozing off and, feeling tired herself, she went to her own room. To her relief it looked blessedly the same as always. She started to pick up her overnight bag.

"I'll help with that," Mam insisted. "You sit down and rest."

Margaret wanted to protest this but didn't. Instead, she sat at the foot of her bed, just watching as Mam meticulously removed items from her bag, putting them away.

"I'm so happy to have you and Baby Peter here with us." Mam set her hairbrush on the dresser. "Seeing him in the nursery just now, well, it just took me back. It reminded me of when I had my first baby. In so many ways, it was just like what you're going through, Margaret. The war was on, your dad was overseas. Jack was overseas too. That's why Louise and I set up housekeeping together. In a little apartment above my parents' store. Louise used to watch Peter for me while I worked down there. It helped us both to save money. We probably complained about living like church mice back then, but really, it was a delightful time."

"Yes, you've told me about it before." Margaret felt slightly envious to imagine the two young mothers sharing an apartment, helping each other and living like grown-ups . . . not still with their parents like she was doing.

Mam slipped the emptied overnight case into Margaret's closet, then turned to her with a smile.

"I'm sorry for rambling, darling. It's just that seeing you with your baby, well . . ."

Because it still hurt to bend at the waist, Margaret was trying to use one foot to push a shoe off the other foot.

"Here, let me help." Mam kneeled down, quickly removing her shoes.

"I hate feeling so useless," Margaret confessed.

"You're not useless, darling. You're just weak from everything you've been through. Good grief, you've endured toxemia and a caesarian operation. It's taken a toll on you. But, like Dr. Groves told you the other day, you just need to give yourself time."

She felt the tears coming. "All I want, Mam, is to be Baby Peter's mommy—and Brian's wife. I just want—*I want a normal life!*" Margaret started crying again. She hated being so emotional, but for the past two weeks, because of her in-laws, she had kept her feelings inside.

"I know you do." Mam put her arm around Margaret's shoulders. "It's what we all want."

"But it feels like—" She choked on a sob. "Like everything I want keeps slipping between my fingers. Every plan I make—it just falls to pieces. Nothing ever goes right." She pointed toward the nursery. "And—and I'm afraid I'll lose that too."

Mam handed her a handkerchief. "Lose what, Margaret?"

"My baby!" She blurted the words out with a loud sob.

"What?" Mam frowned. "Why would you think that?"

"I feel like—like I must've done something terribly wrong. As if God is punishing me. But I try to be good—I go to mass and confession and I say my—"

"God is not punishing you, Margaret." Mam pushed a loose strand of hair from her face. "You're just going through a hard time. And, my goodness, you've got a beautiful son to show for it. Certainly you don't think that's punishment."

Margaret looked up at Mam. "But don't you see what I mean?"

"Not exactly." Mam still look confused.

"Well, you just said it yourself, Mam. You said how Peter and I remind you of you . . . and your first baby."

Mam nodded. "Yes, you do."

"What if we're *just* like you?" Margaret blotted her tears with the hanky. "What if my baby grows up and what if he goes to war and what if he gets killed . . . just like your son?"

Mam's face seemed to pale. "Oh my . . . Well, no, I don't think so . . . No, no, of course not. That won't happen—"

"You never thought you'd lose Peter, did you, Mam? When he was a baby and you rocked him in that chair, did you ever dream he'd go to war—just like Dad was doing at the time—and that your baby would never come home?"

"Well, no . . . . Of course not."

"What if history repeats itself again, Mam? What if my Peter is—"

"Oh, Margaret." Mam wrapped her arms around her, rocking her slightly as if Margaret was a little child again. "Don't you know that kind of thinking can make a person crazy? You can't let your mind go to such dark places, darling. It's not healthy."

"But what if—"

"What if? What if? What if the sun refuses to shine? What if the stars fall from the sky? What if tomorrow never comes? What if? *What if?*" Mam let out a weary sigh. "I'm well aware everyone says I worry too much. And I know it's true." She sadly shook her head. "Perhaps that's why I'm the person to say this—*stop it, Mary Margaret, stop it right now!*"

Margaret blinked in surprise.

Now Mam took Margaret's face firmly in her hands, peering directly into her eyes. "You were named after me, darling, and it seems you've inherited some of my tendencies along with my name. But I can truthfully tell you—from my own personal experience—worrying does not make anything better."

"I know." Margaret sniffed.

Mam pursed her lips as she put her hands on

her hips. "Worrying is a nasty habit to get into, Margaret, and it's very hard to get out of." Her brow creased as if she were thinking hard. "Worrying is like digging a hole. A hole that you are standing in. Every time you worry, you dig down deeper and you throw out another shovelful of dirt . . . but eventually you look up and realize all you've done is dug yourself into a deep dark hole . . . a hole you cannot climb out of."

Margaret considered this. It actually made sense. "How do we stop it, Mam? How do we *not* worry?"

"Father McMurphey has told me—more often than I care to admit—that prayer is the answer. He says instead of worrying, I should be praying. That I need to give my burdens to God. And then I need to leave them in God's hands—not keep snatching them back."

"That sounds easier said than done."

"I agree." Mam smiled. "But I'll tell you what—how about if we help each other with this problem?"

"How?"

"If I see you worrying, I will try to remind you to pray instead. And I give you permission to do the same for me." She touched her forehead. "You know how I get my headaches?"

"Yes."

"I've wondered if they come from worrying."

Margaret nodded slowly. "I've wondered the same thing. It does seem your headaches are worse after you've been very worried."

"So, if you can help me to remember that, I will try to help you." Mam grasped Margaret's hands, gently pulling her to her feet and helping her to remove her cardigan.

"It's a deal."

"And now I want you to take a little nap." She helped Margaret into bed.

"I am pretty tired."

Mam tucked the comforter up around her chin. "And since you're going to start caring for Peter yourself, you should learn a little trick."

"What's that?"

"Rest while the baby's sleeping."

Margaret nodded sleepily. "Thanks, Mam. For everything." She sighed and closed her eyes. It really was good to be home.

# Twenty-Eight

*Late November 1942*

Colleen had no delusions about the amount of hard work involved in making a motion picture. Partly because she'd had lead roles in high school plays, partly because of her brief and trying stint in the propaganda film, partly because she voraciously devoured stories in movie magazines, and partly because of the lectures she'd received from Georgina during the two weeks prior to production. But she had really hoped that once the actual shooting began, it would be a combination of hard work as well as some fun.

She'd also hoped that the fact that she was in the cast of this major motion picture, even as a costar, might garner her a smidgeon of respect. But after two weeks of rehearsing and filming, that did not seem to be the case. And some days, like today, it felt like it was never going to get better.

"I feel like Darla hates me," Colleen confided to her hairdresser. It had been a particularly stressful morning trying to nail a musical number with Darla and some backup dancers who just weren't getting it. And it seemed everyone on the set was on edge. They were all taking a short break now, getting a bite to eat and their hair and makeup freshened up for the next go around, which Colleen really hoped would be a "take."

"Of course she hates you," Diane said in a hushed tone.

"Really?" Colleen turned to look at Diane.

"Hold still." Diane pushed her shoulder back into the right position as she combed Colleen's hair into a fresh ponytail. "We need to get this thing tidied up. The last thing you need is for it to fall out just when you all get this scene right."

"You really think she hates me then?" Colleen stared into the mirror, watching Diane's reflection as she worked. The hairdresser simply nodded, focused on her work, with bobby pins wedged between her lips.

"Why?" Colleen frowned at her own reflection. She looked like she was Molly's age in this juvenile costume of a red gingham shirt and overalls, but they were filming a barnyard scene. Although Darla got to wear a pretty pink polka dot dress with a skirt that showed off her legs when she danced. "I've gone out of my way to be nice to her. I've always admired her. I even told her so the first day we met."

"So?" Diane curled the dampened tail of hair into a loose roll, securing it with pins, which she would eventually unfurl into a pretty curled ponytail that she'd lacquer with hairspray.

Colleen was used to the routine by now but hoped she wouldn't be sporting the "perky ponytail" for the entire movie. According to the script, young Lucy would eventually grow up a bit.

"So why does she hate me?" Colleen asked quietly.

"Because you're young and pretty." Diane glanced around. "And because she knows that Robert's been eying you. She's jealous."

"But she's married."

"Haven't you heard?" Diane whispered. "They separated right before we went into production."

"So are you suggesting she's interested in Robert?"

"Isn't it obvious?"

Colleen frowned. "But he's a happily married man with two little kids."

Diane laughed. "This is Hollywood, Maureen. No one is happily married here."

It still took Colleen a moment when someone called her Maureen. Most of the crew called her Miss Mulligan. But she'd invited her hairdresser and makeup girl to call her by her first name. "Even so," she said quietly. "I'm not the least bit interested in Robert like that. Even if I was, I would never go after a married man."

Diane laughed even louder now. "That's what they all say . . . at first. It's amazing how quickly things change."

"I won't change," Colleen declared.

"I'm done for now," Diane told her. "But Stella is waiting."

Colleen stood but before she could leave, Diane put a hand on her shoulder. "While we're on the subject of Darla's dislike of you, she's also worried about how you've enchanted the producer—"

"That's nuts. Leon keeps yelling at me. According to him, I do everything wrong."

"I know he yells." She nodded. "But it's the way he yells."

"Maureen," Stella called. "We're on a tight schedule here."

Colleen went over to the makeup station, still trying to absorb the information Diane had just shared. She wondered how much she could trust Diane. Georgina had warned her that every movie set was a political minefield and that the smartest actresses kept themselves to themselves. But Stella was about the same age as Colleen's parents, and for some reason Colleen trusted her.

"Something troubling you, doll?" Stella used a brush to reapply Colleen's lipstick. It was a soft rose color, very natural, and suitable for an ingénue. Something that mattered in this Technicolor musical.

"Oh . . . I just get the feeling that Darla doesn't like me." Colleen knew she was baiting Stella, but she wanted to know if her observations would match Diane's. "No matter how hard I try, she treats me like—well, dirt, basically."

Stella did a quick glance around as well. "Darla *doesn't* like you," she said quietly. "And because I *do* like you, I'd warn you to watch your back with her."

Colleen felt a ripple of concern. "What do you mean?"

"I mean when the star takes a strong dislike to the costar, well, you can guess which one gets sent packing."

"Packing? Do you really think I could get dismissed? Just because Darla doesn't like me?"

Stella simply nodded as she picked up an eyebrow pencil.

"What about the expenses? Would the producer really want to go back to the drawing board? To redo all those scenes with another actress?"

"He may not *want* to. In your case, Leon really doesn't want to. But he'd do it to keep the star happy—and to get the film wrapped up in time. He'd have no choice."

"Even though I have a contract—"

"Surely your agent explained about who has all the power in a contract, doll. You're the underling here. You've got no real clout."

Colleen grimaced. Georgina had pointed out that a contract was more binding for her than it was for Pinnacle. "They hold all the cards, honey," she'd informed Colleen at signing time. "To start with anyway. We hope to change that . . . in time."

"So what do I do?" Colleen said as much to herself as anyone.

"Watch your step." Stella blew the powder puff into the air, then began patting it onto Colleen's forehead. "And keep a real safe distance from both Robert and Leon."

"It's not hard to keep a distance from Robert since I hardly have a scene with him. Even when I do, Darla is right there, upstaging me and playing the romantic interest."

"Just don't let Robert's romantic interest wander your way," Stella warned. "And don't let yourself get caught alone with either of those boys." She lowered her voice. "They both have reputations as notorious womanizers. Maybe not with the presses, but with us folks who work on the inside. Just don't say you heard it from me, doll, because I'll deny every word." She patted her stiff titian red hair. "I've been working these sets since before the talkies, and I expect to still be here even after you've moved on."

"Hopefully that won't be anytime soon."

Stella chuckled. "I hope so too, doll. I like you. I think you got real talent."

"Thanks." Colleen smiled gratefully.

"You going home for Thanksgiving?" Stella pulled a red enamel cigarette case out of her smock pocket, offering Colleen one.

"I'd just have to be back here the next day." Colleen paused to light her cigarette. "Doesn't seem worth it."

"You got anyone to spend the holiday with?" Stella blew out a stream of blue smoke.

Colleen just shook her head. "But that's okay. A day of rest may be welcome."

"You know Bette Davis?"

Colleen laughed. "I wish!"

"Well, she's looking for pretty young actresses to help at the Canteen."

"The Canteen?"

"The Hollywood Canteen. Bette set it all up herself. It's like a USO. But Bette only uses starlets for hostesses. Then she opens it up for servicemen on leave or stationed in Hollywood. Gives the boys a chance to rub elbows with movie stars. Bette has local restaurants donating food. I hear the eats there are pretty good too."

"That's very generous." Colleen nodded. "I've always been a fan of Miss Davis."

"Well, you should go to the Canteen," Stella told her. "You're a starlet."

"Not really." Colleen shrugged. "No one knows my name."

"You're pretty enough, doll. Names probably don't matter to lonely soldier boys. Just show up in your dancing shoes and a pretty dress, and I'm sure Miss Davis will let you in."

Colleen wasn't so sure.

"I know what I'll do. I'll call Bette's makeup gal. She's a friend of mine. I'll let her know you'd like to help out. How'd that suit you, doll?"

"Really?" Colleen wanted to hug her. "You're like my fairy godmother."

Stella laughed heartily. "Leave your phone number, and I'll call you to confirm that Miss Davis knows you're coming."

"Thanks!"

Now Diane came over with a can of hairspray and, quickly unpinning the ponytail, she styled it into a nice curl, then coated it with the smelly spray. "Perfect."

Colleen could hear Leon calling them back to the set now, but as she returned, she remembered the warnings she'd just gotten from both Diane and Stella. She would be watching her step—with everyone.

Molly had been disappointed Colleen hadn't made it home for Thanksgiving yesterday. But at least they'd had the Hammonds and Mrs. Bartley with them. And, of course, it was wonderful having Margaret and the baby here. Sure, it wasn't the same as a year ago, but it was still good. And Margaret seemed to be improving daily. Not only was she getting out of bed every day and getting dressed, she was caring for her baby too. This allowed Mam to go to work with Dad. And then, after school, Molly would come home and help Margaret with the baby. All in all, their household seemed to be functioning fairly smoothly.

"You got a V-mail letter from Brian," Molly announced as she came in with the mail.

Margaret looked up from the stove, where she was heating a bottle for Peter. "I'll read it right after I feed the baby."

"And I got a letter from Bridget." She held up the envelope. "And it's a thick one too."

"Oh, good. Will you read it aloud while I give Peter his bottle?"

"Sure." Molly used a kitchen knife to slit it open. As eager as she was to read it, she made herself wait until Margaret was seated with the baby.

"Okay," Margaret said eagerly. "Read away."

Dear Molly and family,
Thank you for your last letter. And thank you for the photographs of Margaret and the baby. I agree with you, Molly, our nephew is absolutely beautiful. I'm so glad to hear Margaret is doing better.

As you know, my unit had been reassigned to a field hospital after our brief visit in New Zealand. The location is similar to our last hospital, but it's on a different island. And I must say this location is an improvement. We even have a coconut grove behind us. My tentmates and I are trying to grow a small vegetable garden, but it's a battle against the insects.

We are kept extremely busy with our patients. They seem to arrive more quickly than we can release them. It looks like we'll need another tent ward put up soon. Because of the increase of patients, I just heard that we will get a few more nurses, which will be good. We will also get two more doctors. One of them will be my friend Dr. Cliff Stafford—

"Dr. Cliff is coming back," Margaret said eagerly. "Oh, I'm so glad for her."

"Yes," Molly agreed. "Bridget had seemed blue in her last letter. I thought perhaps she was missing him."

"Keep reading, please."

I was surprised at how much I missed my little walks and chats with Dr. Cliff. However, I know I'm not the only one looking forward to his return. Suffice it to say, he is popular among the nurses. Sometimes I wish I had Colleen around to give me a few beauty tips. I'm sure she's learning all sorts of new things in Hollywood. I wrote her a letter but have not heard back. Although I know that she was never much of a letter writer and she must be very busy. So I appreciate it, Molly, when you give me your little updates. I still think of you as my personal war correspondent.

Now, in answer to your question about my spare time. First of all, there is not much of it! When I do get a day off, it is often raining. We call those footlocker days because we nurses tend to open our footlockers and go through all our belongings, looking at photographs, rereading old letters, flipping through books and magazines and so on. Then we neatly repack it.

I also spend my spare time in the wards. I see how lonely some of these boys are, but when we're working we don't have time to visit. So sometimes I go back in and sit with a wounded soldier. I might write a letter or play checkers or just chat with him. Similar to what a Red Cross volunteer would do. Except we don't have them here to help out.

Occasionally we nurses will get invited out to dinner by officers who want a bit of female companionship. Not for romance, mind you, but simply for socialization. But if we have a choice between dining with the army or the navy, we always choose the navy. Their food is much better!

We also get to watch movies at the open air theater some evenings. We sit on benches, boxes, or even our helmets. On a rainy night, and we have many, we nurses have learned to wear our bathing suits beneath our raincoats in order to keep our clothes from getting too soggy. Can you imagine doing that in a San Francisco theater? I do hope Colleen's movie comes out while I'm still here. I would love to brag to my friends that Maureen Mulligan is my very own sister.

It is nearly time for my shift to begin, so I will sign off. I love you all and wish you a happy Thanksgiving. I've heard that we will have something special in our mess hall on that day. I doubt that it will be turkey, though!

Love always,
Bridget

"She sounds happy," Margaret declared as she lifted the baby to her shoulder for a burp.

"She really does." Molly refolded the letter. "Do you think she's in love with Dr. Cliff?"

Margaret nodded. "I do."

"Do you think he may be in love with her?"

Margaret's mouth twisted to one side. "I don't know about that. Bridget has a lot of competition with all those other nurses."

"Wasn't it interesting that she wanted Colleen's beauty advice?"

"I'll say. Our Bridget never seemed to care much about her appearance."

"I know." Molly frowned. "Maybe I'll write to Colleen—to see if she has some advice for Bridget."

"Good luck getting Colleen to write back to you."

Molly glanced at the phone. "Maybe I'll call her then."

"Long distance?" Margaret's brows arched. "Dad won't like that."

"I can pay for it myself." Molly went for the phone, then stopped. "Except that I know she's working today. That's why she didn't want to come home for Thanksgiving. They were scheduled to film in the studio the next day."

"Maybe you can call her on Sunday."

"Yes." Molly slipped the letter into her skirt pocket, knowing her parents would be eager to read it. "I better get to the store now. I promised Mam I'd be there before noon."

"Well, the store is never very busy on the day after Thanksgiving," Margaret told her. "I doubt they'll really need you."

"I know, but I thought Mam could come home early if it's slow." Molly pulled on her coat, then paused to pat Baby Peter's head. "You take care of your mama, little man." She grinned at

Margaret. "If I had my camera handy, I'd snap a photo. You two look so sweet together."

"Thanks, Molly. Maybe later."

"Enjoy your letter from Brian." Molly pulled on her knit hat. "Maybe you can read it to us at dinner tonight." She waved good-bye, then headed outside to where the fog was damp and heavy and cold. She thought about where Bridget was right now—so different than here. She tried to imagine her brave sister, nursing wounded soldiers back to health. And although Molly hadn't mentioned it to Margaret, she knew that because of the great losses in Guadalcanal— including the sinking of the USS *Juneau* two weeks ago, where the legendary five Sullivan brothers were all lost—the hospitals down in the South Pacific had to be overly crowded.

As she walked toward town, Molly prayed for Bridget's continued good health and safety. And for Patrick's and Brian's too. And then she decided if Colleen was too busy to give Bridget beauty tips, Molly would do the research herself. Colleen had left a lot of old fashion magazines in her room. Molly had stacked them in the attic when she helped set up the nursery. But she could bring them down and peruse them. She could clip or copy the tips that seemed appropriate for a nurse in the South Pacific and send them in her next letter.

# Twenty-Nine

*December 1942*

The Mulligan household was quieter than usual on the one-year anniversary of the attack on Pearl Harbor. Although no one spoke of it, Molly knew what was on their minds as they sat around the breakfast table. Later that evening, Dad announced the good news about the USS *New Jersey* being launched that day. "It's the largest battleship in the US fleet." He described the mighty ship to them as they sat in the front room after dinner. "It'll help us win this war."

"As will these." Margaret dangled an olive green sock from her knitting needle. "According to Louise, soldiers with warm, dry feet have a better chance of winning a battle."

"That's true," Dad said. "I know from my own experiences in the last war."

"How many pairs have you made now?" Molly asked her.

"This is my fifth pair," she said proudly. "I'm so glad Louise encouraged me to take this up while I stayed with her. I sent three pairs with Brian's Christmas package, and I'll donate the other two pairs to the Red Cross. Although I doubt they'll get to the soldiers by Christmas."

"I sure hope Bridget gets her Christmas package in time," Mam said. "I'm afraid we mailed it a bit late. Louise told me she sent Brian's and Patrick's packages a whole week before Thanksgiving."

"The post office said the chances were good," Molly reminded her. "And even if it gets there a few days later, we know Bridget will still enjoy it."

"It was sweet of you to send her those cosmetics," Margaret said to Molly. "And those silk scarves."

"They were just some items Colleen forgot to take to Hollywood with her. It was her idea," Molly said.

"I don't see why our Bridget wanted those silly things." Dad frowned with disapproval. "She's already a beautiful girl. She doesn't need all that gobblety-goop."

The women just laughed.

"If it makes her feel pretty, what's the harm?" Molly asked him.

"And if it helps her catch Dr. Cliff's eye, we won't complain now, will we?" Mam said with a wink.

"If Dr. Cliff has good sense, he'll know that Bridget is a catch," Dad declared. "Even without Colleen's beauty products."

"Molly, are you really certain Colleen plans to be home by Christmas?" Mam asked for what felt like the tenth time. "She actually said that to you?"

"Yes, Mam. She promised. And she asked me to pick her up at the airport at two o'clock on Christmas Eve. Don't worry," she said to Margaret, "Colleen will be bunking with me. She knows her room's been turned into a nursery."

"Well, if she's really coming home for Christmas, I think I'll talk to Father McMurphey about getting Peter Brian christened," Margaret declared.

"Good idea," Mam told her.

"Colleen said she has to be back for filming by Monday the twenty-eighth." Molly glanced at Dad. "And she's hoping to drive Peter's car back to Hollywood on Sunday. She said you'd made a deal with her to buy it."

"Are you really going to let her take the car?" Mam asked Dad.

"That's right," he confirmed. "She's paying a fair price for it, and the truth is we can use the money right now. Besides, with gas rationing, we're better off with just one car in the family."

"Colleen can't wait to have her own car down there," Molly told them. "She's been taking taxis to the Hollywood Canteen in the evenings. She said the cost is adding up." Molly had already told them about how Colleen volunteered at the club Bette Davis had started for the local servicemen. It sounded like a USO club, only a lot fancier. According to Colleen, she'd been rubbing elbows with all sorts of interesting actresses. And they all sounded much nicer than snooty Darla Devon, although Colleen had asked Molly not to repeat that.

"Did Colleen say how the filming is going?" Margaret asked.

"I think it's going okay. And I nearly forgot, she told me about going to the premiere of a new movie called *Casablanca*. She said it was the best movie she's ever seen."

"I read something about that film in one of Colleen's movie magazines," Margaret said with interest. "Doesn't it have Humphrey Bogart in it?"

"Yes. She saw both the stars, Humphrey Bogart and Ingrid Bergman, at the premiere." Molly considered this. "I wonder just how many movie stars she's seen in real life by now. Do you think she's keeping a list?"

"Knowing Colleen, she's probably writing it all in her diary," Margaret said.

"Well, I'm glad she's enjoying her time down there." Mam set her own knitting project aside. "It seems she's finally moved beyond her sadness over losing Geoff. It was hard seeing her like that."

"Speaking of Colleen," Molly began carefully since the timing seemed right. "She's invited me to come down there."

"She's invited all of us to come visit her," Dad reminded her.

"Yes, I know. But she specifically asked me to *drive* down there with her. Right after Christmas," Molly said.

*"What?"* Dad lowered his newspaper.

"That way she wouldn't have to drive by herself," Molly quickly explained. "And she offered to pay for my plane ticket to come back home—before school starts, of course. Can you imagine? It would be my first time flying in an airplane."

"I don't know." Mam frowned. "You're not even seventeen, Molly."

"I know. And Colleen is only nineteen," Molly said lightly.

"I think Molly should go," Margaret declared.

Molly looked hopefully at her. Margaret's response was unexpected but most welcome.

"Molly is always helping everyone," Margaret continued. "She works so hard at school and at home and in the store. Why not let her have a little fun for a change? We all know she's a responsible girl. Everyone always says she's old for her age. Why shouldn't she go down there?"

Mam and Dad asked Molly a few more questions, but with Margaret's encouragement, they finally agreed to this plan. Molly jumped up, hugging all three of them. "This is going to be so great!" And then she excused herself to go do homework—and to write Colleen a quick note saying that she could come visit.

*Christmas Eve*

Colleen waved to Molly as she got off the plane. At first glance, she hadn't even recognized the attractive young woman waiting on the tarmac. Molly looked so grown-up in a dark blue suit that had once belonged to Colleen—and taller too. As Colleen walked toward her "baby sister," she felt relieved the rest of her family was too busy with the store and the baby to come meet her plane. The truth was, after six weeks of intense filming, Colleen was tired. She hoped her visit at home would be somewhat relaxing.

"You look so glamorous." Molly hugged her. "But then, you always do."

"You don't look too bad yourself." Colleen gave Molly a nod of approval.

"I tried to dress up for you," Molly confessed. "Here, let me take that." She reached for the cosmetics case.

"You're a doll." Colleen gave her a squeeze. "And I'm so glad you get to drive back to Hollywood with me next week. I was afraid Dad would put his foot down."

As they went to retrieve Colleen's suitcase,

Molly explained how Margaret had come to her defense. She filled her in on other bits and pieces of Mulligan household news and, before long, Molly was driving them back into the city.

"I thought about something on my way home," Colleen said. "Something I forgot to ask you about before I went to Hollywood."

"What's that?"

"Because of all the excitement over Margaret's baby and my quick departure, I never got to hear all the details about your big homecoming night. All I know is that you weren't chosen as queen. But you never told me how it went with the Stockton boy. Are you and he dating now? Is he your boyfriend?" Colleen gave Molly a teasing poke in the shoulder.

"No—not at all!" Molly's eyes narrowed. "I have no interest whatsoever in Charlie Stockton."

"Oh?" Colleen knew there must be more to this story. "What happened?"

Molly bit her lip like she was trying to decide how to answer. "I, uh, I don't know . . . . Nothing really."

"Look, Molly, this is Colleen here. You can be honest with me. I doubt there's anything you could tell me I haven't heard before. Or experienced personally."

Molly glanced at her, then nodded. "Well, it would be nice to talk to someone about it."

"What happened?" Colleen demanded.

"So . . . Charlie was acting like I really was his girlfriend," Molly said somberly. "Even though I told him I just wanted to go with him to the dance as a friend. But he kept putting his arm around me. And he was trying to kiss me and acting like I was his personal property."

"That sounds like a Stockton to me."

Molly nodded. "I tried to act like it wasn't a big deal at the dance, and I knew I'd never go out with him again. But when he took me home, well, he insisted on walking me to the door. Of course, with Margaret's baby being born and everything, no one was home. And so Charlie started getting, well, sort of fresh with me. You know what I mean?"

"I certainly do." Colleen wanted to punch this boy right in the nose. "I hope you told him to knock it off."

"I did tell him. But he wasn't listening." Molly's voice choked slightly. "It turned into sort of a fight. He kept grabbing me, trying to kiss me, saying that I was his girlfriend and he expected more of me. You know?"

"Pull over," Colleen insisted with alarm. "Let me drive."

Molly did as she was told, but as soon as Colleen was behind the wheel, Molly started to cry even harder. "He was so mean to me, Colleen. Like he'd turned into a—a monster.

Like Dr. Jekyll and Mr. Hyde. He was so rough that he even tore my dress—the beautiful dress you—you made for me." She sobbed. "He ruined it. I had to hide it in the back of my closet so no one would see it."

"But how about *you,* Molly? Did he hurt you? I mean, besides trying to take unfair advantage of you and acting like an ill-mannered gorilla?"

"Mostly he hurt my feelings," Molly told her. "And I was embarrassed. I didn't really want to tell anyone what happened. I would've told you, but—well, there wasn't a right time. I decided I just needed to forget the whole thing. Put it behind me. You know?"

"Yes. I suppose that's the best thing. And never ever speak to the monster again."

"But then at school . . ." Molly started to cry again. "Charlie went around and told everyone lies about me."

"Lies?" Colleen knew where this was going. "Did he make you look like you'd done things you hadn't? Did he ruin your reputation?"

"Yes." Molly nodded eagerly. "He told them I was a bad girl, Colleen. And I wasn't. I really wasn't."

"That little monster! I could kill him!"

"It's been so humiliating." She used a hanky to wipe her tears. "I mean, sure, it's died down by now. Well, mostly. I know some girls still whisper behind my back. Dottie doesn't. She believes me. But others act funny around me. They treat me differently."

"I know exactly what you mean, Molly. Exactly."

"Did something like that happen to you?"

Colleen nodded. "Yes. But I wasn't as smart as you. I allowed it to change me. I tried to act tough—like I didn't care what they said about me. But that only seemed to seal the deal for everyone. I became the girl with the reputation. Even though I did nothing to earn it. My defense was to look fabulous and hold my head high—and act like it made no difference." She glanced at Molly. "But I still hurt inside."

"I'm so sorry," Molly told her. "I never knew any of that."

"No one did. Not even Margaret, and she was still in school with me at the time. The only other person who has heard this story besides you is . . . Geoff." Colleen felt a lump in her throat. "And he understood completely. He believed in me."

"He was a good guy, Colleen."

"I know."

When they got home and out of the car, Colleen hugged Molly tightly. "I'm sorry for what happened to you, Molly," she said. "But you're handling this much better than I did at your age." Even so, as they carried her bags to the house, Colleen still wanted to punch that stupid Charlie Stockton right in his stupid nose.

Having a baby in the house was making Christmastime a lot more fun. At least for Margaret. Oh, she knew that Baby Peter was oblivious to the trappings and trimmings, but he did look adorable in the little red and green velvet outfit that Louise had made for him. Margaret chuckled to herself as she held him up. Hopefully, Molly would get some good pictures to send to Brian.

"Look at the little Christmas elf," Colleen said as she came into the nursery. She gently tapped a chubby cheek. "Just as handsome as ever, aren't you?"

"Want to hold him?" Margaret frowned at Colleen's elegant black satin dress. "Or are you worried he might spit up on your beautiful gown?"

Colleen held out her hands. "The little prince can spit on me if he wants. Hand him over."

Margaret laughed. She hoped Peter wouldn't ruin Colleen's dress, but you could never tell with babies. Margaret had enough stained pieces of clothing to prove that.

"Auntie Colleen has been missing her little man," she cooed to him.

"Did you have a good flight?" Margaret asked.

"It was just fine." Colleen peered at her. "I hear that you helped talk Mam and Dad into letting Molly drive back with me after Christmas. Thanks."

Margaret shrugged. "I think Molly deserves it."

Colleen nodded. "If you weren't so busy with the baby, I'd suggest you come too, Margaret. Maybe someday."

Margaret smiled wistfully. "Yeah, maybe so."

"So how are you doing?" Colleen asked. "You look good."

"It was a little rough at first," Margaret admitted. "But having family around to help . . . well, it's been a huge blessing."

"And what do you hear from Brian?"

"He sounds okay in his letters. I know he's in North Africa somewhere . . . he can't say where . . . I'm guessing it's in the thick of the action." Downstairs the phone was jangling noisily, probably someone calling to say Merry Christmas, but even so, it was disconcerting. Margaret wouldn't admit it, not even to Mam, but whenever the phone or doorbell rang at night, she would always brace herself for bad news. "And I know it's dangerous," she continued to ramble as she listened to Dad answering the phone. "But I've been trying not to worry so much. Mam and I are reminding each other to pray instead of fret. It's become our motto."

"That's a good one."

"Hey, Colleen," Dad yelled from downstairs. "Telephone for you."

Colleen handed Margaret back the baby. "I wonder who that could be."

Margaret felt a wave of relief as she held Peter. It was not the War Department on the other end. And, really, did they ever call on the phone? From what she'd heard it was usually a telegram. Not that she expected any. And, once again, instead of delving into worrisome thoughts, she said a prayer for Brian to remain safe—and to have a happy Christmas.

Colleen was surprised to hear Geoff's mother's voice on the other end. "Oh, hello," she said brightly. "Merry Christmas."

*"Colleen,"* Ellen Conrad's voice sounded higher pitched than usual. "I have some news."

"News?"

"About Geoff."

*"What?"* Colleen wondered if she'd heard her wrong.

"We just received a telegram—from the War Department." She actually laughed now. "A Christmas present, really."

"What do you mean?"

"Geoff is *alive.*"

Colleen felt slightly faint, and reaching around for the straight-backed chair that was by the phone, she collapsed into it. "I—I don't understand."

"I know it's shocking to hear. But I had to call you."

"Yes, of course." Colleen was trying to absorb this. "Geoff is *alive?*" Suddenly everyone in the room—her family, the Hammonds, and Mrs. Bartley—stopped talking, and now they were all staring at Colleen with wide-eyed interest.

"Yes! That is the *good* news." Ellen's voice seemed to grow more somber.

"Is there some *bad* news?" Colleen took in a quick breath.

"According to the telegram, when Geoff's plane went down in the ocean, he managed to save his crew by using the life-raft, but then they were captured by the Japanese. He's a prisoner of war, Colleen."

"Oh . . . my." Colleen felt like she could barely breathe. "But he *is* alive? You know this for an absolute fact? Geoff is alive?"

"That's what the telegram states. I don't even know how they found out, but the telegram sounded certain. And they don't give the specific location, only that he's being held captive somewhere in the Philippines."

"Geoff is alive." Colleen repeated those three words again, still trying to take it in. "He's alive."

"We're so thrilled about it, and I knew you'd be happy too."

"Yes, yes, thank you, I am. But I'm so stunned—I can barely think straight. Do you think he's okay? Do you think he's been injured or harmed or anything?"

"The telegram had no information about his condition. Only that he's alive and imprisoned. But Geoff is a strong person—both physically and mentally," she said with confidence. "I can only expect that he's going to get through this, Colleen. That he's going to come home to us."

"Yes!" Colleen agreed eagerly. "Of course he will."

"Merry Christmas, dear."

"Merry Christmas to you too, Ellen!"

"And we'd like to invite you out here, Colleen. We'd love to see you . . . and celebrate . . . if you can get away from your family for a bit."

"I'd love to come," Colleen told her.

"How about dinner tomorrow at two?"

"I can do that." Colleen felt certain her family would excuse her from tomorrow's dinner at the Hammonds', considering the circumstances. She thanked Geoff's mother again and then hung up. "Geoff is alive!" she cried out. *"He's alive!"* And now, as they all gathered around, she told them the details of the telephone call. Christmas Eve at the Mulligan house was quite the celebration that evening—with no one happier than Colleen!

Molly offered to go with her to the Conrad farm, but Colleen already felt guilty for removing herself from today's celebration at the Hammonds'. "Thanks," she told her sister. "But our family needs you with them today. And my visit with the Conrads should be a happy one this time."

But as she drove Peter's car, which was actually her car now since she'd given Dad a check for it, she felt a slight bit of apprehension. She knew Geoff's mother would not approve of Colleen's acting career. Ellen had not concealed her dislike of Hollywood, movies, and actors. Colleen wondered if it would be wrong not to mention such things during their visit. After all, today should be about celebrating. On the other hand, it might be a smart move to disclose this slightly sensitive information while Geoff's mother was in good spirits.

By the time she pulled up in front of the big white house, Colleen was still uncertain—to tell or not to tell, that was the question. She checked herself in the car's rearview mirror, making sure her lipstick wasn't too strong. She'd purposely gone light on makeup today. And she'd borrowed a rather conservative dress from Margaret—a dark green velveteen with a full skirt and three-quarter length sleeves. Something she hoped Geoff's mother would approve.

"Welcome, welcome!" Geoff's grandfather opened the front door wide. "We're so glad you could join us today." He hugged Colleen, then offered to take her coat.

"Dear, dear Colleen!" Geoff's grandmother

hurried into the foyer. "You're looking lovelier than ever too." She hugged Colleen.

"Thank you, Mrs. Conrad."

"I insist you must call me Grandma. Just like Geoff does." She turned to her husband. "And you should call him Grandpa." She smiled brightly. "We're all so terribly happy that you could join us. Grandpa even made a batch of eggnog to celebrate." She nudged her husband with her elbow.

"Can I get you some, Colleen?" His blue eyes twinkled.

"Sounds lovely."

"Oh, there you are!" Ellen joined them. She looked surprisingly festive in a red cashmere sweater set and tartan skirt. "Thank you for coming, Colleen. I'm so glad to see you again." She opened her arms to embrace Colleen—a first for the two of them.

"I still can hardly believe it," Colleen said as she removed her gloves and hat, setting them by her purse on the foyer bench. "I keep wanting to pinch myself."

"I know what you mean. I woke up several times last night, trying to determine whether it was real or not. But I had the telegram right on my nightstand so I could read it whenever I needed." Ellen linked her arm in Colleen's, leading her to the living room. "I've got it in here for you to read too."

With the ladies settled on the sofa, Colleen slowly read the slightly worn telegram, taking in each word, which was almost exactly what Ellen had told her last night. "It's really true," Colleen said with a slightly choked voice. "He *is* alive."

"Here we go." Grandpa set a silver tray with four silver cups of eggnog on the glass-topped coffee table. He waited for the ladies to take one and then held up his cup to make a toast. "Here's to Geoff," he began, "a true survivor—and a hero. May God bring him quickly home to us."

"To our dear boy," Grandma said a bit more somberly. "May God keep him safe and deliver him from the hands of the enemy."

"To my son," Ellen said. "To his strength and bravery and perseverance—and to a safe journey home."

They looked at Colleen, waiting expectantly.

"To my beloved Geoff," she said quietly. "May God bring him home to us. *Soon!*"

The room got quiet as they sipped their eggnog. Colleen knew that they, like her, probably had mixed feelings. On one hand, there was much to celebrate—Geoff was alive! On the other hand, the press had made no secret that Japanese prison camps were brutal and inhumane. She'd recently heard a serviceman at the Hollywood Canteen saying that a Japanese prison camp was a "fate worse than death."

"So, Colleen," Grandpa said pleasantly. "Are you still working at the airplane factory? That must be exciting, getting planes ready for the military."

Colleen knew she couldn't lie to Geoff's family. "Actually, I quit working at the factory in October. About the same time my sister Margaret had her baby." Now for a bit, she told them about Margaret's toxemia and difficult delivery and beautiful baby boy.

"So you're helping your sister and her baby?" Grandma asked with arched brows. "Playing auntie?"

"I did help her for a while." Colleen swallowed. "Then I returned to, uh, to work."

"At your parents' store?" Ellen asked with interest.

"No . . . I'm doing a different kind of work." Colleen tried to think of the best way to say this. "You may remember how I had an interest in acting." She quickly told them about the short film she and her family had participated in. "I really didn't think I'd done a very good job in it, but an agency in Hollywood felt I had potential. They invited me down for a screen test."

"Oh, my." Grandma's eyes lit up. "How exciting for you."

Ellen didn't look quite as enthused. "Did you go?"

Colleen nodded. "You see, I'd been so terribly sad about losing Geoff. It was as if I had turned into someone else. My family was actually getting concerned. But going down to Hollywood, doing the screen test, well, it sort of brought me back." She smiled stiffly.

"So, excuse my ignorance, but what exactly is a screen test?" Grandpa asked. "What is it for?"

"It's how a motion-picture studio determines if an actress would be good in a movie," his wife told him. "Don't you ever read any of my ladies magazines?"

"Not if I can help it." He chuckled.

"Well, they often have stories about film stars. I find it all rather fascinating." She smiled at Colleen. "So tell us, dear, how did your screen test go?"

Colleen returned her smile. "It went well. Pinnacle Studio offered me a film contract. It's only a supporting role. It's a musical romance film. But it's also about the war effort. And it stars Robert Miller and Darla Devon."

"Robert Miller?" Grandma's eyes lit up. "We saw him in that movie last summer, Edgar. The one about the Nazi spies and—"

"So this film contract?" Ellen's brow creased. "Did you accept it, Colleen?"

Colleen nodded. "I did. We've been filming about six weeks. It will probably wrap up in late February."

"But what if Geoff comes home?" Ellen asked her.

Colleen considered her answer. "Then I will drop everything to welcome him back."

"Meaning you'll quit the film?" Ellen asked.

"No, of course, not. If I did that, it would ruin it for everyone. And I have a contract to keep."

"Of course you do," Grandma told her. "And I'm certain Geoff would understand."

"I think he would." Colleen firmly nodded. "He believed I could be an actress. He was always supportive of my dream to be in a movie."

"What about your plans to marry?" Ellen asked. "Would you carry on with your film career and be Geoff's wife?"

"Oh, Ellen," Grandma said. "Don't you think you're getting the cart ahead of the horse?"

"I agree." Grandpa waved a dismissive hand. "These are decisions that Geoff and Colleen will need to make."

"I still want to marry Geoff," Colleen assured them. "If he still wants to marry me."

"Of course he will," Grandpa declared.

"We'll just have to sort it all out," Colleen said quietly, "when Geoff comes home."

"And we have no idea when that will be," Grandpa said solemnly. "I've been reading about how it's heating up down there in Guadalcanal, but it's possible that Colleen's movie filming will be finished before Geoff is even released."

"But will you be involved in another motion picture by then?" Ellen asked with a furrowed brow.

"I honestly don't know. No one has mentioned anything like that. I suppose it depends on how this film goes. But if Geoff isn't home and I get another film offer, well, I have to be honest with you. I will probably take it."

"Even though you know he's alive now?" Ellen studied Colleen closely.

"My family has had a very difficult year . . . in many ways." Colleen wondered how much to say. "It's been hard emotionally and financially. I won't get into all the details, but I've been very thankful that I can help them out for a change."

Grandma reached for Colleen's hand, giving it a warm squeeze. "That is so generous, Colleen. Such a good daughter. I know that Geoff would approve of that."

Ellen still looked a bit uncertain, but at least she stopped questioning Colleen, and for the rest of their time together, they returned to celebrating the good news that Geoff was alive.

# Thirty

Margaret hadn't been this excited about going to church since she and Brian got married almost a year ago. But she didn't want to think about their first anniversary today—or how she would be celebrating alone. Well, not completely alone. She had Peter Brian and she had her family.

"Doesn't he look like a little prince," Mam declared as she came into the nursery.

"This christening gown is the nicest I've ever seen." Margaret lifted the baby up so the long gown draped beautifully. "I just hope he doesn't spit up on it."

"Let's put a bib on, just until we get to the church." Mam went to the dresser to look for one.

"Oh, my!" Colleen exclaimed. "Look at you two standing there in the morning sunlight— pretty as a picture." She called out to Molly now. "Bring your camera. You have to get a photo of this."

Margaret felt very chic wearing the pale blue suit Colleen had loaned her for today's event. The waist of the skirt was a bit tight, but with the flair of the peplum jacket, no one would notice that the top hook was undone. At least she got it zipped. Or mostly. She smiled and posed while Molly took a couple of photos.

"I'll save the rest of my film for the church," Molly said as she put the camera back in its case. "And I almost forgot. Mail call." She reached in her pocket to hold up a V-mail. "This one's for you, Margaret."

Margaret handed the baby over to Colleen as she eagerly reached for the letter. "I won't be long," she assured them. "But I'd like to read it before we go to the church."

"We'll go downstairs," Mam told her. "And start loading the car."

Margaret felt relieved as she opened the letter. She hadn't heard from Brian since he'd been relocated to North Africa. She knew there'd been battles down there and had been trying not to worry, but it wasn't easy!

Dear Margaret,
First of all, I want to say happy anniversary, my darling. I hope this arrives in time. Perhaps by our next anniversary, we will be together. I also hope that our son Peter Brian has a fine christening on the day after Christmas. Just know that I will be there in spirit. You both are always in my prayers.

I could tell by your last two letters you are worried about me being in active duty. I was so very eager to get out from behind my desk, I suppose I didn't fully appreciate the seriousness of the battlefield. I can say that has changed now. I am helping to lead a fine infantry unit of young men. Two of them are only seventeen! The responsibility of getting all these men home safely rests heavily on my shoulders, but I believe I'm up to the task.

I'm going to make a confession to you, Margaret. I experienced a certain amount of fear during my first battle. I was caught off guard, but from what I hear, that is perfectly normal. A healthy amount of fear helps to keep a soldier on his toes, it helps to keep him alive. And I do plan to stay alive, my darling. I plan to come home to you and my son. So, please, don't be anxious over me. Instead, you can pray for me and my unit.

I have another confession and I pray this one won't cause you to worry. Although I plan to come home, I know that is out of my hands. So I want to say this to you, just one time. I am not afraid to die. I trust God knows best. I leave it in His hands. I pray you do the same.

On New Year's Eve, I will be thinking of you. I will remember my beautiful bride walking down the aisle of Old Saint

Mary's, I will remember the short time we had together. And I will be looking forward to the next time we meet.

Love always,
Brian

Margaret refolded the V-mail, slipped it into her skirt pocket, and, removing a lace-trimmed handkerchief Louise had given her for today, she dabbed a tear. She knew Brian hadn't meant to make her sad. He simply was trying to be honest. She held her head high. And she could take it. She was a wife and mother now, and it was time to be strong.

As Margaret rode in the backseat with Molly and Colleen, she braced herself for all that might go wrong at the christening. The baby might start howling, although she'd just fed him, so she didn't think that would happen. Or he might spit up all over his pretty gown, or make a stink and soil his diaper. Or she might do or say something wrong. Anything was possible. But as Dad parked in front of the church, she felt herself relax. Really, it didn't matter if things went "wrong." The important thing was that they were all here together. What would be would be, and there really wasn't much she could do about it.

"Ready?" Colleen asked as she helped Margaret out of the car.

"I am if you are." Margaret grinned at her.

"It's not too late for you to change your mind," Colleen said quietly. "You can ask Molly to be his godmother if you like."

Margaret laughed. "Don't try to get out of this, Colleen. You agreed." She glanced over at Molly. "Besides, I don't need to ask her. She'll act like a godmother whether it's official or not."

Colleen nodded. "You're right."

To Margaret's surprise and relief, the christening ceremony went off without a hitch. Nothing whatsoever went wrong! The baby was calm and even seemed to smile at Father McMurphey. Colleen said her vows in such a reverent way. Even if she was acting—although Margaret knew better—everyone believed in her sincerity. Molly took a lot of photos, many of which would be sent to Brian as soon as they were developed. And, all in all, it was a thoroughly enjoyable time.

Afterward, as family and friends gathered at the Hammonds' for a late lunch, Peter Brian was the center of attention. Everyone took turns holding him. And Margaret managed to get him changed out of his beautiful gown and into a baby blue suit before he spit up. And then she just laughed about it. Everyone was in high spirits. Really, short of having Brian home with them, it could not have gone better.

By the time she was putting the baby to bed

that night, she felt just as tired as he looked. "You've had a big day, little one," she said quietly.

"Can I tell him good night?" Colleen asked as she slipped into the dimly lit nursery. "Molly and I will be leaving very early tomorrow, so I might not see him again."

"Of course." Margaret stepped aside, watching as Colleen bent down to kiss his cheek.

"Good night, darling boy," Colleen whispered. "You and your mommy and daddy will be in my prayers." She winked at Margaret as she stood. "Just like I promised in church."

"Thanks." Margaret hugged her. "For everything."

Colleen patted Margaret on the cheek. "And you, dear sister, please take good care of yourself and your baby."

"I'm trying," Margaret assured her. "And for that reason, I'll tell you good night. Because I am thoroughly exhausted."

"Promise me something, though," Colleen said suddenly.

"What?"

"My most favorite movie will be releasing in a few weeks. It's called *Casablanca* and it has Humphrey—"

"Yes, yes, I already know about it."

"You have to go see it, Margaret. It's about the war and it's set in North Africa and the acting is just brilliant. And it has the best song—it's called 'As Time Goes By.' You'll love it."

Margaret held up her hand. "I promise to see it, Colleen. Wild horses won't keep me from going."

"And then I'll call you up and we'll talk about it. Okay?"

Margaret nodded happily. "You got it!"

As Colleen slipped back out of the nursery, Margaret marveled at how much she loved all her sisters. Oh, she had always loved her other sisters. Bridget and Molly had always been easy to love. But Colleen? Sometimes Margaret had wanted to take her over her knee. Now she was already missing her again. But she knew Hollywood couldn't keep Colleen forever. Someday she'd come back home to them. In the meantime, Margaret would try to be patient . . . and she'd pray for her.

As Colleen drove her "new" car down the serpentine highway on the outskirts of Los Angeles, she asked Molly to try the radio again. "We should be getting something by now," she said.

"I'm so excited about being here," Molly said as she turned the dial, listening to the crackling sounds.

"We'll be there in time for a late lunch," Colleen told her. "And then I'll drive you around to see some of the sights."

"There." Molly stopped turning the dial and music filled the car. "Oh, I love that song! I've been trying to learn the lyrics. They're so interesting."

"Turn it up!" Colleen said eagerly. "That's from *Casablanca*!"

As usual, Colleen had a hard time fully getting the first parts of the song. It was about all the confusing things going on in the world and how they could wear on a person. But when it came to the first chorus, both she and Molly sang enthusiastically along with it. Together they limped through the next few lines and finally sang the last chorus loudly together.

It's still the same old story,
A fight for love and glory,
A case of do or die.
The world will always welcome lovers
As time goes by.

"What a great song." Colleen slowly shook her head.

"Yes, I love it."

"I just hope that's really true," Colleen said quietly.

"What do you mean?" Molly reached over to turn the volume down. "What's true?"

"That the world will always welcome lovers. I'm not sure that Geoff's mom is like that. I don't think she particularly wants to welcome me."

"But I thought you mended your fences with her. And you were there at Christmas, celebrating about Geoff." Molly frowned. "Why wouldn't she welcome you now?"

Colleen waved her hand toward the valley unfolding below them. "Because of Hollywood. She doesn't approve of me being here."

Molly patted Colleen on the shoulder. "Well, it's a good thing you're not going to marry Geoff's mother then, isn't it?"

Colleen couldn't help but smile. "Yes, I must agree with you on that."

"The important thing is what *Geoff* thinks about it. And you've said that he was okay with it before. Besides, we don't know how long it'll be before Geoff gets out of the prison camp. You may be done with your movie by then." She sighed loudly. "But I hope he gets freed a lot sooner than that. I've really been praying for him, Colleen."

"Thanks." Colleen slowed down for the traffic ahead. "Keep praying, Molly. For all of us. I'm praying too. Praying that this war will soon be over . . . but I have a feeling it's going to be awhile."

"I know. I wish that Hitler and Hirohito and Mussolini would all just fall into a deep black hole and disappear from the face of the earth forever," Molly said wistfully.

"Unfortunately, it doesn't work that way. It's going to take all of us—our guys overseas and everyone on the home front—to end this thing." Colleen reached for Molly's hand. "But it helps to know we're all in it together."

" 'It's still the same old story . . . ' " Molly started to sing heartily, and Colleen quickly joined her, finally ending with "As time goes by," followed by giggles.

"You're going to love Hollywood," Colleen told Molly.

"I can't wait!"

As much as Colleen knew she'd enjoy showing Molly the sights, she could imagine the day—hopefully not too far off in the distant future—when she would be giving Geoff the full tour.

Books are produced in the United States using U.S.-based materials

Books are printed using a revolutionary new process called THINKtech™ that lowers energy usage by 70% and increases overall quality

Books are durable and flexible because of Smyth-sewing

Paper is sourced using environmentally responsible foresting methods and the paper is acid-free

**Center Point Large Print**
600 Brooks Road / PO Box 1
Thorndike, ME 04986-0001 USA

**(207) 568-3717**

**US & Canada:**
**1 800 929-9108**
www.centerpointlargeprint.com